Also by Tracy J. Cass
Labor of Love

Praise for _Labor of Love_

"In her debut novel, T. Cass has shown us the ups and downs, the joys and sorrows that being in love puts us through. This read was enjoyable and true to life. I look forward to reading the future works of this up and coming novelist." **~Reviewed by Renee Williams for The RAWSISTAZ Reviewers**

"New author T. Cass immediately distinguishes herself from others in this realistic and frank look at the labor of love...a well written and enjoyable read. I look forward to reading more from this author." **~Reviewed by Toni for O.O.S.A. Online Book Club**

"I could not believe this was a debut novel. I was compelled by the storyline and drawn in by the characters. The author writes with such realism and simplicity, it is easy to have a love affair with each page." **~Pierce Publishing Company**

"A charming, funny look at love and the many obstacles we face when we've found it." **~J. Monique Gambles, author of When the Drama has Ceased**

All That Matters
By Tracy J. Cass

NINE TWELVE Publishing
Fort Worth, Texas

NINE TWELVE Publishing
P.O. Box 6643 Fort Worth, TX. 76115

ISBN: 978-0-9764634-2-9
ISBN: 978-0-9764634-6-7 (eBook)

Published by NINE TWELVE Publishing
P.O. Box 6643
Fort Worth, TX 76115

Library of Congress Control Number: 2021923557

Cover Concept: Tracy J. Cass
Cover Design & Logo: Kiosha Collins

Printed in the United States

Love forgives a multitude of sins. ~The Bible •*ish*

Part One
Break Up to Make Up

Chapter 1
Jaslyn

Just My Fuckin' Luck

How is it that you can spend an entire lifetime not having known someone, but the minute you meet, you see them everywhere you go? Especially when it's someone you'd give your last dollar never to see again?

That's the way I feel about my ex-boyfriend, Sampson Tate. I can't lie; I still have feelings for him, but he hurt me too bad to even entertain that nonsense. You see, the problem is that he was cheating on me. I caught him locked in an embrace with an old sweetheart, Alicia Matthews. You can call that trivial if you want, but a man never gets over his first love, and Alicia was his.

It's ironic that Sampson and I spent our lives growing up in Texas together but never managed to meet. We were both raised in Fort Worth, a big city with small town ways. Everybody knew each other, knew of each other, or knew someone that knew you. Imagine having a conversation with someone and incidentally mentioning a name, say for example, Raynelle Watson. All of a sudden, some stranger next to you gets excited and interrupts your conversation. "Excuse me, do you know Raynelle?" You say, "Yes, ma'am. I do. She's my brother-in-law's stepdaddy's cousin." Then they say, "Girl, that's my cousin, too! We almost kin!" To an outsider, this exchange would definitely be considered a country conversation, but this is what we loved about our city. The diverse cultural settings of art galleries, concert halls, restaurants, and bookstores surrounded by neighborhoods like mine which were mixed with the flavor of a hometown appeal made black and white alike proud to call Fort Worth home. Even the hood was a place of pride, or should I say, especially the hood. The effort to overcome poverty and crime drew you and your neighbors in so tight that you developed a distinct homage to that way of life and to the area in which you grew up.

I grew up on the Southside. Sam was reared about ten minutes away on the Eastside of town in a neighborhood called Stop Six. We even knew some of the same people. I went to college with his brother, Solomon, and his best friend, Jawaan, married my cousin, Tamika. Our paths just never crossed until we met at their wedding. Then we fell in love, and then, we broke up. Now that I never want to see him again, I see him all the *fuckin'* time. *What's up with that?*

If I don't see him, then I'm constantly running into someone that knows him and who is more than willing to offer tidbits of information about how well he's doing. I graciously grin and bear it. Say the obligatory, "Well, good for him," bit and try to move on, but truthfully, that shit grates on my nerves. What's a girl to do? Be rude and tell the bearer of *Sampson News* that I really don't want to hear that shit. I think not. I was never one to let others see that they were getting the best of me even though it may have been true.

Anyway, every time I turned around, Sam was there—at church, the grocery store, parties I attended for old friends. He was even at a conference I attended a while back. It was given to new entrepreneurs by the chamber of commerce. A year had passed since our break-up. I no longer wanted to sit around feeling sorry for myself, and the demise of our relationship was the motivation I needed to get me started on opening a shelter for battered women. My job as a therapist paid well, but there were issues that I wanted to address with battered women that I felt my center didn't really make a priority, especially for minority women. Women stay in abusive relationships because they may not have anywhere to go. Any shelter satisfied that need, but I wanted to address the holistic needs of abused women. In addition to providing housing, Davenport House (Yes, named after yours truly. A little vanity never hurt anyone!) would also provide economic and job training seminars, spiritual counseling from the religion of their choice, as well as standard self-esteem and self-love workshops. The shelter would focus on self-actualization because what good would all of those workshops be if it did nothing to help the women make their dreams and goals reality? Each woman would also be required to participate in physical fitness and self-defense classes four days a week. So, the next time any man, or person for that matter, wanted to physically abuse them they could open up a can of whoop ass to make sure it didn't happen again. My philosophy: Treat the whole woman so they could begin to make better life choices; not just relationship choices. Nothing ingenious about it, but still, I wanted it to be my own program.

I went to the conference to get some much-needed information on writing business plans, finding financing options, and creating an effective brand for my business. It never entered my mind that Sampson would be there. He owned an advertising firm, and if not considered a huge success, it was at least profitable. Well, now I really am being petty...his shit was the bomb, and he knew it. So did everyone else.

When I entered the hotel where the conference was being held, I walked up to the registration table in the center of the lobby to sign-in and pick up my conference materials. After I checked in, I looked in the conference brochure to locate my classes. As I skimmed the pages, whose name did I see? It was like I had bionic vision. My eyes skipped all the other names and zeroed in on his:

November 3, 2004

Breakout Session #8: *Branding Your Business*

Speaker: *Sampson Tate*   **Company**: *Tate & Associates*

Time: *9:30 a.m.-11:30 a.m.* **Location**: *Conference Rm. 215*

I looked at my registration, and sure enough, I was registered for Breakout Session #8 at 9:30 a.m. in room 215. *Just my fuckin' luck,* I thought. I was turning around to leave when I hit a wall. You guessed it, Sampson's chest.

"Hello, Jaslyn. You're looking lovely this morning," he spat through a jaw that was locked tighter than the Federal Reserve.

I didn't feel lovely, I felt like trash. Veiled as a compliment, Sam's icy greeting was clearly a dis.

If it weren't for bad luck, I wouldn't have any luck at all. "Shit," I mumbled.

"What was that?" His eyes were hard and cold.

"Nothing." I lied to keep from looking like the fool that I was, and then I added my own version of the veiled compliment, "You're not looking too bad yourself." First off, my jab didn't sound nearly as insulting and antagonizing as his; it actually sounded like I meant it. *I have got to bone up on the bitterness,* I thought. Really, I should have gotten the award for understatement of the year. He always did look good, and that day was no different. He was draped in a navy, three-button suit and white shirt. From the looks of it, he must have been best friends with Hugo Boss. The suit clung to his body. Not too tight but close enough to show off his solid build. I had to do a pussy check to make sure my girl wasn't reacting. She bounced around a little bit, but the panties were still dry; she hadn't betrayed me yet. I was still holding it together. *Thank God.* I squared my shoulders and tilted my head in an effort to appear collected.

He smirked at me. "You're not leaving, are you?"

"No. Actually, I was just going to the ladies' room before the session started."

"Good. I wouldn't want you to leave because you're uncomfortable around me. That would be a terrible waste of the $350 you paid to be here."

"Thanks for the concern, but I have no reason to be uncomfortable around you. Your presence here doesn't faze me in the least." I lied but continued the game he started. He wanted to upset me. It was working, but I refused to let him see that, so I added, "Furthermore, I'm here to learn, not worry about you."

"I apologize. You just seemed to be surprised when you saw me."

"Well, yes, that's true. But weren't you surprised when you saw me? Besides, I didn't see your name on the website when I registered."

He shrugged. "Last minute addition. The original speaker cancelled three days ago. I hope that's not a problem for you?"

"Of course not." I lied again. *Can he see my nose growing?* I decided to leave before I started writing my own version of Pinocchio. "People are starting to come

5

in. I'd better hurry up and go to the ladies' room so I won't be late. You go on ahead. I'll be there in a few minutes."

"Okay. See you in a few." He went into the conference room, and instead of leaving like I originally planned, I headed for the restroom. I used this as an opportunity to check my appearance. No one wants to get caught by their ex-boyfriend not looking their absolute best. It gives the appearance that you couldn't make it without them. Tell the truth, whenever you see an old flame who looks like he has no job and was thrown out with yesterday's garbage, you're secretly delighted. Relishing a brief moment of self-satisfaction, thinking, *Ah ha! That's what his dumb ass gets. I knew he couldn't keep his shit together!* I clearly didn't want to give Sampson the impression that I was suffering without him.

I walked into the restroom, confident that I could allay any fears of physical inadequacy. However, when I looked in the mirror, I was horrified. It was the middle of November, so I was dressed in a pair of black wool slacks, a matching sweater, and a waist-length, black leather jacket. I was always pleased with my image in black. It made me look sexy, that wasn't the problem. The ensemble fit nicely. I loved to workout, especially riding my bike; so, I was pleased with the athletic, size-ten physique I managed to maintain. That wasn't the problem. My hair had recently been streaked with highlights and fashioned with a new pixie cut. It glistened with the care my stylist lovingly gave it. That wasn't the problem. My make-up was flawless. Not too much. Powder, eyeshadow, eyeliner, mascara, lip-gloss. Just enough to give that "fresh face" look. That wasn't the problem. I looked up and to my chagrin…I was wearing my glasses! My many nights as a child spent reading by the closet light when I should have been in bed, along with the years of computer use in college, and the detailed reading of case files as a therapist had caused undue stress on my sensitive eyes. On my last trip to the optometrist a few months ago, the diagnosis was that if I didn't want to go blind by the time I was sixty then I needed a pair of reading glasses. It wasn't that severe, but I still needed the glasses. I could have gone with contacts; however, I knew I would either lose them or blind myself trying to put them on. So, I chose the glasses thinking I would only pull them out when necessary, as was the case this morning. I hastily put them on to read my registration information. Stunned by the revelation that Sampson was my teacher, I forgot to take them off. I was pissed, I hated those damned glasses. Only a few people even knew I wore them—my secretary who liked to barge in my office unannounced and my two best friends, Shellie and Lisa. They were my girls, and I knew they didn't give a damn about me in a pair of bifocals. So, whenever I was relaxing at home while reading a book and they happened to stop by, I never worried about taking them off.

Maybe that's why he was staring at me so hard. He wasn't mad. He just wasn't used to me in those damn glasses. Who was I kidding? He was livid. Although he cheated on me and not the other way around, Sam was definitely pissed. Hell, he probably didn't even notice the glasses.

I sighed, pulled off the Ralph Lauren tortoise shell frames and threw them in my purse. I drew another deep breath to pull myself together. I had to hide my exasperation and nervousness.

Satisfied that I looked good and was now the picture of indifference, I started toward the workshop, making a mental note to sit in the middle of the conference room. Sitting in the back would seem too obvious that I was trying to avoid him, and sitting in the front would be too close for comfort. Unfortunately, I had lingered a moment too long in the ladies' room. The conference room was packed, and I had to sit in the first seat in the front row...directly in front of the speaker. *Damn!*

Maybe it wouldn't be so bad.

Sam pulled his phone out of his pocket, flipped it open as if he was checking the time, slammed it shut, and then said snarkily, "Come on in, Ms. Davenport. It's not too late for you to join us. We're just getting started."

This wasn't going to be bad. It was going to be awful. *This Negro had the nerve to call me out for being late!*

I sat down, pulled my notepad out from my briefcase, crossed my legs, and prepared to take notes. I refused to put my glasses back on. I'd just have to do the best that I could. I promised myself to schedule an appointment to get contacts or Lasik eye surgery as soon as possible.

I said a silent prayer, determined to concentrate on the information provided and make the session go by as quickly as possible. I wasn't that successful. I spent the next two hours daydreaming and reminiscing about me and Sam making love. I kept licking my lips, crossing and uncrossing my legs. The pussy checks weren't working anymore. As a matter of fact, I stopped doing them. I was doing all that I could to pretend that I was actually paying attention to the workshop. I just prayed that it would be over soon.

Chapter 2
Sampson
Get Out

I never thought I would have said this, but my brother and my friends were getting on my fucking nerves. I was trying to be a good friend by letting them stay with me, but my patience was running short. Tamika had put Jawaan out. I didn't know why, and I didn't want to know. Malik was strapped for cash after he lost his job as a police officer, so he needed a place to stay. And Solomon, my younger brother, was hiding out from some stalker that had been harassing him at church and was looking for a new place to live. *What the hell?*

My condo was pretty big but not big enough for all of them. Solomon slept in the guest bedroom. My third bedroom served as my office, so Malik slept on the couch in the living room, and Jawaan slept on an inflatable bed right next to him. They were nasty as shit. It was unbelievable, but every day, I thought to myself, "If I have to tell one more grown-ass man to pick his fucking socks up off the damned floor, I think I'm going to shoot myself!" And the food! Oh my God, the food bill was enormous. You'd think they would offer to pick something up from the store? Hell no!

They had been staying with me for over a month, but I was ready for their asses to go. I marched in from work one day with that very thought on my mind. I was going in firm. Resolved in my mission to be rid of the nuisance that I called family. My speech would be quick and to the point. "All you niggas get out of my fucking

11

house!" Especially if I had to pick up Malik's nasty, dirty, musty socks again…I was going to kick his ass *and* then tell him to get the fuck out.

I would not be moved. I was ready. No sob stories. No pleading. I wasn't trying to hear, "Man, just give me a few more days. Tamika just needs to cool off, but if I go home now her crazy ass will just start trying to fight all over again." Yeah, you guessed it, that's how Jawaan had managed to maneuver his way into my home. A few days had turned into a few weeks, which had turned into a few months. They all had legitimate reasons for needing a place to stay, and I didn't mind because, truthfully, other than my Aunt Tootie and Uncle Junior, they were the only family I had.

Aunt Tootie and Uncle Junior took me and Solomon in when I was five. My aunt caught Sylvia, her sister, and my mother, in the bathroom shooting dope. They had a big argument. Aunt Tootie put my mother out, and Solomon and I never saw her again.

Malik Wallace and Jawaan Turner, on the other hand, had been my best friends since the fifth grade. We've done everything together. From getting trims at the barbershop with Mr. Turner, a tradition we continued to honor, to chasing women together *and* getting over them together. We fuss, fight, laugh, and love together, and I'd give my right arm for either one of them. I just don't want to live with them! I can't get grown men to understand the meaning of common courtesy. You would think that things like that were pretty basic. They're not.

Solomon…Lord, I love him to death, but he does shit like check my voicemail. Prime example. I came in from work one day, and he said, "You had a message from Naomi."

"Oh, yeah," I said. I raised my eyes in anticipation. My mouth started watering. I was excited. Naomi was a real freak and would do just about anything without much provocation. "You talked to her? What did she say?"

"No, I didn't talk to her. I checked your messages. She said to call her."

Just like that my mouth went dry. I cherished my privacy, and Solomon had crossed the line.

"Dude, that shit ain't even cool. You have your own voicemail on the phone. Why are you checking my messages?"

"It was an accident."

"Accident my ass! Stay out of my business, man."

"Look, I was just looking out for you. I thought Jaslyn might have called, and I didn't want you to miss the message."

Jaslyn was my ex-girlfriend, and it's a long story that I'll get into later. It didn't end well. Let's just say that whenever Solomon brought her name up, and he always brought her name up, I would get an immediate migraine. I should have been over her, yet I was still seething. I never appreciated him mentioning her name, but he always did.

"I haven't seen or heard from Jaslyn in...in...in ages!" This wasn't exactly the truth. A month ago, I taught a class at a business conference, and she was one of my students. Although we were cordial to one another, we didn't leave the class feeling all warm and fuzzy, either. As a matter of fact, she was so cold towards me I knew there was no way for us to get back together.

*Not that I was thinking of getting with her again anyway...*I shook that thought out of my mind and resumed my assault on my brother. "Why would she, all of a sudden, start leaving messages now? And if she did, don't you think I can check my own messages and return her call if I wanted to?"

"The "*wanted to*"is the problem?"

"Don't you have anything better to do? You don't know what the fuck you're talking about and stay out of my fucking business!" No one but Malik knew why we broke up, he would never say anything, and that's the way I wanted it to stay. To tell the truth, people being in my business was part of the reason we broke up. He didn't need to know that, and he wasn't going to know that. But he kept right at it.

"Sam, Jazz was the perfect..."

"Shut the fuck up, Solomon! Just shut up and leave me alone!" I was so mad I was literally spitting. I couldn't let him finish. I didn't want to hear any more about her being the perfect woman for me. I knew that already. The problem was getting her to understand that, and thinking about it only made me angry. I hated talking to my brother like that, but he didn't know what he was saying. I walked to my bedroom, and before I slammed the door, I yelled, "And stop checking my fucking messages!"

We'd been going at it like that every day for the last two weeks. Him trying to tell me how to live my life and me cursing him out.

But not anymore. I was about to end all that with a 400-year-old message that was championed by the white man, "Niggas, go home!"

14

I pulled up to the condo ready to do battle. I stepped out of my truck determined and focused. As I walked the ten or so yards that stretched from my parking space to the steps of my front door, I felt a sense of relief wash over me. I would have my house to myself again. There would be peace in the valley. No more listening to Jawaan argue with Tamika over the phone at six a.m. in the morning. No more listening to Solomon's gospel music blaring through the front door whenever I came home from work. And no more knocks on the door during all hours of the day from Malik's booty call partners who were dying to be serviced and willing to drive thirty damn minutes to my condo in Las Colinas to come get him.

I was exhausted. Sleep was no longer a viable option for me, and I couldn't keep up the pace. So, as soon as they packed their shit and got out, I was going to take a much-needed nap.

My evictions would be the first thing on my agenda when I entered the house. In anticipation, I had a little more spring in my walk as I bounded up the steps and put my key in the lock. As I entered, the phone was ringing. I wrestled with the keys to open the door and raced to catch it. *Heaven forbid if someone had to leave a message.* I picked up the receiver.

"Yeah!"

I heard a gruff and disheveled voice answer. "Sampson, this is Junior." Lord, it was my Uncle Junior. I didn't have time for his drunk ass today, and he sounded like he was really out of it. For a while, my Aunt Tootie and Solomon had managed to convince him to stop drinking. It sounded like he had started again. *I told them that his sobriety wasn't going to last long.* Although Junior

Wilson helped raise me, he was one of my least favorite people. Married to my aunt, Uncle Junior would never be a candidate for husband-of-the-year. To say he used Aunt Tootie as a punching bag is an understatement. For the first thirty years of their marriage, not only did he beat on her, but he cheated on her and fathered a small Zulu nation. And he didn't stop when he got shot and had to wear a prosthetic leg. As Malik put it, he just became a "pimp with a limp." He only stopped his drinking when Solomon became a preacher a few years ago. Solomon's first act as a minister was to try and save his family. Unlike us, Junior never came to church with us when we had to tag along with Aunt Tootie. It was my firm belief that Jesus didn't know that Junior Wilson ever existed. However, after a couple of talks with Solomon, Uncle Junior started on his path to being a better man, which included ending his love affair with the bottle. He even confessed to me once that he drank because he was a coward. He needed the alcohol to do and say the things he didn't have the nerve to do otherwise. I wanted to believe him, and in some way, I did forgive him for how he treated Aunt Tootie, but I guess throughout the years I had seen too much. In my mind, Uncle Junior was always going to be a baby-making, wife-beating, no-working, lying, sneaky, alcoholic. *What the hell did he want?*

"What do you need, Uncle Junior? Do you need a place to stay too? Did Aunt Tootie finally come to her senses and put you out?" I knew I was being rude, but I was frustrated because I thought he had started drinking again. I also knew that if he were drunk, he would never remember this conversation. I wish that had been the case.

"Sam, Camille is dead."

"What? Stop playing'. You need to stop drinking. I knew that shit wasn't going to last."

"I'm not drunk, Sam. Camille...your Aunt Tootie is dead. She...she had a stroke." He started to sob. I knew he was telling the truth. Everyone who knew and loved her called her Aunt Tootie, but he never did. He never used Tootie because in his hateful, drunken days he wanted to aggravate her and us, so he called her by the birth name that no one ever used. Calling her Tootie was the only way to get me to understand the severity of the situation–my aunt, the only mother I had ever known, was dead.

My evictions would have to wait until tomorrow.

Chapter 3
Jaslyn
A Heavy Heart

When Tamika called me and told me about Aunt Tootie dying, I didn't know what to do or think. Despite our last encounter at the conference, I felt sad for Sam, yet I also felt powerless in how I could comfort him. I had never lost anyone that close to me before, so I couldn't fathom the magnitude of his pain. I knew he was hurting, and I wanted to be there for him. At the same time, I knew I was the last person he wanted to see. I decided to go to the funeral anyway to pay my respects and hope for the best.

The funeral was scheduled for a Tuesday afternoon at the family church in Stop Six. The church was crowded by the time I got there at 11:30, even though services were set to begin at noon. I signed the guest book, left a card on the stand, and then sat at the very back about fifty pews from the family.

I could see Sampson, and right next to him sat Uncle Junior on the right and Solomon on his left. I saw a few more faces that resembled Sam and Solomon. A few men, but mostly female. I wondered if any of them belonged to their mother—if she had come out of hiding and stayed sober long enough to attend her sister's funeral. I was also wondering if she *was* there, how was Sampson dealing with her reappearance? That would probably break him in two, to lose the mother that raised you and find the mother that left you all in the same week.

I opened the obituary and stared at the woman who single-handedly destroyed the best relationship I'd

19

ever had. I wanted to blame her for all of my problems with Sam, but truthfully, I couldn't put all the responsibility on her. I couldn't fault Alicia either. I really had to blame myself for everything that had gone wrong in our relationship. I'd had my heart broken so many times in the past that I couldn't trust any man, not even a good one like Sam. Maybe if I had dealt with my trust issues before getting into that relationship then Aunt Tootie and Alicia would not have been able to come between us, but it was hard to trust him considering our circumstances.

I looked around at the blue décor of the church. The pews were decorated in blue cloth and oak trimming. An oak cross was hanging from the ceiling at the center of the choir stand. Three stairs led up to the pulpit, which was an oak podium that had blue cloth draped on the top and sat on top of blue carpet.

Once the funeral began, I was surrounded by a sea of whimpering faces. Soft, quiet tears rolling slowly down the sides of each cheek, mixing in with Fashion Fair, black mascara, or aftershave lotion, and haunting guffaws of loved ones who realized that this friend would never return. Remarks from family and friends took nearly an hour because everyone wanted to use this as an opportunity to explain every single detail of their acquaintance with Tootie: how they laughed on the front porch together, how she used to shoot pool back in the sixties, how she loved red fingernail polish, or how she would only cut her hair on a full moon because it would make your hair grow. The comments ran the gamut, but some really were meaningful and made me regret the fact that I never really got to know her.

After forty-five minutes of speeches and resolutions, Sampson approached the podium which stood to the right of the pulpit and next to the piano. He wasn't crying, but his eyes were red and swollen. It was difficult for him to talk; his voice sounded shaky and gruff, but there was a resolve in his face that let me know he could get through what he had to say. He pulled the mic up to his mouth and bent his head slightly and said, "Hello, everyone." The congregation responded in unison, "Hello."

"Uncle Junior, Solomon, and I want to thank all of you for your kind words and sentiments. We truly appreciate you coming today to join us in this homegoing celebration for my aunt. Your presence and support have truly been a blessing to our family. Unfortunately, we have to end remarks at this time so the pastor can proceed with the eulogy." The twenty people who were still standing in line reluctantly took their seats, but Sam continued to speak. "If you'll forgive me, I want to close with a few comments of my own. I'm going to say a few things and then take my seat.

"As you all know, Camille Wilson raised me and my brother after our mother deserted us years ago. So, although we call her "Aunt" Tootie, she was most certainly our mother. If not in blood, then definitely in spirit. In my mind, that guarantees her a spot in Heaven. If not for the fact that she raised us, then she certainly deserves a place next to Saint Peter for the things she taught us. Like, 'Love the Lord with all your heart.'" A few amens went up throughout the sanctuary. "She taught us that being a black man was a privilege and an honor, and that our strength was a blessing not a curse and to never let anyone convince us otherwise." The

21

applause from the crowd grew louder as more people began to clap and shout in support of Sam's comments. "Aunt Tootie showed us that love was a sacrifice as she gave up so much to raise us when our own mother couldn't, or wouldn't, do it." By this time, the entire congregation was on its feet in praise of the woman they knew and admired.

Sam waited for the group to quiet down then added, "I'm saying all of this to share how much she meant to me and my brother. Aunt Tootie was my rock. Lord knows she wasn't perfect. She'd cuss you out in a minute and gossip was her middle name." The members of the congregation laughed in agreement. "All you had to do was ask. If she didn't know, she'd find out. She'd just call her best friend, Miss Bertha, and between the two of them, they'd get the story straight."

In the midst of the laughter, a loud wail went up inside the church. "*Tootie! Lawd have mercy!*" I could only imagine that it must have been Bertha who had been touched by the memory of conspiring with her best friend. I didn't even want to think about losing one of my sisters, Shellie, or Lisa.

"No, Aunt Tootie was far from perfect, but she was all we had, and I will truly miss her. I'll miss her laughter when she was happy, her tears when she was sad, her scolding when she was mad, and her hugs when she was proud. She meant everything to me. My heart is heavy, and I don't know what I'll do without her." There was not a dry eye in the church, especially mine. In the middle of his speech, he began to weep, and when he cried, I cried. Finally, he lowered his head as he walked back to his seat, and I felt the barrier that I had constructed around my heart begin to crumble. I was in love with him all over again. *Aw, hell! Did I ever stop was the question?*

I wanted so much to comfort him, but I didn't know how to go to him. To repair the irreparable. Sam wasn't the only one with a heavy heart, but I had a totally different reason. So, I left before the funeral was over, before I gave myself the chance to admit that maybe I had made a mistake a year ago.

Chapter 4
Sampson
Making Things Right

"Hold Up, Sam!"

"What's up, man?"

"Before you go out there, there's something I need to tell you."

I'd gone into the bathroom to relieve some pressure from the beer I'd been downing all evening. Aunt Tootie had been dead for two weeks, and I was trying my best to keep it together. At best, I felt...fragmented. That's the only way to put it. Nothing was right in my life. I refused to give in to the notion that I might be depressed, so I chose to refer to my current state of conditions as "fragmented." Things weren't in place like they should be, but in time, they would, *should*, come together. Now just wasn't that time. I had no idea when that time would be; therefore, I was drinking a lot more than normal to ignore the fact that my life was out of order. *Stupid...I know.*

It was New Year's Eve, and my boys volunteered to take me out for drinks to try and get my mind off everything. It wasn't working. I was becoming a bit too liberal with the alcohol, but it was what I needed at the time. Nothing was working to numb the pain I was feeling, and I was about to tell Malik and Jawaan that I was ready to leave. I'd stepped out of the restroom back into the overcrowded club that was dimly lit. The noise was giving me a headache. The cacophony of patrons attempting to cut loose, celebrate, and fill the empty spaces that had built up in their lives throughout the year compounded an ever-increasing migraine. I *really* was just ready to leave because I had no longer had anything to celebrate. However, Jawaan seemed determined to tell me what was on his mind.

"What is it?"

"Look, I had no idea she was going to be here, so don't be mad at me."

"What are you talking about?"

He was stalling, and I couldn't figure out why. But as soon as he opened his mouth to tell me what was going on, Jaslyn walked around the corner from the main dance floor and was about to enter the ladies' restroom. She was just as stunned as I was. She hesitated in her approach. Behind her stood "the crew"— Shellie and Lisa. Looks of curiosity passed between them to assess the situation. An arched eyebrow. The shrug of a shoulder. *Were they trying to avoid the war in Iraq? Or was this going to be more like Armageddon?* Jaslyn continued her approach until she stopped in front of me. No words passed between us. Only emotions. Surprise, disappointment, sadness, pain, anger…and attraction. And for a brief moment, anticipation. All those things were communicated between us in a silent moment. Finally, she said "Sampson," and nodded in my direction. "How are you?"

"Fine." I said. Then I settled back into my solitary emotion of hatred. I was ready to move on.

I tried to move past her when she said, "I heard about your Aunt Tootie. I was really sorry to hear that she had passed away."

I stopped walking and turned to face her. I wanted to say, "*Don't do that. Don't be nice to me. I enjoy hating you, and I want it to stay that way."* But instead, I said, "Thanks."

I moved toward the bar and ordered a shot of Jack Daniels. The beers were no longer doing it for me. I wanted to be indifferent, yet my anger kept manifesting itself in immature thoughts and questions: *How dare she express any sort of sympathy for me? And why was she here tonight? Of all nights?* I wanted to go, but now, I couldn't leave. My anger was the fuel that ignited my desire to stay. I wasn't about to have her think that I was leaving because of her. So instead, I perfected the faзade of a veritable player. You know, the "Man, fuck that girl" image. Drink in my hand. Swagger in my step. Lust in my look.

Instead of sitting at the bar blubbering over my drinks, I tried to dance with every fine–ass woman in my vicinity. Most were women that I had turned down earlier in the evening. After each rejection, they had suggested, not too subtly, that I was a stuck-up bastard, but I didn't give a shit. After a free drink or two, they didn't seem to mind the fact that I was an asshole. I had to show her that I had moved on. After dancing for a solid hour, it was definitely time to refill my glass. I ordered another shot of Jack. Downed it, and then ordered another. I was feeling good. The liquor was starting to warm my blood, and my body felt loose and languid. I wasn't drunk, but I was nice. I downed my third shot, looked up and realized that Malik, Jawaan, Shellie, Lisa, and you guessed it, Jaslyn, surrounded me. There was no avoiding her. We were at a club with over two thousand people spread out over three floors, and there was no getting around this woman. Before I knew it, our friends had made their way back to the dance floor with various partners, and we were at the bar alone. As I sat there, I thought about how good it was being with her, in her presence, and her bed. She was a generous lover, and it had been a while since I had slept with someone so giving. I felt the muscle between my legs begin to grow, and my pants tightened against the pressure. For a moment, I didn't care about the history between us. The reasons we were no longer together. My nature was talking to me and telling me that it was time to revisit the wealth of her body, so I acted on instinct and, at least for the evening, put all the drama between us aside.

"You wanna dance?" I asked, my speech slightly slurred.

"Do you really think that would be a good idea?"

"You scared?"

"Of what?"

"Me."

"No!" she shouted just a little too loudly.

"Well, then what's wrong with us dancing?"

"We haven't spoken to each other in over a year."

"Really, it's only been a couple of months. You remember the conference in November, don't you?" I knew that things were icy between us the last time we saw each other, but I was willing to put all of that behind us for the sake of my penis. "Besides, what's that have to do with anything?"

"Nothing. I'm just saying."

My aggravation was starting to show, "Saying what? Look, do you wanna dance or not?"

"Fine."

"Okay, fine." But neither one of us moved.

"What are you waiting on?" she finally asked.

"I'm waiting on you."

She pushed her seat back, and I stood to help her. I looked at her dress—the deep cut at the cleavage to accentuate her breasts and collar bone, the fitted skirt hugged the curve of her thighs—and that muscle between my legs got just a little bit harder.

On the dance floor, we remembered that we never had a problem with rhythm or synchronization. We danced to a reggae song reminiscent of the sensual tunes of The Wailers. It did nothing to relieve the tension or my sexual frustration. I pulled her into my arms. I wanted to feel her and smell her. And without a thought, I kissed the top of her head just like I used to. I heard her sigh, and I knew she was feeling the same way I was feeling.

I wanted to fuck her, but Jaslyn wasn't that kind of girl. *What could I do? What could I say to convince her to be that type of girl?* Probably nothing…but I had to try.

"I've missed you, Jazz." I didn't want to admit it, but it was true.

"I've missed you, too, Sam." And although she probably didn't want to admit it, I knew that it was the truth for her, too.

I pulled her closer to me as the music drew us closer emotionally and reminded us of a time when we knew where we stood with one another.

"Let's go someplace and talk."

"Where?"

"My place, your place. It doesn't matter. Wherever you feel comfortable."

"What are we going to talk about?"

"Us."

"Why?"

"Because it's time. Look, don't play with me. We need to do this, and you know it."

"Humph! I love your persuasiveness. Need I remind you that I'm not particularly fond of mind games? I'm sure you probably want to do more than talk. And if you do, then just say so, but don't lie to me."

I thought about her statement for a moment. Jaslyn had a bad habit of putting up this brazen front like nothing bothered or hurt her. I *could* take a chance and tell her the truth, but frankly, whether she wanted to admit it or not, she didn't want to hear that I just wanted to have sex. If I admitted it, her defenses would go up like a barbed wire fence at a Texas prison, and we would be back at square one. Again, I thought about who she was and what it would take to get her in my bed. I *could* lie and insist that I just wanted to talk. Didn't work the first time, chances were, it wasn't going to work a second. Instead, I kissed her. I let my tongue linger on her lips, and when she tried to protest, I let my mouth apply soft pressure. I pulled her closer, almost lifting her off the ground as my tongue plunged deeply and passionately with hers. She knew right then what I wanted from her, and the decision would be hers to accept or reject. But instead of demanding that she answer me immediately, I decided to wait. I wanted her mind to marinate over what we used to do.

I pulled away from her and whispered in her ear, "Don't say no. Not right away. Think about it."

"Sure," she mumbled.

I walked to the bar and ordered another drink. The liquid mimicked the heat and warmth of my body. It felt good, so I ordered another. When I dispensed with that drink, I had the dreadlocked bartender give me a cold beer because the dance floor was hot. He handed me the drink and asked, "Are you alright?"

"What the hell are you talking about?"

"Man, that's like your fifth shot of Jack, and you've been downing beers all night. You sure you ain't drunk?"

"Hell, naw!!"

"Whatever. I *will* take your keys, so you better slow down."

"I'm payin'. That's all you need to worry about, a'ight?" I just wanted his buffed-up, Bob Marley lookin' ass to leave me alone. He was huge, and with a head full of dreadlocks, he looked like a Rastafarian on steroids. I was talking shit, but I knew that he meant every word.

"You heard what I said."

"Yeah, whatever."

I grabbed the beer and turned around to go dance. My head started spinning, and I tripped. I didn't fall, but I had to regain my composure. When I steadied myself, I wanted to give the Rasta bartender my drink back. It had to be the alcohol because I couldn't believe my eyes. It was like dĕja vu in reverse! I was staring at Solomon kissing Jaslyn. They kissed and then she handed him a slip of paper. I wasn't crazy. I'd been in the game long enough to know what was on that paper. And unlike the shit she accused me of, this shit was real.

I couldn't take it. I was about to kick somebody's ass.

I strolled up to them. "What the hell is going on?"

"Sam...," Jaslyn was the first to speak.

"You tryin' to fuck my brother?"

"What?" they both asked.

"I should have known your ass would do something like this," I pointed to Jaslyn. "Here I was trying to hook you up and..."

She cut me off. "Hold on...hook me up? You weren't doing me any favors. You were trying to hook yourself up!"

"What? You think I just been sittin' around waitin' on your ass? My dick is raw from all the pussy I've been gettin'!"

Malik tried to intervene. "Sam, that's enough. You are going too far, man! You're starting to sound like me. And trust me, the world does not need two of us."

Jaslyn pulled herself together long enough for her to reply. "Naw, that's alright, Malik, don't stop him. He's trying to convince himself, not me. You know what, Sam? I don't care how much pussy you've been getting or will ever get, no one or nothing will ever be as good as me! You need to get it together and stop talking crazy."

"Talking crazy? Who's talking crazy? I'm telling the truth, and I'm going to do more than that if you keep fucking around with my brother!"

"What the hell are you talking about?" she said, throwing her hands in the air.

"You know what I'm talkin' about. It doesn't shock me that you'd do me like that, but I am surprised at you, Solomon!" I spat. "Tryin' to fuck my girl? What? You can't find decent pussy in the church house, so you have to run up behind your brother?"

Solomon finally spoke. "Shut up, Sampson! Preacher or not, I'm not gone let you keep disrespecting me. Nigga, I'm from Stop Six just like you!"

"Now you finally have something to say. It's cool. I'm finished. I just have one last warning. Be careful. If you didn't already know, Jaslyn's known for breakin' a nigga off and leavin' him hangin' like a chump with his dick in his hands. Oh, and just so you know…before you got here, she was dancin' all up in my face, so think twice before you hit that!"

"He ain't hitting shit!" Jaslyn screamed before Solomon could respond. "And you need to shut up before you make an even bigger ass of yourself…you know what? Bye! I'm takin' my ass home. Shellie, Lisa, I'll holla at y'all tomorrow."

Lisa started grabbing her belongings, too. "Hold up, Jaslyn. We'll go with you. You don't need to walk out of here by yourself."

"No, that's alright. I want to be alone right now, and I have my pepper spray if anyone tries to bother me. I'll call you guys later on." She grabbed her purse and keys and walked outside.

Everyone sat in silence staring at me, especially Solomon, who had focused on me with a mixture of pity and anger. He was starting to get on my nerves.

"What, nigga? What the fuck you lookin' at?"

"You tell me because it damn sure ain't my brother."

The waitress passed by, and I ordered another drink.

"Boy what's wrong with you? Were you smoking crack when you went in that bathroom?"

"Whatever." My vocabulary was stunted. Shame was beginning to engulf me because I couldn't formulate a whole sentence.

"You can blow me off if you want to, but you know, as well as the rest of the damn club, that the scene you just caused was entirely uncalled for."

"Solomon, you can say what you want, but I'll be damned if I let my girl try to talk to my brother and not say anything about it."

"Do you know what type of idiot you sound like right now? Hit on me? Why on earth would Jaslyn be hitting on me? And where did you get such a ridiculous idea?"

"She's probably trying to make me jealous. I saw her kissing all on you and giving you her phone number. That's where I got the idea from."

"Jealous? You are so stubborn...and stupid! She was hugging me because we're friends. Remember I have known her longer than you. She wasn't giving me her number so we could hook up; she wanted me to call her because she admitted to making a mistake when she broke things off with you. She wanted to talk about how she could make things right with you, dumb ass. Even though I still don't know why she broke up with you, although after tonight I can only imagine, I, like a dummy, was willing to help her. Lord forgive me...got me all up in a club cursing. Shit!"

I ran my tongue across my teeth and mumbled an undignified, "Humph!!"

The waitress came back with my drink. I threw it back quickly and let the warm liquid slide down my throat.

Although Jaslyn and I didn't meet until Jawaan and Tamika's wedding, she and Solomon were classmates at the University of Texas at Arlington. After the wedding, we became friends and started dating. In the beginning, we were both trying to avoid being in a serious relationship because we'd been hurt by other people, but our attraction was so strong we couldn't ignore how we felt about each other. Despite my fears, I fell in love with Jaslyn. Madly. I know that's not very *playa* of me to admit, but it's true. I loved that damn girl with all my heart, and I knew she felt the same way about me.

I really felt like we could make our relationship last, but Jaslyn's fear of being hurt really prevented her from ever fully trusting me. Once we became involved, one of my old girlfriends, Alicia Matthews, started coincidentally calling and coming over. I explained to Jazz that it was nothing. That I dated the girl in the eighth grade. *The eighth fuckin' grade!* And, I hadn't talked to her since she stood me up at my eighth-grade prom. She was a bridesmaid in Tamika and Jawaan's wedding, they had been friends and had maintained their friendship throughout the years. But, I hadn't seen her or talked to her until the night of the wedding. Jaslyn said she believed me, but it didn't help that my Aunt Tootie, who didn't care for Jaslyn, was giving Alicia information about me and my advertising firm, Tate & Associates. Let's just say Alicia saw a cash cow and tried to milk it. I wasn't having it. You'd never know that the way she called and constantly dropped by my house unannounced. She even managed to leave a pair of underwear for Jaslyn to find.

Jazz broke up with me after she came over to my condo, and Alicia was there trying to seduce me. It was nothing. We were outside; the girl threw herself at me, and I turned her down. In the middle of it all, Jaslyn pulled up, and to her, it looked like something. I tried to explain, to tell her things were not the way they seemed, but she wasn't listening. She was too hurt to even consider any other explanation besides the one her eyes were telling her, which said that I was sleeping with my ex-girlfriend. I was devastated, and I haven't been the same since.

Since it seemed I was clearly committing the same crime as she did, I tried to save my pride by adding, "That explains the hug and the phone number, but what about the kiss?"

"Kiss her? It was a kiss on the cheek, jeez! In your alcohol–induced stupor, there's no telling what you *thought* you saw," he emphasized as he pointed at my drink.

I looked around at everyone, and they were all staring at me with disgust and contempt. Malik was the first to speak.

"Man, you fucked that shit up! Really, I wish you two would just get over yourselves. You act like you're the only two people in the world who've ever been hurt before. You and Jaslyn are just alike. You need to stop licking your wounds and talk to each other instead of constantly assuming shit!"

This time Jawaan, who was usually my salvation, didn't even come to my rescue. He nodded his head along with everyone else and said, "Yep. Fucked that up real good."

I knew they were right, but in my mind, the situation was already in shambles. I finally found the nerve to defend myself.

"You can't fuck up something that never had a chance in the first place. She fucked up a year ago. I just closed the deal. And you know what? At least now she knows what the shit she did to me feels like."

As usual Malik, the perpetual clown, always found a way to make us laugh. "I swear you must be the biggest fool on earth. Sam, get therapy!" He didn't know how close he came to the truth.

I didn't know about therapy, but I needed something. And, at that moment, alcohol was all I had. I went to the bar and ordered another drink. As I waited for my liquid therapist, one thought passed through my mind: *Blessed is the heart of the commitment-phobic for they shall live a life of solitude.* And I knew I was one of them. My pain had been isolating me, and the only time I felt any semblance of peace within the last month was the five minutes I had danced with her. How was I going to turn this mess around? I accused the girl of being a slut, sleeping with my brother, and I insulted her in front of her friends. What was I doing? I was killing myself. Killing my heart. But I wasn't ready to die. Malik was right, we needed to talk. I needed to apologize, and I didn't want to wait another night. But before I could leave, they started the countdown to 2005. I looked around at my friends and throngs of people looking forward to another opportunity, another year, to get it right.

"Five...Four...three...two...ONE! Happy New Year!!" Streamers, balloons, and hats rained down in celebration as the crowd downed glasses of champagne. I grabbed a glass from a waitress walking in front of me because I needed a few more drinks in my system to get up the nerve to try to make things right with Jaslyn.

Chapter 5
Jaslyn
Butter on Burnt Toast

When we danced together that night, I knew perfectly well what Sam was doing. He may have wanted to talk, but that wasn't what was on his mind that night. I knew that Sampson wanted to have sex with me that evening, but I couldn't stop myself from enjoying his nearness. Instead, I lied to myself, creating an illusion that I could separate sex from love. *It's just physical,* I said. With another man, maybe. But with Sampson, those two things, for me, would be two sides of the same coin. I was giving him my sex *because* I loved him. Yet, I would take the risk. I would allow myself to sleep with a man who had placed me in the same category as Cruella Deville. To him, I was the epitome of pure evil. But I didn't care. I was willing to do it because I knew I had what he needed. I chose to give in to him in an effort to correct the grievous error I had committed when I ended our relationship. So, I hedged my bet. I would use my body as a bargaining chip for forgiveness and hope the gamble paid off. However, when he started tripping and accused me of trying to hook up with Solomon, all bets were off...until he showed up at my house.

When Sampson arrived at my house at three in the morning, I shouldn't have answered the door. But I wanted to.

Love is a strange phenomenon. I've learned that love and hate are just different degrees of one emotion; hate is love intensified. In one moment, we love someone; but in the next, we hate them. Under the right circumstances, hate can easily return to love. I was hurting because of the hate I saw in Sampson's eyes when he accused me of trying to have sex with his brother. The accusation alone would have never bothered me. I've been accused of much worse, and sometimes, I'm actually guilty. But it was the hate smoldering behind those sad, brown eyes that bothered me. I knew, at one point, Sam loved me; now, he hated me, and I had no one to blame but myself. I was hoping that on the way over his hatred for me had somehow returned to love. That's why I opened the door. I was ready for him to love me again.

But that is not what I got.

When Sampson showed up at my house, he was a drunk, incoherent mess! So why on earth did I open the door, you ask? Again, because I wanted to.

When he came into the living room, he started rambling on, apologizing with talk of getting back together. At one point, I even thought I heard him say that our relationship was a good thing.

"Jazz...," he began. "I'm...so...sorry." He leaned over and patted the side of my face.

"I know, Sam. It's okay. I forgive you, now go home."

"No...you don't understand...how...sorry...I am. I was wrong for saying you fucked Sol..." He stopped, slurring his speech and trying to get his thoughts together. He shook his head as he said, "Damn wrong..."

"Okay, Sam." I was close to tears, and I just wanted him to leave. "I forgive you. Now, *please*, go home," I pleaded.

"I'm really sorry...for everything." He paused. Then confessed, "I love..."

I knew he didn't realize what he was saying, so I tried to cut him off. "No, Sam! Go home. You don't know what you're saying."

"I know what I'm saying, damn it! I love you. Always have, always will," he sang, the effects of the alcohol had his emotions all over the place.

My mind was telling me to send him home, but my heart heard what it wanted to. I mumbled a feeble, "Sam, please...".

"You love me, too...don't you, Jazz?" His glossy eyes gazed into mine looking for an answer that he already knew—I still loved him, but I was too scared to be with him.

And then, it happened. He kissed me. He leaned in, placed both of his hands along the sides of my face, and kissed me. His body fell into mine, and he wrapped me in his arms. I winced from the stench of his breath and the alcohol that reeked from his pores. I struggled to remove myself from his embrace, but the more I moved, the more he kissed me. The more he kissed me, the tighter he held me. Before I knew it, we were in my room and in my bed and his foul breath and body odor no longer seemed to matter. And I was like butter on burnt toast, no good. Because even in his drunken state, Sampson was an exceptional lover. It was quick...and guttural...and nasty...and rough. But damn, the shit was good! And I needed it. Yet, when we finished a wave of guilt and shame swept over me that made me regret each and every moan I'd muttered.

Of all the mistakes I've made sexually, that was the biggest. Sam awakened the next morning in a state of panic. He'd been sleeping soundly for a few hours, but I had tossed and turned all morning. When the sun began to rise, I decided to make breakfast. I thought a good pot of coffee and a hot meal would be just what Sampson needed to help ease the hangover I was sure he'd have. I walked into my bedroom from the hallway. I had just left the kitchen to wake him. As I entered the room, he was rubbing his eyes. He looked at me and smiled. But then, as if aware of some horrendous revelation, he sat straight up. He looked around as if he were paranoid and lost.

"Oh, shit! What did we do? Please, tell me we did not have sex last night!"

"What?" I blinked and shook my head in confusion. It looked like I was going to need a cup of coffee, too.

"We didn't have sex, did we?"

"You don't remember?"

"No. I just remember dancing with you last night, but that's all."

"You don't remember anything? Not even cursing me out and calling me a hoe in front of my friends?"

"I called you a hoe?"

"Not exactly, but you might as well have. You accused me of trying to fuck Solomon."

"This is unbelievable," he whispered. "Well, how did I end up here... naked...in *your* bed?"

"After your unwarranted accusation," I paused to let the statement hang in the air for a moment in order for him to feel the full impact of how he treated me, "I left and came home. Later on, you came over to apologize. Evidently, like me, Solomon didn't take too kindly to being accused of stabbing you in the back."

"So, after I apologized, we had sex?" he asked incredulously. *I cannot believe this Negro does not remember having sex with me. With me! Can you believe this shit?* I wanted to tell him the truth, but for some reason I just couldn't.

"No, we didn't have sex, Sam, damn!"

"Then why am I naked?"

"You passed out, alright? Your ass was so drunk you couldn't drive home, and I didn't have the heart to make you leave." At least I confessed to part of the truth. He *was* drunk and couldn't drive. After we had sex, he *did* pass out. I was only leaving out part of the truth, I reasoned. *It wouldn't hurt. Would it?* "I undressed you and put you in the bed. I slept on the sofa."

"Whew! That would have been a huge mistake."

"Look, I don't need dick that bad to take advantage of you!"

"I didn't mean it like that." He threw the covers back and slid out of bed with his early morning hard-on greeting me like a soldier saluting the flag. He started putting on his clothes, moving and talking to me at the same time. "I just meant that sleeping together right now would have made things more complicated than they are already."

"I know that!" I shouted. He stopped and looked at me. "Just go home. Last night, you insulted me, and you continue to insult me by calling me desperate today. I'm sick of this shit. Get out of my damn house!"

"You're taking this the wrong way, Jazz. And I didn't say you were desperate. I…"

"You insinuated it. Same thing. Get the hell out!" He was now entirely dressed except for his shoes. He started looking around the room to find them. I was standing next to them. I snatched them off the floor and shoved them into his chest.

He tried to appease my ever-growing temper. "Jaslyn, we need to talk. Seriously. Now's not the time or place, but we need to talk."

"Whatever! Go home!" I grabbed his elbow and led him out the bedroom and down the hallway toward the front door.

"I'll call you, okay?"

The infamous parting words of the standard booty call.

"Yeah, whatever." I said and then slammed the door in his face. *What the fuck just happened?* I got played.

Chapter 6
Sampson
What Did I Do?

"Wake yo' sorry ass up!"

Malik was standing over my bed with this smug grin spread across his face. I wanted to slap him. I looked at the glowing red light of the digital clock on my nightstand. The numbers told me that it was almost two in the afternoon. I wasn't ready to get up, though. My head hurt, and I was exhausted. Malik's presence irritated me.

"Leave me alone, fool! Can't you see that I'm sleeping?"

He laughed. His voice reverberated on my temple like a gong crashing against a cymbal. I winced as my head began to throb.

"Yeah, I can see that, but you know what? I don't give a shit! Get yo' ass up! Get out that bed and go in there and talk to your brother."

I thought about all the things Jaslyn told me that morning about my behavior at the club. I groaned, as much from the discomfort from my hangover as I did from the fact that I would eventually have to face my baby brother. I massaged my temples.

"Don't nobody give a shit about yo' head hurting'! You didn't give a shit about nobody's feelings last night, so get on up. I'm not gonna be dealin' with the two of you walkin' around here lookin' all cross-eyed at each other cuz y'all mad. You need to take care of this shit. And now!"

He was really starting to get on my nerves.

"You know what? You don't have to deal with anything. *You* can leave *my* house whenever *you* get ready."

He laughed again. Everything was a fucking joke that morning.

"You know, I should be offended, but I'm not one of those cats who cares what other motherfuckers think about him. So, get yo' black ass out the bed and go talk to your brother!" He kicked the side of the bed and walked out of the room.

I pulled the cover over my head and tried to go back to sleep. The light from the sun cut through the room and penetrated the normally protective shield of my blanket. As I attempted to close my eyes tighter to fight the piercing sunlight, I overheard Jawaan arguing in the office adjacent to my room. He and Tamika were at it again.

"Damn it, Tamika! If I had known something like this was going to happen, don't you think I would have told you?"

There was a long pause. Finally, he confessed, "Look, I didn't plan on something like this happening. It did though, and I can't change it. I wish I could, but I can't!" He paused again. "Who told you I was at a club...You know who I was with...Sampson, Malik, and Solomon...Yeah, Solomon went out with us, too...I don't know...Stop tripping, Tamika. That has nothing to do with it...Yes, I still love you. Can't we work this out? Just let me come home." He was pleading. I felt bad. I didn't know how to take it. I had never heard any of my friends sound this vulnerable before.

As I was dealing with the fact that my friends were fallible, I heard him yell, "Now you're just being silly! Look, I can't talk about this here. I'm coming over there...You can't tell me that...Fuck that shit! That's my damn house! I'll be over there in twenty minutes!" He slammed the phone down, and I heard his keys jingling as he headed for the door.

What was that about? I wondered. It had been three months since he'd been staying with me, and I still had no idea what was going on between them. I made a mental note to sit down with my friend in the near future and talk to him about what he had been up to in his marriage. Normally, I wouldn't even ask, but since it seemed he may be taking up permanent residency in my home, I felt like he at least owed me a partial explanation. In the meantime, my sleep had been all but ruined, so I took Malik's advice and got out of the bed. I showered, brushed my teeth, and put on a clean white t-shirt, a pair of blue sweats, and Adidas running shoes. When I finished, I sat down on the bed. I thought about heading to the gym because I wasn't ready to talk to Solomon just yet. I needed a few more minutes. I put my head in my hands, thinking. *What was I going to say?* I felt like an asshole. And if I handled things as badly as I handled them with Jaslyn, I would only make the situation worse.

Before I could figure out how I wanted to approach him, Solomon opened the door to my room.

"What's up?" he asked.

"Nothing. What's up with you?"

"Same ol, same ol'." He stood in the doorjamb. I remained at the foot of my bed. We looked at each other for a few moments. I stared at my reflection. My brother. A mirror image of me except a little leaner and a bit darker. He was also dressed in sweats and a t-shirt. His curly afro was an exact replica of mine. We were almost exact images of each other except for his clean-shaven face, which was a representation of his strait-laced attitudes and behaviors. My brother was a preacher, and for all intents and purposes, he lived up to the expectations most people had of their ministers. He didn't drink, smoke, or do drugs; he didn't lie, and he didn't cheat or steal. When he wasn't working, he spent most of his time at church teaching bible study classes. You never saw him fooling around with a bunch of different women. Quite frankly, he was celibate. Malik often accused him of being gay; he felt that any man that wasn't trying to get in a woman's panties had to be a homosexual. He wasn't. Solomon just believed in God and tried his best to practice what he preached. I couldn't fault him for that. As a matter of fact, I gave him mad props for it.

I, on the other hand, was not quite as devoted. I believed in God, and in recent years, I started going to church and praying again. My personal relationship with the Lord was growing, but I was a neophyte in my spiritual walk. There were definitely some things I still needed to work out. Yet, my brother was always by my side praying for me and helping me through whatever situations I found myself caught up in, which is why I felt so ashamed about my behavior towards him the night before.

He shifted his feet then looked at the floor. Finally, he said, "I just came to see if you had any deodorant."

I chuckled softly knowing that wasn't the truth, grateful he was trying to let me off the hook.

"Are you just now getting dressed?"

"Yeah. It was a long night. I'm not too used to that, so I slept in. Didn't you sleep late too?"

"I guess you could say that. Anyway, it's in my bathroom. In the medicine cabinet."

He walked in the room toward the bathroom. I spoke to him while he searched for the desired product.

"You know you're too old to be borrowing that kind of stuff. Aunt Tootie taught you better than that. You should have your own."

"I know. I just ran out. I'll pick some up at the store later today." I heard him fumbling around but couldn't see him. He finally added, "Hey, where is it? I don't see it."

"Top shelf. Right Guard spray. You see it?"

"Yeah. Thanks." I heard him pop the top and start spraying. I took the coward's way out. It was easier to talk to him face-to-face without actually having to *face* him. So, while he was in the bathroom spraying on an inordinate amount of deodorant, prolonging the job much longer than was necessary, I said, "Yo' man, I'm sorry about last night. I had no right to act that way or talk to you that way. I know that you would never do something like that to me. I was tripping. Hard."

He stopped spraying, walked out of the bathroom, and stood just above me. I was staring at my floor. Although I couldn't see him, I felt his presence.

I heard him say, "It's cool, man." With that, he patted me on the back, and we were back to normal. I stood up, pulled him to me with one arm, and hugged him with the other.

I sat back down on the bed. As he was leaving, a thought crossed my mind.

"What were you doing at that kind of place anyway? Isn't there some type of rule that prevents preachers from going to clubs and parties or something like that?"

"No, stupid! And it's not like we were at some swingers' club!" We laughed together. He walked over and sat down on the edge of the bed next to me. Then he explained, "Man, I'm just going through some stuff."

"Like what?"

He sighed. "Well, before I decided to preach my life was on track. I knew the difference between right and wrong. Things were black and white. I knew exactly what to do and how to do it. But lately..."

I interrupted him; he was starting to sound like a politician. "What are you talking about? Stop talking in circles and be straight with me."

"I have never been faced with so many opportunities to do wrong in my life. I feel like an NBA player. The money. The *women*! Man, the women are out of control. They just throw themselves at you. And I'm talking about Christian women. Calling all hours of the night asking for "special prayer." They treat me like I'm Teddy Pendergrass or something. I swear sometimes when I'm preaching, I'll look out into the sanctuary, and I'll see at least one woman who's looking at me like she wants to throw her panties at the pulpit. It's like, 'Damn lady, you *are* at church!' Anyway." He sighed then began again, "Then there's the prestige. People try to wait on you hand and foot. I got old-head preachers telling me stuff like the best way to make money is to work a revival. It's disheartening. Don't get me wrong. Everyone in church is not like that. Most people are genuinely trying to build a relationship with God, and live by his will, but those few that ain't sincere…Whew! I didn't expect it to be like this at all. That on top of Aunt Tootie's death…it's wearing on me. So, when Jawaan told me that he was taking you out to get your mind off of everything, I volunteered to go, too. I needed a break. I didn't know what to do."

"Didn't you think about this type of stuff before you made the decision to be a preacher?"

"Hell, no! When I made my decision, it was purely spiritual. I wanted to help spread the Word, not have sex or get paid. I can do that without serving in the pulpit."

"Hey, I'm not accusing you of anything. I wouldn't dare make that mistake twice in one day." He smiled, and I was glad. He was really down, and I wanted to help but didn't know if I could.

"Look, you know the reasons you chose this lifestyle, but that doesn't mean that every person who chooses this way of life chose it for the same reasons as you did. As a preacher, that's one of the issues you are going to have to constantly deal with. From men and women. Now, if your decision to be a preacher was spiritual, then you shouldn't let the shortcomings of others, mine included, cause you to go to places that you wouldn't, or shouldn't, go to, or do things you wouldn't normally do. You're going to have to deal with that in a different way. How, I don't know."

"I know, man, I know. That doesn't mean that things don't get hard on me from time to time. I just needed a break. A different atmosphere."

"I understand man, but I don't know if going to a club was it. I wish I could help you more."

"That's cool. Thanks for trying."

"Well, at least one good thing came from you being there. If I hadn't accused you of trying to get with Jaslyn, I would have definitely had sex with her when I left."

"Well, you did that anyway. Didn't you?"

"No. I didn't."

"But didn't you spend the night with her last night?"

"Yes, but we didn't have sex."

"You mean you didn't do anything with Jaslyn last night? Not even a kiss?"

"No, asshole. Stop rubbing it in."

"Why are you just coming in today, then?"

"She said I was so drunk I passed out."

"Are you trying to tell me that Sampson Tate was lying next to a fine, sexy, beautiful woman and didn't have sex with her?"

"Shut up, will you? I'm relieved, though. I already feel bad for the way I treated her last night. If I'd had sex with her, that would have just made things worse. She did me wrong, but she doesn't deserve to be treated like that."

"What? Does that sound like forgiveness I hear?" He held his ear as if he were listening for something.

"I didn't say all that. But when I first saw her this morning, I was so happy. It was like all the shit we've been through had vanished. I saw her face, and I was in love just like that. Didn't even remember not loving her. All the negative drama between us...it was like it never existed. And it felt *good*, you know? Then I realized where I was and panicked. I just don't want to put my feelings out there like that again. Then we started arguing. It was crazy. But, in my heart I was thinking, hoping, that if we take it slow maybe we can figure out a way to work things out between us. We haven't even resolved what happened between us. Having sex on top of that would only exacerbate the problem. I love the girl, man, I'm just mad at her.

"You've been mad for a long time."

"I know."

"Try talking to her."

"I did."

"And?"

"She wouldn't listen to me."

"So. Try again. And again. And again. Until she believes you or forgives you, whichever comes first.

"You just said you still love her, and chances are, she still loves you. Why else would she be interrogating me about my drunk brother in the middle of a club with all those other eligible, and might I add sober, men?"

"You do have a point?"

"And why else would she let you spend the night, or should I say morning, at her house? We had just exchanged phone numbers, remember? She could have called one of us to come get you. Or even better, she could have called you a cab since she does know where you live."

"I never thought about that."

He looked at me and laughed. He shook his head and said, "I still think you two had sex."

"What makes you so sure of that? You don't think a man and a woman can be together without having sex? Isn't that what you've been telling me these last few years?"

"I *know* a man and a woman can be together without having sex; I just don't think that the two of you can," he said chuckling.

"Ha. Ha. Very Funny. Don't you think I would remember something like that?"

Then he raised his eyebrows, realization spreading across his face.

"You're not even sure yourself, are you?" I didn't say anything. "Are you?"

He started to laugh harder.

"That's sad, Sam."

"Man, she said we didn't. Why would she lie?"

"Maybe because she was embarrassed. Maybe because she was hurt that you didn't remember. Maybe because she didn't want to admit she'd just had sex with someone who was so drunk he probably pissed in his pants."

"Jaslyn knows I wouldn't judge her like that. She wouldn't lie about something like that. She's not that type of person." Of this, I was certain, and I wasn't going to let Solomon or anyone else convince me otherwise.

But then, he added, "Look man, I'm not trying to scare you. I'm just saying after dealing with these women at church, I've learned that women do all sorts of crazy things when their feelings are involved. I really wouldn't put anything past anybody. I like Jaslyn, but just like any woman, any person, she'll do whatever she has to do to protect her feelings."

Then he stood and walked out of my room.

Chapter 7
Jaslyn
Decisions, Decisions

Hello! Hello!!! Where are you?...Is there anyone there?

That's me throwing a search party for my period! The last time I'd had sex had been about a month ago, and we all know who it was with. *Lord Jesus, I cannot be pregnant,* I prayed. I was hoping against all hope that my life, as I knew it, was not about to end, but I needed to be sure. I was nervous and scared as hell. *What is it about babies that makes you want to kill yourself?* Well, it wasn't that bad, but it was pretty close.

I didn't want to be alone. I couldn't think clearly, and I desperately wanted someone to hold my hand to face what seemed like the death sentence. I thought of my sisters, Carol, Francine, and Melissa. I couldn't call them. They all had families and were busy. I was sure they would come, but I really didn't want my family to know what was going on until I had my head together. They would surely tell my mother, who would then begin asking questions about the father. And I certainly wasn't ready to answer questions about my relationship with Sam.

I thought of Lisa and Shellie. Lisa and I had grown up together. She lived across the street from me, and we were practically family. We met Shellie when we all attended college together in Arlington. Shellie was my roommate, and she quickly became part of the Davenport family, too. I could trust both of them to stand by me during my crises since they had been there for me during all of my other life–altering events—catching my college boyfriend sleeping with a man, bailing me out of jail when I vandalized his car, my relationship with a married man, and watching Sampson cheat on me with his ex-girlfriend. I decided to call Shellie because Lisa had just started as the lead producer for the newest hip-hop station in the area. It was her ideal job (making her dream of one day meeting DJ Quik a reality), and I didn't want to impose. Besides, Shellie was the perfect choice because she kept a stash of pregnancy tests for emergencies such as this one. I dialed her cell phone. She answered. "What's up?"

I lost it. Unable to prevent the sobs of anguish waiting to erupt, I started crying.

"What's up, girl? What the hell is wrong with you?"

I continued to cry. She let me shed a few more tears. Finally, she asked, "Are you done?" Her tolerance for crying and weakness were pretty low. She'd let you get a few tears out, but then, she was back to the business of solving the problem.

I sighed.

"Yes."

"Good. Now let's get a handle on the situation. First, you need to calm down. Then you need to tell me what's wrong. And stop crying. Nobody hit you, so there's no need to cry. Or did they? Let me know, and I'll get my gun." Shellie was a card-carrying member of the NRA and was extremely proud of her concealed handgun license and .40 caliber Beretta; although, there was never a need for her to use it...yet. She continued, "You know I don't mind busting a cap in a nigga's ass!"

I laughed knowing that she was serious. I gained strength from the laughter and discovered the courage to finally say, "I think I'm pregnant." That was home girl code for *'Bring your ass, and your test over here right now!'*

"I'll be over there in ten minutes. Damn! I just might have to shoot somebody!" She yelled before hanging up.

Shellie arrived with the necessary equipment, and sure enough, the dot turned blue.

I looked at my friend who seemed as disoriented as I was. I could tell by her expression that she wanted to comfort me but didn't know what to say. I started crying again. But instead of the hysterical sobs from before I let the tears roll down my cheeks as I sat silently, contemplating my next decision. My next choice. Choice…pro-choice. I knew exactly what I wanted to do.

Shellie sat next to me on the bed, patting my back for comfort.

"What are you going to do?"

"Call the clinic." That was home girl code for *I'm not having no damn baby!*

Chapter 8
Sampson
Sam To the Rescue?

"Bitch you STANK! You need to go to the doctor and see what crawled up in yo' ass and died!"

"Fuck you, bitch! I'll kick yo' ass!"

I looked in at Jawaan's class as two teenage girls stood almost chin-to-chin like a Tyson-Holyfield rematch. "Shantrell and TrayVondra! That's enough! Sit y'all asses down and be quiet before I kick both of y'all's behinds!"

"Yes, Coach Turner."

"Sorry, Coach."

"Look, I don't know what kind of problem you two have with each other and I don't care, but you will leave that mess outside of my classroom. Do you understand?"

"Yes, Coach," Shantrell answered reluctantly. TrayVondra, however, wasn't giving in so easily. She didn't say anything, just sat at her desk with her arms tightly crossed over her chest and a frown that clearly said, "It ain't over!"

When the bell rang for class to be dismissed, Jawaan announced, "Guys don't forget your homework. You'll need it to review for your test on vectors this Friday. Now, everyone may leave except TrayVondra."

As the group of seniors filed out of Jawaan's class, TrayVondra stood and whined in protest. "But Coach!"

"But Coach nothing. Sit down, TrayVondra."

The girl huffed, sat down, and crossed her arms in defiance. I waited patiently outside as Jawaan conferred with his student.

"TrayVondra, I expect more from you than to bring that petty bickering inside my classroom."

"But, Coach," TrayVondra continued to whine, "Shantrell is always walking around like she is better than everybody, and that bitch know she stank!"

"Excuse me!"

"I'm sorry. What I mean is that the girl know she smell bad, and that shit just ain't right!"

"Look, whatever issues Shantrell is having with her body can be handled a little more diplomatically than that. Couldn't you have pulled her to the side?"

"Yes, sir."

"I know you could have. You did that to be mean, and that's not right, either. I wouldn't want anybody doing that to you."

"Ain't nobody gone do me like that cuz my ass don't stank!"

"That's another thing. You will respect me and my classroom. The next time you curse in front of me or anywhere near me, I will write your ass up on a referral. Do you understand that?"

"Yes, sir."

"Good."

"But Coach, can I say something?"

"What, TrayVondra?"

"You cuss?"

"I know that!" TrayVondra looked scared; Jawaan tried to calm her down. "I'm sorry, TrayVondra. I'm having a difficult time right now, okay. I don't mean to curse at you, but remember, I am grown. And you know how they say, 'Do as I say, not as I do?' They say that for a reason. I'm human. I make mistakes. Everything I do is not going to be perfect, but I will tell you what's right, okay?"

"Okay."

60

"And I mean it, TrayVondra. If I hear you cursing again, I'm going to give you extra laps during practice, and then I'll write you up on a discipline referral. Now get to class."

"But Coach…"

"*What,* TrayVondra?" Jawaan was clearly getting frustrated with TrayVondra's incessant whining.

"I need a pass to class."

"No, you don't. That's punishment for acting a fool in my class. Now get it!"

TrayVondra took off running out of the classroom and down the hall. A whirl of fuchsia and blond streaks coupled with the sparkle created by the rhinestones on her denim jacket and jeans, TrayVondra quickly forgot the lesson she'd just received about her language as she yelled, "Move, bitch!" to a fellow classmate that was blocking her path. Jawaan dropped his head in defeat, accepting that getting TrayVondra not to cuss was a battle he probably wouldn't win.

I walked into the classroom.

"Damn, man. Kids talk that way in front of their teachers?" When we were kids at Dunbar Middle School in Fort Worth, I remember testing our verbal flexibility with forbidden language but never in front of adults.

"In front of adults? TrayVondra's known for cursing out students *and* teachers. Hell, she even threatened the vice-principal two weeks ago. Man, that wasn't shit. I stopped them before they really got started. The bad thing about it is that TrayVondra is one of my honor students!"

"*TrayVondra?*" I asked, laughing.

"Don't laugh, boy. You remember my name is *Jawaan.* And did you forget about *Malik?* Our names

61

aren't exactly common. You're the only one of us with a white man's name!"

"Touchǐ. But my name is biblical, thank you."

"Man, stop playing? I didn't ask you to come here to make fun of my students."

"Speaking of, why am I here?"

Jawaan called me at my office and asked me to come to the school during his planning period. He said he needed my advice, and it couldn't wait. My office was in downtown Dallas, about ten minutes away from Jawaan's school. He taught calculus at a high school about ten minutes away in South Dallas. I decided to go during my lunch break, so I took a late lunch and arrived at his classroom at around 1:30 in the afternoon. He was taking his time answering me, so I asked again, "What's up, fool? Why did you need me to come all the way over to South Dallas?"

"I got a lot of shit going on, and I think it's about to blow-up today."

"Okay."

"I know you've been wondering what's up between me and Tamika, and I appreciate you not asking?"

"Right."

"I don't know how to say this."

"Just say it, man."

"I'm about to lose my job."

"What? Whatever, man. They need teachers too damn badly, especially math teachers. No one gets fired from teaching, and Tamika wouldn't leave you for that. "

"They will fire a teacher for having sex with the students, and Tamika would leave me if she believed it."

"What the hell? You mean to tell me that you're sleeping with one of these kids!"

"Keep your voice down. I don't want everybody in my damn business. And no, I am not sleeping with any of my students, but the accusation is all that matters."

"Okay, I'm confused. Why do you think you're going to be fired for something you didn't do, and why would Tamika believe it?"

"Sam...ever the eternal optimist. Let me explain. There's this senior, Jackie Fenton; she has a crush on me. I didn't think anything of it because not many of these girls have father figures at home, so they latch on to anybody that shows them the slightest bit of attention. She started coming to my room every day at lunch telling me about her problems. Stuff with her family, boyfriend, school. She has a baby. Her mother is really sick, and she and her boyfriend were always arguing. I mean she would tell me everything, man. I gave her advice, you know, to try to mentor her. But then Jackie started telling everybody that I was her Daddy, and she started hanging out in my room every period. I didn't want to hurt her feelings, you know, so I let her do it.

"Well, one day Tamika comes up here to have lunch with me. I guess Jackie got jealous because after that, the girl starts acting crazy. She starts telling me how much she cares about me, what she can do for me and *to* me. I tried to let her down easy. Let her know that I was her teacher and that we could never be together. I explained that it was morally wrong and professionally unethical. I told her that I could be fired and would probably go to jail if I even considered getting into a situation like that with a student.

"She starts crying and shit. She threatened to kill herself if I wouldn't be with her. So, I tried to calm her down. I hugged her, you know, to let her know that everything was going to be okay. What the hell did I do that for? The damn girl kissed me!"

"Did you kiss her back?"

"Hell, no! I put her out and told her not to come back to my room anymore."

"Damn, man! Did you report what happened to the administration?"

"No."

"Why not?"

"I don't know. I figured she'd let it go and forget about it. I never imagined that it would go this far."

"What happened next?"

"Jackie's an office helper in the front office. The damn girl gets my phone number out of my personnel file and proceeds to call my house. Unfortunately for me, when she called, Tamika answered the phone. She proceeds to tell Tamika about how we're sleeping together and shit, how good I kiss, and that we had sex in the house. She even described my place to prove that she'd been there."

"When did you take her to the house?"

"Never! Aren't you listening? She's lying."

I took a deep breath and exhaled before I proceeded. Jawaan, normally the calm and collected one of my friends, was losing control and not making sense. I needed him to pull it together. "Look, I'm not accusing you of anything. I believe you. I'm just trying to sort out what's going on. That's all. So, help a brother out and fill in the gaps. How was she able to give Tamika details about where you live?"

64

"I'm sorry."

"No problem. Keep going," I nodded.

Jawaan took a deep breath. He walked over to his desk. He picked up a framed picture of him and Tamika sitting in front of the fireplace at his house. I thought he was going to cry; instead, he brought the photo to me. I looked at them together. Even seated, you could see the stark differences between them. His lean six-foot-three-inch frame sitting next to her petite five-foot body. They were sitting on the sofa adjacent to the mantle. She was sitting in his lap. Her head, framed in short tight curls, was resting against his shoulder. His sharp, slanted eyes were gazing down on her as he smiled. The fire cast a glow against his light brown and her golden skin. If ever there was an image of love, this was it, and I immediately felt bad. When Jawaan and Tamika were married, I was a staunch opponent of the union, even more than Malik who thought that every male living or dead should be a player. His motto: "Never give up your player card, even in death. If you can pimp a hoe from the grave, dammit she deserves to get pimped, so do it!" I wasn't that bad, but Tamika gossiped too much, and even with a college education, she was ghetto. But now looking at this picture, I realized that my friend really loved his wife. An image of Jaslyn and me sitting together like that flashed before me, and I was instantly envious.

"I've had that picture on my desk since the day we were married. We were at my house having dinner with my old man. It was the day he gave me his approval of my choice to marry her. She didn't know it, but I did, and I was elated. You know how much I love my father, man." He paused briefly to sigh. "We were having a good time, so Pops took the picture, had it framed, and gave it to me as a wedding gift. I keep it on my desk to remind me of what we share and how much she means to me. I never thought it would be the downfall of my marriage."

He took another deep breath. There were so many questions I wanted answered, but I decided against interrupting him this time. This was his story to tell. In his own way, he would reveal all that he wanted me to know.

"Tamika and I are sitting in the living room. All I could figure was that during one of Jackie's visits to my room about her so-called "problems," she memorized that picture. All she needed to do was to tell Tamika a few of the details, and I'm out the fuckin' house."

"And Tamika believed her," I sighed.

"Exactly. Anyway, I was cool with being out of the house. I kinda understand where Tamika is coming from, I mean I'd be upset too if I thought she was playing me for some seventeen–year–old kid. Besides, I figured once Tamika calmed down that I could convince her that I'm not some damn pedophile!

"But I am not okay with being out of a job. This girl is threatening to go to the principal and tell him that I kissed her and about our so-called relationship. She told me that she was going to his office in the morning if I don't meet her after school today. I don't know what to do?"

"Calm down, Jawaan! It's your word against hers," I assured him.

"Not when it comes to public education. They're going to believe her first, especially since she was seen in my room everyday by just about everyone. They'll have to investigate. In the meantime, I'll probably be placed on administrative leave. Even if I'm found

66

innocent, my reputation will be so screwed up I won't be able to get a new job, and I won't be able to face anybody at work.

"Shit, man!"

"I know. I'm stupid, right?"

"No, not stupid. Just naïve."

His voice cracked signaling his fear as he said, "Just help me, Sam. Please!"

My mind was racing as I fought to find some type of answer for Jawaan. *Why were my friends always calling me when they got themselves in trouble?* They'd all been living with me because of various housing situations—a few years ago, Malik called me when he was arrested in a strip club in his police officer's uniform and lost his job; Solomon needed a new place because of some stalker at church; and now, Jawaan has found himself in some R. Kelly type shit and needs me to throw him a life preserver. *Shit, who am I? Jesus? Who's going to help me when I have problems?* I didn't know, but I knew that they all needed me. I was going to do my best to be there for them.

I shook my head and said, "I will, I will. First thing, don't meet that girl anywhere."

"You don't think I'm some type of pervert, do you?"

"Not until today," I joked.

He finally laughed and nodded in relief that I wasn't judging him.

"Tomorrow, you're going to take a sick day. If you're not here, she probably won't do anything. My guess is that she needs an audience. She wants the pleasure and attention of you being here when the shit hits the fan. Do you have a lawyer?"

"Yes. Through the teacher's union. We get free representation."

"Good. Call them first thing in the morning so they can start to help you figure this mess out. And if you don't get the help you need, let me know and I will hire an attorney for you. Cool?"

"Cool. But what about my wife?"

"What about her? Shit, I say good riddance! If she doesn't trust you enough to stick by you, then you deserve better. I never liked her ghetto ass anyway."

"Hey, man! That's still my wife. She may be ghetto, but I still love her, okay?"

"Your choice," I replied disdainfully. "Let's get your name cleared first, and then we'll work on Tamika. I promise. Regardless of the bitter taste it will leave in my mouth, I'll help you get your wife back."

Relief washed over his face as he pulled me in for a hug, "Thanks, man!"

Chapter 9
Jaslyn
Dreams About Fish

I didn't call the clinic; I didn't know what I wanted to do. Everything was so messed up now. I loved Sam, and I wanted us to be together. However, I didn't want him to be with me out of pity or a sense of responsibility. I had always been a proponent of the Pro-Choice Movement, even vowing to definitely exercise my choice to terminate if I ever came close to finding myself in this type of situation. Now, the reality of my life had me thinking that this might not be the best choice for me.

I really had no reason to terminate the pregnancy. My excuses in the past for not having children had been that I wasn't stable; I didn't make enough money, and I wasn't married. But here I was a grown woman with a house, a job, and a decent salary. I couldn't lie to myself about not having a stable living situation. All of my reasons were no longer valid, except for the fact that I wasn't married to my child's father. And as things stood, there was nothing I could do about that.

I had to deal with that issue before I made a final decision about this mess I found myself in. What would make a woman have a baby by a man who might not want her to do so otherwise? To bring into the world the product of a drunken night of sex? An alcohol–created love child? How would I ever explain to my child the story of his or her birth? Your dad was so drunk he just climbed on top of me to do his business as Miss Celie would say. Or how about, I'm sorry, son, but you were an accident. You were never meant to be here, and your dad still doesn't remember having sex with me or telling me

69

he loved me. I wasn't thinking of any of that the day I decided to cancel my appointment at the clinic. Oh yes, appointment. *Didn't you hear me when I said I didn't want no damn baby?*

Anyway, the day I made my decision to embrace motherhood, I was in the shower admiring the body I worked so hard to keep, more determined than ever to let nothing make me lose it, especially a baby. I was lathering up, getting ready to wash my womanhood, when I noticed amongst the blackness of my femininity a sliver of light. A light so fine and silky. A shadow of gray. In the middle of the forest of black called my vagina, I caught sight of my mortality. A gray hair. Of all the places in the world to find gray hair, my vagina would not have been my first choice. I didn't even have gray hair on my head yet. Then it hit me. Time was running out on me. Life was going on about me and I was stagnant, I was still in the same place I was in ten years ago. I wasn't married, which isn't a necessity, but hanging with my homegirls until the wee hours of the morning isn't what I called leaving a lasting legacy. What would my epitaph read? *She kicked it...HARD!* I didn't want to go out like that. My sisters had all started families and were moving on. Carol had three kids, Melissa had twins, and Francine had a toddler. They were all married. Francine, much to my chagrin, married Morris, her "baby's daddy" even though he was a loser. He couldn't keep a job and was too lazy to hustle like Damon, Melissa's husband. But hey, Francine was happy, and that's really all that mattered.

And whether they wanted to admit it or not, Shellie and Lisa had also moved on. They were starting to date seriously, narrowing down the pool of eligible men to those worthy of their time and energy. For them, this was a gigantic step from using men to pass the time of day. One day, I thought I heard Lisa use the word "boyfriend," and I almost choked. I was happy that they were moving on with their lives, but what about mine?

At thirty-three years old, that gray hair was my life. I was getting closer to death, and I was doing it alone. I realized then that this might be the only chance I had at forming some semblance of my own family.

My body was creating life. My life. Sam's life. And truthfully, I wasn't sure if I wanted to end it. The culmination of, if not our love, then our relationship would be here in less than nine months, and I wanted to see what it would be like. But would Sampson feel the same way? Did he want a baby right now? Was he ready to be a father? Did he want *me* to be the mother of his child? Unfortunately, I wasn't ready to hear the answers to those questions.

I was ready, however, to make a decision. I was having *my* baby. Damn what Sam wanted or what he was ready for. I wouldn't give him the opportunity to tell me he didn't want our baby because I wasn't going to tell him about it. *Why risk the disappointment his rejection is sure to bring?* I reasoned. Furthermore, if he never knew he had a child, he would never feel bad about not being a part of its life. So, in essence, I was doing him a favor.... or so I thought.

It was a Sunday afternoon, and I was looking forward to just sitting at home and relaxing. No work and no drama. Definitely *no* drama. I knew the situation I was in, but honestly, I really didn't want to deal with it all for

71

a while. Sundays are my mental break days. On this particular Sunday, I spent the day watching football, reading the paper, and doing my nails. The excitement of the football game helped me to blow off some of the pent-up frustration I had been harboring, and doing my nails began my initiation process for soothing my spirit. I always ended the ritual by having a steaming hot bath with aromatherapy oils—my favorites were vanilla and jasmine—and having a hot cup of cocoa with whipped cream on top. I had just finished doing my nails and was about to run the water for my bath. My phone began to ring, and I was immediately aggravated. *Everyone knows about my "Ritual Sundays," so who the fuck is calling my house. It had better be important,* I fumed. I usually cut the ringer off, but I guess I had so much on my mind I completely forgot to shield my serenity from the outside world. I made a point to cut it off as soon as I ended this phone call.

I picked up on the second ring.

"*WHAT!*" I snapped.

"Damn, girl. What's gotten into you? Can't you say hello?"

It was my sister, Melissa. She knew I hated it when she called me on Sundays, but she did it anyway to fuck with me.

"*Hello.* Now, what?"

"My goodness, aren't we cranky today."

"Melissa, you know how I am about my Sunday's. Why do you continue to interrupt my day of peace? Don't you get enough of aggravating me throughout the week?"

"First of all, if you brought your ass to church on *Sundays* instead of sitting at home acting like a broke down version of Tina Turner, all 'nam myoho-ing' and shit, I wouldn't have to call you on *Sundays.* Second of all, no, I don't get enough of aggravating you through the week. You're my baby sister, it's my job to get on your nerves, and I take my job very seriously. Finally, I only called to deliver a message."

I laughed at her and finally decided to just talk, because we could go on like this forever, and I wanted to get back to my mental break. Surely, whatever message she had couldn't be so bad. It was probably from Carol and Francine expressing a similar sentiment about me not coming to church but with a little more tact. Well, at least Carol would have more tact. Francine probably added a few more curse words, so they chose to go somewhere in the middle by having Melissa call.

"Hello, Melissa. How are you? Nice to hear from you. Is everyone all right?" I asked to get her off my back. "Was that better?"

"Yes. You see, it didn't cost you a dime to be nice to me."

"Yes, big sister. You are so right. I do apologize. Would you please forgive me?"

"Okay, stop being an asshole and let me deliver my message.

I chuckled inside knowing I had successfully turned the tables from aggravated to aggravator.

"What's up?"

"Grandma had a dream about fish, and she wants to talk to you."

"About what?"

73

"I don't know. But you know they say when old people dream about fish somebody's pregnant."

"What the hell?" I started sweating. There went my mental break.

Melissa continued. "Yep. She called Mama and said she had a dream about fish and then told her she wanted to talk to you. You pregnant?"

"I'm not driving an hour and a half to the country to talk to Grandma Pearl about fish!"

"You don't have to. She's here."

"Here?" A wave of nausea washed over me, and I had to inhale to keep from vomiting.

"Yep. She came home for a visit and said she wanted to see you. Are you pregnant?"

"Who brought her home?"

"Uncle Willie picked her up yesterday."

"And y'all just now calling me?"

"Well, you know how Grandma gets when she's tired. She didn't want to talk to a lot of people yesterday, so Mama just let her chill. I didn't even know she was here until today. Besides, we figured you'd at least come to church this Sunday since you haven't been in weeks. Anyway, answer my question, bitch. Are you pregnant?"

Why couldn't I just tell my sister the truth? She had two kids of her own. She would understand. I was almost six weeks pregnant, and I still couldn't form my lips to say it. If I didn't speak it, it wasn't true.

"Stop being silly."

"Whatever. All I know is Grandma Pearl told Mama she had a dream about fish, and she wants to talk to you, so they made me call you."

"Stop repeating yourself, would you?"

"I will when you answer the question."

"Melissa, that's an old wives' tale. Please tell me you don't believe that do you?"

"All I can say is that she had a dream about fish the first time Carol got pregnant and wanted to see her. She had a dream about fish when I was pregnant with the twins and asked to see me. And, she had a dream about fish when Francine got pregnant and came to see her. Now she's dreaming about fish and wants to see you. So, you tell me, what do you think I believe?"

"Bye, Melissa. Tell Mama I'll be over in a couple of hours."

I heard her yell, "You still haven't answered the damn question," just before I slammed the phone down in her face.

After my phone conversation, I soaked in my bath for about thirty minutes. I was going to need all the peace and relaxation I could get in order to outsmart my shifty, eighty-eight-year-old grandmother. It was a medical marvel that Grandma Pearl was still around. She had a hearing aid-in her right ear and was slightly blind in the left eye. She used a walker to support a hip she had replaced, and she had been operated on at least six times in the last three years for various ailments and injuries. She still ate like the Southern Belle that she was. And I'm not just talking about Sundays. It wouldn't be strange to go to her house on a Tuesday afternoon, and Grandma Pearl would have hot-water cornbread, oxtails, greens filled with salted-pork, beans flavored to taste with bacon, topped off with a glass of tea so sweet the sugar settled at the bottom. She'd outlived three husbands and six of her twelve children, and if you asked her how she was doing, she would answer (after you had to repeat it five times), "Just glad to be here, baby. Just glad to be here."

Yet, when she wanted to be, Grandma Pearl was an agile, astute, quick-witted sleuth who could run circles around Perry Mason, Matlock, and Sherlock Holmes if necessary. It was going to take all I had to hold up under the pressure of her dark-eyed gaze and tell her that she wasn't going to have another great-grandbaby. I didn't know what the problem was, but I was not ready to share this bit of my life yet. Maybe, once the baby was born, I could mail her a greeting card. *Congratulations, Grandma, on the new addition to your family! You and the fish were right.* All I knew when I left the house an hour later was that I was not going to stand in front of my grandmother, the matriarch of our family, and tell her that I was going to be a mother. Because the inquisition would not stop at that question. That was only the beginning. I would surely have to answer questions about the father and why we weren't married, and I wasn't ready to do that. So, I was prepared to lie to Grandma Pearl while hoping and praying she didn't detect the truth beneath all the bullshit I was about to feed her.

I walked into Virginia Davenport's home and coughed. Along with my mother, my grandmother smoked a pack of Kool's a day, so the air was thick with tobacco.

"Hey, Mama. What's going on?"

I walked over to her and gave her a hug. She nodded and said, "Mm–hmm." My mother wasn't big on affection, so I knew that meant, "I love you, you need to come see me more often, and we missed you at church today."

"I know. I'll be there next week," I responded out loud. I really did plan on going to church next week, but she and I both knew that I was probably lying. Sunday was the only day I had to just chill, and our pastor tended to be a little long-winded. I knew I needed to make my presence known in the house of the Lord, but I just wasn't ready to give up my downtime yet.

"Where is Grandma Pearl?" I was ready to get this over with.

"She's in the back. Go on back there. She's up. She's just watching *Gunsmoke*."

I headed toward the back bedroom. *Stay strong, stay firm; she can't break you*, I told myself trying to get ready for the senior citizens' answer to the Terminator.

I opened the door. She was sitting in a recliner next to the bed and sure enough there was a marathon of "Gunsmoke" on TV Land. The sound was reaching decibel levels that competed with NASA space shuttles. "Hey, Grandma Pearl! How are you doing?" I yelled trying to make sure she heard me.

She turned to look at me. She stared and focused in on me with her good eye.

"Jaslyn? What you yellin' so loud for, I can hear you?" I told you she could hear when she wanted to.

"Sorry. I just came to say hello. How are you doing?"

"Fine. Just glad to be here, baby. Just glad to be here." My grandmother was under the impression that each day on this earth was probably her last, but truthfully, she was so strong she would probably outlive us all.

I walked over to the television and turned it down. The shootout was giving me a headache.

"Go ahead and turn it off. I wasn't watching it anyway. I was sitting here dozing."

I hit the power button and then sat down on the bed in front of her.

"What's going on, Grandma Pearl? Melissa said you wanted to see me."

"Who's the daddy?"

I was stunned. This old girl was sly. It was going to take more than strength and a couple of lies to outwit her. *Next phase...denial.*

"Wh...what...what are you talking about?"

"Girl, don't play dumb with me. I had twelve kids, twenty-one grandkids, and six great-grandkids, and I had a dream about fish every time one of 'em was born. I know you didn't think you was gone come up in here and try to fool me, did you?"

Man, she was good. I sat there in shock. Mouth agape like Macauley Culkin in *Home Alone. Hell, what was I going to do now?* I thought of an old trick I used when I would visit Grandma Pearl in the summer, and I didn't want her to whip me. I started crying.

"What the hell are you cryin' for? You wasn't crying when you were getting pregnant?"

As she said it, I remembered this trick never worked when I was little, either. She would always say, "Oh, I'm gone give you something to cry about!" Then, she would proceed with an ass whipping. This time she said, "Maybe, you were crying, but them was good tears. Hmph! I miss them kinda tears." She started laughing, and I did too. My grandmother was a trip and a half. When I was a child, she would never come close to saying anything like this. But as she got older, I guess

78

she felt she had earned the right to say whatever she wanted, and she always did.

"Grandma Pearl, you are so crazy. I love you, though." I stopped laughing, took a deep breath, and answered her question. "The father is a guy I used to date a while back. Things didn't work out. This was just an accident.

"That's a hell of an accident!" She shook her head in amusement. "Do you love him?"

"Grandma, I told you. It *was* an accident. We haven't dated in a long time."

"Jaslyn, who do you think you're foolin? You don't let a man inside you like that unless you have feelings for him. Unless, that is, you're a tramp. Are you a tramp?"

I gasped. I couldn't believe she asked me something like that. "No ma'am!" I finally said.

"I know it, cuz yo' mama didn't raise none. I know you feel something for the boy otherwise you would have never slept with him. I just want to know how deep those feelings are. Now back to my question. Do you love him?"

"Yes, ma'am." I started crying again.

"Now, stop all that crying. Ain't no need for all that. You know my nerves bad."

"Yes, ma'am." I sniffed to stifle my tears.

"Does he love you?"

"I don't know. He used to."

"Then what are you crying for?"

"Because everything is so complicated."

"If you love him and he loves you, then what's the problem?"

"I said he *used* to love me."

She nodded her head in thought, then finally asked, "Does he know yet?" *Damn, this woman is shrewd*!!

"No, not yet."

"Why haven't you told him?"

"Because I'm scared."

"Scared of what?"

"That he doesn't love me anymore."

"Well, I can understand that, but you should have thought about that before you laid up with him," she explained as she kicked back in her recliner.

"Young people these days are so impulsive and emotional. If you had thought that out beforehand, then everything wouldn't be so *complicated* as you say. You don't have time to be scared. That's nonsense. You need to tell that man about his baby. Period."

"But Grandma, I don't know what he's going to say,"

"Shit, ain't nothing for him to say, now is there?" And with that, we were through talking and she went back to sleep in the recliner.

Chapter 10
Man's Biggest Downfall
Sampson

"Man, pussy don't have a face! It's all the same in the dark!"

"It might not have a face but it sure as hell has a smell!"

"Chicago, man, that was gross!"

That was our friend, Chicago. Malik and I were having lunch with him at the food court in the mall when out of nowhere Chicago sees a girl he swears he would never have sex with. The girl wasn't exactly attractive, and she had a few extra pounds in some of the wrong places. She wasn't completely unattractive, so Malik was standing firm in his belief that all pussy was good pussy! Chicago was of a different opinion, however.

"It might be gross, but it's the truth," he continued.

"Whatever, man! You're just foul!"

"Seriously, Malik, I could smell her ass coming from a mile away. I ought to know what she smells like, I hit it twice."

"If she smelled so bad, why did you have sex with her... *twice?*" I had to interject at this point. I should have known better; that was carte blanche for Chicago to delve further into his foulness. He was a bit of a clown with a knack for nastiness. On a daily basis, he used his customers as targets to hone his comedic skills at the barbershop where we got our hair cut. Our barber and the shop's proprietor, Womack, only tolerated Chicago because he was one of the best barbers in Fort Worth, and he brought in thousands of dollars in business each week. On several occasions, Chicago almost lost a few customers because without a bit of hesitation, or tact, he always hit his point home. He was the only person I knew who could be worse than Malik when it came to having a talent for being crass. Through years of edge-ups, drama, arguments, advice, political debates, and playing the dozens, Chicago had become one of our dearest friends.

"The first time I didn't know any better. I met her ass at a club. I was drunk, high, and horny, and it was dark."

"See that's where your ass messed up; alcohol and desperation don't mix. Does it Sam?"

"Ha-ha, asshole!" I told Malik about waking up naked with a hangover at Jaslyn's. After he finished laughing, he had the same opinion as Solomon. But I still refused to believe that we had slept together, and I had no recollection of it.

"Will you two listen to the story?" Chicago asked.

"Go ahead, Chicago. This fool is stupid," I said.

"After I slept with her, I swore I would never let another drop of my sperm swim in that vaginal sewage again." At this point, I twisted my nose in disgust, and Malik looked as if he were about to lose the shrimp fried rice he'd just eaten.

Our demonstrations of disgust were to no avail. Chicago continued, "Man, for real. I hit it, left, and didn't call her ass again. She kept on calling me for about two months after, but the scent was too fresh in my memory to even consider calling her back.

"Two years later, I saw her at the Fourth of July parade in Como. All I can say is that THC is a motherfucker because my memory is fucked up from smoking all that herb. She walked up to me and says, 'Chicago, when we gone hook-up?' I was like 'Girl, we can hook-up tonight!' Again, I was high and horny; I forgot I even knew the girl. I remembered her ass as soon as I got a whiff of that stank coochie though. Whew! That shit was foul. Like a really bad porno movie. I was like 'Damn, it's *Stank Ass Part II*!'"

Malik was in tears from laughing as he said, "Dude...you are so...so fuckin' stupid!!"

I tried to contain myself as I said, "You know I hate to ask you this question because I'm afraid of the answer, but curiosity has gotten the best of me..." I inhaled deeply and then exhaled before I finally asked, "Did you stop?"

"Hell, no! I held my breath and kept right on hittin' it. Other than the urge to vomit every now and then, the shit was pretty good. But then, guess what?"

"What, nigga?! I can't take no more of this," Malik cried through tears of laughter.

"Right before we finished, the bitch farted! I swear she must have had Parmesan cheese or cabbage for lunch because it was awful. I finally came, and then I fainted from the stench. I guess between her stank coochie and her stank ass, I couldn't take it."

"Man, that shit is nasty!" Malik clutched his stomach to control a wave of nausea.

It was Sunday afternoon, and we'd gone to early morning service at church. Chicago invited us to lunch, so we decided to hit the mall to grab something to eat and then do some shopping. I needed some new running shoes, and those two fools looked for any excuse to be at the mall to pick up women or go shopping. When it came to clothes, we were almost worse than women. Malik with his dark skin, fashioned himself as the Morris Chesnutt of the ghetto. Chicago was also good looking but a little over the top with his wardrobe. The knock-off Versace shirts and pink and white Stacy Adams were a bit too much for my taste. He kept his hair braided in the latest cornrows, and at that very moment, I was staring at a twenty-nine-year-old man with blue and gold beads dangling from the back of his neck.

Before long the conversation turned a bit more serious. Chicago shifted the mood when he interrupted our laughter with some news.

"All jokes aside, I didn't just ask y'all here to hang out. I have something I want to talk to y'all about."

Malik put his drink down, and I asked, "What's up, man?"

"I have some bad news and some good news. The bad news is that Womack is retiring; the good news is that he wants to sell me the barbershop."

Chicago was sitting in between the both of us, so Malik and I slapped his shoulders simultaneously and said, "Congratulations!"

Chicago smiled and said, "Thanks, but I'm a little nervous."

Malik took a sip of his drink, and then asked, "Why?"

"Because I'm a barber, not a businessman. It takes more than cutting hair to know how to run a shop. I'm a simple dude, you know? I love women, weed, and a fly ass wardrobe. Womack handled the business— paying bills and collecting booth rent. Now, that's all on me. I don't know if I'm ready for all that."

I offered my support. "Man, don't worry about that. You're ready! How long do you have before Womack retires?"

Chicago paused in between a bite of food. "About a year. He said he's buying an RV so that he can travel across the country with his wife. His old ass needs to sit down somewhere," Chicago shook his head and laughed.

Malik nodded his head and said, "Nice!"

I said, "That gives you a full year to learn everything he knows. Even when he retires, you know Womack is only a phone call away. He will help you just like he always has, like he has helped us all. He's probably just tired of the day-to-day grind, you know? Plus, you have us; we will help you, too."

Malik interjected, "Speak for yourself. I don't know shit about running a barbershop."

Chicago's shoulders slumped immediately, so I shot Malik a look that said, *Shut the hell up!* He apologized with, "I'm just kidding, man. You know I will help you. I'm happy for you!"

He lifted his shoulders, and his eyes perked up as he said, "I appreciate that, man!"

Chicago started laughing again and immediately went into another nasty, freaky tale, but I zoned out. Hearing about Womack's decision to retire and travel the country with his wife had me reflecting on my own love life.

While I was having fun with the fellas, I was secretly longing to be somewhere else. I certainly had better things to do than hang out at the mall with two grown ass men, but I needed to clear my mind of a few things. Specifically, Jaslyn, Jaslyn, and Jaslyn. Since our argument at her house and my conversation with Solomon, I couldn't stop thinking about her and everything that happened. It had been a few weeks since the incident, and I really wanted to talk to her about it all. Some of my anger was starting to wane, and my feelings for her seemed to be resurfacing. I was determined to take it slow, but I was hoping that she was feeling the same way, too. I called her several times, but the answering machine always picked up; she never returned my calls. After a few weeks of rejection, I was about ready to move on; however, I *was* contemplating giving it one last shot. I didn't know what I was going to do, but at the same time, I didn't want to just give up on what we shared. But my resiliency was reaching its limits.

When my mind returned to the table, I realized two things—my friends were crazy, and I was still in love. However, if Jaslyn didn't make up her mind to talk to me soon, I would be moving on. Life was too short to waste time on unrequited emotions, and there were too many available women out there for me to waste time worrying about one. So, I resolved in my mind to make one more attempt at reconciliation because through it all, Jaslyn was still my girl. But if it didn't work, I would be done fooling with her ass.

Just as I decided on my course of action, Malik taps me on my shoulder.

"Hey, ain't that Alicia Matthews? Look, over there. She's walking toward us."

I turned my head and sure enough, she was approaching the table. Spit began to accumulate in my mouth, and it lingered like the taste of a sour melon. That's what Alicia did to me; she left a foul taste in my mouth. On the surface, she was as sweet as candy, but shortly after the initial sweetness, you realized the melon wasn't any good. The girl was definitely sexy. Even now as she approached the table in her cream linen Capri pants and her pink muslin top, I was disgusted with myself for having to fight the hard-on that was growing in my pants. I always considered her attractive physically; it was her personality that was the turn-off. Let's see, how can I say this without sounding bitter...she was an uppity gold-digger with a penchant for manipulation. *Did that do it?*

Let me explain. A year ago, she stopped at my house unannounced and asked to use the bathroom. Instead, the silly chick sneaks into my bedroom and leaves her underwear in my dresser for Jaslyn to find. After Aunt Tootie told her how much money I had, the girl was determined to ruin my relationship with Jazz and get me back. A couple of days later, Jazz pulls up and sees what she thinks is a kiss and breaks up with me. Needless to say, I really can't stand this girl.

"Hello, Sam. How are you?" she says to me.

"Fine." I wanted to keep the conversation as short as possible.

"I'm doing fabulous. I hope you don't mind me stopping by." *See, this is the kind of shit I'm talking about. Did I ask how she was doing?* I was purposely being rude, praying that she would go away. It didn't work.

Malik could see the irritation growing on my face, so he tried to run interference. "What's up, Alicia? Long time, no see."

"Malik, right? It really has been a long time. What's up with your friend? He's being rather rude, today."

"Well, let's think about this," Malik took a bite of his food, swallowed, and put his fork down. He settled back in his chair, crossed his arms, and sneered as he said, "Between the eighth-grade prom, a pair of panties, and his last girlfriend, you've stood him up, set him up, and broke him up. Are you really shocked that he doesn't like your ass? Or are you just stupid?"

"Malik, Malik. Still the asshole, I see." She dismissed him with a slight wave of her hand, then turned to me. "Sam, I know you're angry with me, but I really would like for us to be friends again."

"I don't think that's going to be possible. Now, if you'll excuse me. I need to go to the men's room." I stood to leave, almost knocking over a teenager with more tattoos than Tommy Lee. She grabbed hold of my arm to stop me, applying a small amount of pressure. I flinched as she touched me. Nostrils flaring in hostility, I stared at her hand to let her know that she had crossed the line.

She released me then proclaimed, "Look, I really would like for us to get along. At least well enough to do business together.

"Business? What kind of business?" I spat.

"The company I work for is beginning a new ad campaign, and I'm in charge of hiring the agency. I could drag out the bidding process eventually hiring a Fortune 500 company that won't do half as good a job as a smaller company hungry to make its mark. Or...I could shorten the process and ensure that an old friend gets to handle the campaign, all but ensuring its longevity in the business world." She inserted a pause to emphasize her point. "But I can only do that for a friend."

My ears perked up. If there was anything that could make me put aside my differences with Alicia, it was the idea of making money. "Keep talking."

"There are some details we need to hash out—the concept, deadlines, budget, contract details—things of that nature, but basically, we're talking about the possibility for you to earn at least seven figures here. Let's talk about everything over dinner."

As a reflex, I recoiled in disbelief, "Dinner?" *Was there really a dinner or was she just trying to fuck me?*

She was amused. "Come on, Sam. It's only dinner. A business dinner. My boss will be there, and we can eat out."

"Fine. I'll have my secretary call you to finalize the details."

Alicia reached in her purse and pulled out a business card. Her fingers brushed against mine softly as she slid the card into my hands. She leaned in close and whispered, "Call me," letting the words linger on her lips as the sounds kissed my eardrums lightly. And then, she turned and strutted off just as easily as she had come.

Malik and Chicago were glaring at me.

"Sam, you don't believe that chick, do you?"

"Chicago, it's just business. As a black man, I can't rest. I have to take advantage of every opportunity I get. Even if that means having dinner with people I don't particularly like. Business is business. Besides, for a million dollars, I can put up with a few chicken heads!"

"Alright, playa. All money ain't good money. Remember that."

"I gotcha, man. Trust me, I got this. She can't do anything to me unless I let her, and that shit ain't happening."

Malik watched us as we debated the situation. He was blank, and for Malik, that was not a good sign. Usually, he was immediately transparent in how he felt about something. He was either completely judgmental, or he just didn't give a shit. But you knew one way or the other how he felt, yet at that moment his eyes, his entire body, was completely empty. Devoid of any opinion. I couldn't take it. After years of offering his opinion without asking, he decides at this moment to be silent. I was pissed. I had to know what he was thinking.

"What?" I barked in frustration.

"I didn't say anything."

"I know. That's the problem. Come on, Malik. I know you have something to say."

"Really, I wasn't going to say anything. I was just thinking about something."

"Thinking about what?"

"Man's biggest downfall."

"What?" I shook my head in frustration. "What are you talking about?"

"Man's biggest downfall. Every powerful man was destroyed by one of two things, sometimes both. But rest assured in the demise of great men, there was always one of two common denominators present."

I laughed. He was starting to amuse me with his pseudo-philosophical meanderings.

"Really, man. Don't laugh. If you think about it, many a man falls victim because they're too cocky to pay attention. There's Mark Anthony, John the Baptist, Jesse Jackson, *Kwame* Jackson, Bill Clinton, hell *Bill Cosby*.

Shit man, even me! But it never fails...the terrible two always get you.

"Malik, what are you talking about?"

"Money and pussy, man. Money and pussy. And both of them just handed you their business card."

Chapter 11
Sampson
Just the Beginning

Alicia worked for an Internet trading firm that was expanding its market in Europe. My firm was basically putting together a campaign that would promote the strategies that her company was making to ensure its growth in the market and satisfy investors about the stability the company held in the international market. Alicia and I met several times to discuss the campaign that her company wanted to put together. The first few times were with her boss, and I had to admit she was on her best behavior. The closer we came to finalizing the campaign, the later we worked. So, when she suggested a working dinner, I didn't hesitate. I offered my home as a place for us to meet because I figured there would be plenty of people to supervise us since my "roommates" were still living there. Furthermore, I felt more comfortable on my own turf, so to speak. She couldn't sneak up on me in my own home.

Alicia was always impeccably dressed, so I wasn't surprised when she showed up at my house in her "man-catcher" outfit. I looked at her plunging neckline and her skin-tight mini-skirt and laughed to myself.

"You must have a hot date later tonight?"

"Something like that. You like what you see?"

"Let's just say old boy is going to be really pleased."

"Hmmm. We'll see," she said coyly, then added, "Let's get to work."

"Cool. Come on in. We'll work in my office. My brother Solomon is in his room, but if we're in the office, he'll have the freedom to move around the way he wants."

We went to my office and worked diligently for three hours on the presentation we would be giving to the board of directors for my company's bid. Although Alicia had virtually guaranteed the contract to me, I didn't want to leave any doubt that even though we had a hook-up, Tate & Associates deserved this contract. It was approaching midnight, and I wanted to get some rest before the next day's presentation. Before I could declare that it was time for Alicia to leave, Solomon burst through the door.

He poked his head in and announced, "Hey, man, I'm heading out in a few minutes. I'm meeting some friends. You good?"

I nodded, "Yes. We're just finishing up here; we're good."

He gave me a look of caution— "Okay...then I'm leaving. I'll talk to you later." He closed the door and left us alone in the room.

I stretched, another clear signal that I was ready for her to leave. She seemed to have gotten the hint.

"You seem tired."

"Yep, and it's getting late. If there's anything else that needs to be done, I can handle it on my own from here. I don't want to hold you up from your date."

"Oh, don't worry. That's going to happen either way."

"Is that right?"

"That's right," she said with a smile then added, "Hey, Sam, you remember Orandis Jones?"

"How could I forget that clown?" We both laughed at the memory. If ever I had an archenemy, it was

Orandis Jones. The Lex Luther to my Superman, we competed on all levels. I was poor; he was rich, and his dad owned a chain of grocery stores. Aunt Tootie worked at the dry cleaners; we won't even talk about Uncle Junior. Money wasn't our only point of contention. We competed in chess club, in class, and most importantly, with girls. He was the guy that Alicia decided to go to the prom with instead of me. Alicia and I had been dating for about a month, and I assumed that we were going to the prom together. I soon found out that wasn't the case. According to Alicia, I should never have assumed that she was my girlfriend and would therefore be my date. Instead, she agreed to go to the dance with Orandis, and she didn't inform me until I showed up at her doorstep.

"Whatever happened to him?"

"He's around. Running his daddy's stores. He went to law school but could never pass the bar. So, he went to work for Mr. Jones and has been working for him ever since."

"I guess his daddy couldn't help him with that."

"I guess not."

"Is he still as arrogant as he used to be?" I chuckled a bit, asking the question we both knew the answer to.

"Tries to be. But even that's hard when you realize that you're only successful because of your father."

"What made you ask about him?"

"I don't know, just thinking."

"About?"

95

"That if I had gone to that dance with you instead of him, you and I might be more than just business associates right now."

"Alicia, we were in middle school. I seriously doubt that we would be able to maintain a meaningful relationship for that long. Most people can't seem to stay together more than two years, never mind twenty."

"That's not necessarily true. Look at Tamika and Jawaan. None of us thought they would make it."

"True, but they are the exception to the rule."

"Well, rules *are* made to be broken, as they say."

"Maybe. Maybe not. Things work out the way they do for a reason. Maybe you and I were *never* meant to be together. Maybe we were meant to be *just* friends, you know?"

"Yeah, maybe."

She looked at me and smiled like she knew something I didn't.

I smiled back, but I could tell that we weren't getting anywhere; it was time for this night to be over with. My uncle used to tell me that sometimes men accidentally fall into the pussy. This was one accident waiting to happen, so I tried to clean up this mess before it happened. I finally said, "I guess that's about it. Let me walk you to the door."

"Oh yes, I'm sorry. I didn't mean to keep you."

"No problem." I escorted her out of my office and to the door. As I opened the door, I said, "I'll see you in the morning."

"Yeah, see you soon," she replied then walked to her car.

I saw her out and headed immediately for the bathroom. I needed a hot shower to relax because I was exhausted from working all evening. I turned the shower on and let it run to get it as hot as it could go. As I entered the stall, the bathroom became my own personal sauna. I leaned forward, rested my hand against the tiles, and held my head under the steaming water. As I relaxed, I began to think about Jaslyn. I imagined her in the shower with me. Scrubbing my back. Massaging my shoulders. Eventually her hands would knead their way down to my pelvis until she found my "magic wand" and began to cast a spell on me that I couldn't break. I was enveloped in my fantasy when out of nowhere the shower door opened.

I was standing face-to-face with Alicia who seemed to be engulfed in a fantasy of her own. "What the hell are you doing here?"

"I left my briefcase."

"How the hell did you get in here?"

"Solomon was leaving. I told him I needed a minute to run in and get my briefcase. He told me to lock the door on the way out."

"Well, it ain't in here! Go and get it out of my office."

I turned to try and hide my erection.

"I see something else I want more."

"Look, Alicia, our relationship is strictly business, alright? Now, would you close the door so I can finish my shower?"

She reached out, grabbed my penis and whispered, "How about I help you finish?"

"Didn't you hear what..." Before I could get the words out of my mouth, she stepped in the shower fully clothed and began to kiss me, my penis still in her hands. I was powerless. My mouth could lie, but my dick surely couldn't. It was hard as a bat and ready to strike. I was sick of her games, so I decided to take control. I figured I'd give her what she wanted so she would leave me the hell alone.

"You want me to fuck you. Alright, I'm gone fuck yo' ass!"

"Prove it! Fuck the shit out me, then!"

I slammed her ass against the shower wall and hiked up her skirt. In an instant, I had her panties pushed to the side and my dick inside of her. She screamed out once when I turned her around then dipped down and took her from the back, but she kept taking it and throwing back everything I gave equally hard. I closed my eyes and let an image of Jaslyn fill my mind. I exploded inside of her as the water cascaded down my face and body. I was breathing hard from the steam and exertion. She tried to kiss me, but I turned my head.

"Oh, it's like that?"

"Yeah, it's like that," I said. "Now, would you please, get your briefcase and lock the door on your way out."

"Sam?" She looked at me, and I turned away. "You gone play me like that?"

"You played yourself. I told you this was strictly business. You got what you wanted, now leave." I left her in the shower, went in my bedroom, and locked the door.

After my night with Alicia, I awoke with a scale-ten migraine. The stress of putting together the presentation in addition to the guilt of sleeping with her really didn't allow for a peaceful night of sleep. I tossed and turned until I finally decided at five a.m. to get up and run through the final details of my meeting with the executives from Webb Financial. I worked for a few hours in my office until I felt I had all the pieces in order. Although I wasn't a big fan of the drink, at around eight-thirty, I headed for the kitchen to make a pot of coffee; despite my physical inadequacy, I still had a job to do so any discomfort I held would have to be postponed until after I signed my contract. Caffeine would give me that extra boost I needed to get the day started. As I walked toward the sink, I saw Malik at the stove taking a slow drag on a joint and tending to a skillet of fried chicken. *I do not need this shit right now,* I thought.

"Man, I *know* you are not up in my house smoking weed?"

Malik inhaled and then coughed. He looked at me through squinted eyes with his cheeks puffed out as he tried to hold in the smoke. He held out his hand to offer me a puff on the joint.

"You know I don't want that shit! Why the hell are you smoking weed in my house?" I was astounded at the audacity of this cat...friend or not; he had crossed the line. It was unbelievable. He was standing in the middle of the kitchen with a piece of chicken in one hand and a joint in the other. He'd take a drag on his joint then eat a piece of chicken. That was his pattern—inhale, exhale, eat...inhale, exhale, eat. I'd had enough.

"You heard what the fuck I said, man!"

He inhaled again and then blew out a stream of smoke.

"I know, but you fuckin' with my high," he said calmly.

"*Your* high? I don't give a shit! Have you lost your damn mind?"

"Look, man, I'm broke, and I don't have a place to stay. I got a lot of shit on my mind. Shit like that weighs on a brotha, you know?"

"You know what, Malik? I totally understand," I said and nodded my head simultaneously. "But I'll tell you what, if you don't put that mess out, I swear I'm going to call the cops my damn self! You can't disrespect my house like that, man. That shit ain't even cool."

He laughed, then added, "You just mad cuz 'money and pussy' got hold of your ass last night."

"What?"

"Yeah. Alicia. You didn't think I knew about that shit, did you?"

"Man, we were working. Why are you tripping? Oh, I forgot it's the weed. You need to stop hanging around Chicago's weed-smoking behind and get a damn job."

"Like hell you were working. I'm not that damn high. If you were 'just working,' why is it that when I came home at almost midnight Alicia pushed past me, pissed off, soaking wet with her clothes half off? I figured you fucked her then sent her home. Am I right?"

Something in me wouldn't allow me to lie. I wanted to deny it, but instead I said, "Something like that. But you know what? It's about time for all of y'all—you, Jawaan, and Solomon—to find somewhere to go! I need some damn privacy. First, Solomon lets her in when he's leaving and then you let her out on your way in. Can't a brotha get laid without everybody being all up in his business?"

"Back to your old self I see," he said, ignoring any mention of my request for him to get his own apartment.

"What are you talking about? That girl was all up on me begging for it. I just got tired of her sweatin' me. Now that she's satisfied, maybe she'll leave me alone."

"Oh, don't think you're going to be able to relax. When it comes to that kind of 'money and pussy,' your troubles are far from over."

"What makes you say that?"

"Trust me, Sam, I just know. I just know. This is just the beginning."

He puffed on his joint and took another bite of chicken. Only Malik could adroitly manipulate a conversation until I forgot that he was standing in my house, smoking weed. I shook my head and walked toward the living room as he said, "Oh by the way, Jawaan said for you to call his cell phone. He talked to his lawyer, and he's on his way home to talk to Tamika."

"What the hell? That fool is just intent on going to jail!" I shook my head in annoyance.

"Sam?" Malik called out to me.

"Yeah?"

"How do you think Jaslyn gone feel about you screwing Alicia?" he said laughing.

Agitated, I yelled, "Kiss my ass, Malik…and get a real job!" which only made him laugh harder.

I walked to the couch, sat down, and then picked up the cordless phone from the end table. I dialed Jawaan's number. He answered on the first ring.

"What's up?"

"Didn't I tell you not to go talking to Tamika yet? You're hard-headed, I swear."

"Man, I didn't do anything wrong…and I miss my wife."

Before I could answer, Malik yelled out in the background, "Is that 'Chester the Child Molester'?" he exploded into unadulterated laughter. I tried to cover the phone, but Jawaan had already heard him.

"That shit ain't funny!"

I tried to appease Jawaan's temper. "Calm down, dude. He's high right now. Ignore him."

"High? When did he start getting high?"

"I don't know. He's standing in the kitchen right now, smoking weed and eating a piece of fried chicken."

"What?!" Jawaan was bewildered.

"Yep. So just ignore anything he says right now. Back to you. Look, if you go over there, Tamika's going to go off. She thinks you're guilty, and right now perception is all that matters. Trust me."

"Man, I want to go home. I want to sleep in *my* bed. Eat *my* own food. Watch *my* T.V. and make love to *my* wife."

"I know, but that's not a good idea right now. If you go over there today, you know Tamika is going to start an argument. Things are going to get out of control, and she's *going* to call the police. And who do you think is going to jail? That's right, you! You don't need that right now with the situation you're in at work."

"You're right." I heard him sigh before he added a final, "You're right. I won't go today, but eventually I have to if I want to save my marriage."

"True, but not right now. It's not a good time, wait until things die down a little bit before you go over there. And I know I'm right. Your wife's a drama queen, and she'd love to tell her ghetto ass family about how she had you arrested," I explained laughing.

"Stop playing, Sam! This shit is serious."

"My bad. I'm just trying to lighten the mood. Anyway, have you talked to your lawyer?"

"Yes, I talked to her yesterday. They gave me a woman; I don't know if that's good or bad. Kareema Fontenot-Scott...that's her name. She kept stressing the Fontenot part, like that would assure me that she knew what she was doing. It didn't." I could hear him sighing through the small speaker on my flip phone.

"Well, what did she say?"

"She told me that we aren't going to wait for Jackie to tell on me. We're taking a proactive approach. We're meeting in the morning before school and going to the principal first. She said that this way any accusations she alleges look like retaliation instead of the truth. If I go on record with the situation first, she looks like just another teenager with a crush on her teacher.

"What about the kiss?"

"She said that if all my witnesses confirm that I have never been inappropriate while in their presence, chances are the administration and school board would have to back me. If Jackie has no proof, it's my word against hers, just like you said. Besides, I didn't kiss her; she kissed me, and I am going to make sure they know that!"

"That's great, man. You should be excited."

"I'll be excited when this is over, and Tamika says that I can come home."

"Me too, especially the part about you going home. You have overstayed your welcome." I grinned, and I could tell Jawaan was smiling too. I ended the call and headed into the office so Alicia and I could close our deal.

Chapter 12
Jaslyn
The Gambler

A few weeks after I talked to my grandmother, I decided to tell Sam the truth. My plan was to surprise him at his office, take him to lunch, and break the news in a public place so he wouldn't kill me. Not that he would, but I wanted to make sure. I had to tell him that we needed to start working on us. To explain to him that whether he wanted to or not, we were about to start a family. To beg him to forgive me for lying about sleeping together and explain that I lied because I was embarrassed when he didn't remember what happened. I felt stupid, and my pride wouldn't allow me to admit to what happened. But I was tired, tired of trying to protect my pride. I was tired of lying and definitely tired of fighting what I felt. I needed Sampson to know that I was in love with him and that I was carrying his baby. I needed him to know that so I could stop acting like the fool that I was, so we could move forward and do what was best for our baby.

I arrived at Sam's office a few minutes before noon. When we were dating, Sam would usually take his lunches in the office, so I was betting on him still being there. I knew that my appearance would be a bit awkward, but I was hoping that, like me, he was ready to at least be friends again. And I was praying that for my sake it wasn't too late to start over. But as I turned the corner, who did I see but Alicia Matthews.

She was starting to turn my stomach. *Or was that the baby?* She was looking like her usual stuck-up self. I

105

couldn't understand what Sampson saw in this heifer in the first place. How could she have room enough in her heart to love anyone else when she was using so much of it to love herself?

I hadn't seen her since that infamous day at Sampson's condo, and until now, I was certain that I would never see her again. But here she was, at Sampson's office. I wonder if she's trying to "throw" herself at him again. A multitude of thoughts began to form in my mind about any possible explanation for her presence. *What is going to be his explanation this time for why the girl keeps showing up all of a sudden,* I thought. He couldn't use the excuse that Aunt Tootie was feeding her information anymore. No, he'd have to come up with something better. But...here she is *again.* Standing in the way of my happiness. Positioned in the middle of the mess I constructed. Walking down the hall just as cool as you please, hair flowing down her back, silk dress clinging to her body, Chanel sunglasses placed glamorously over her eyes, and a look of satisfaction spread across her face. I was about to hightail it and turn around, but that's how I ended up in this mess in the first place. Running from confrontation. If I had faced her a long time ago, I wouldn't be having all these problems with Sam.

My thoughts raced through my mind as she approached me. *I'm not running. I'm going to stand my ground. I'm going to stand my ground for my baby. I need to let 'Ms. Thang' know that I'm hip to the game, but I ain't going nowhere. No matter what she tries to do, or say, to make me think she's got a chance with* my *man, I'm not going anywhere at all, so she can forget it.* At least that was the plan. She walked up to me with this smug grin spread across her face. Now I knew what people meant when they talked about the cat that ate the canary. I knew what that grin was supposed to convey–victory. But the girl was putting on an act. Displaying a false sense of superiority. I had a grin of my own to convey. And it wasn't about beating somebody in a "Battle-of-the-Bitches" contest. Mine was a demonstration of faith. I believed…No, I *knew that* Sam loved me. And despite all the crazy shit that we'd been through, all the hurtful things that we'd said, I knew that we would be okay because that love was strong enough to get us through anything if we, if *I*, was just open enough to deal with our problems. So, I let Alicia smile all she wanted because I knew better than to believe someone stupid enough to throw herself at a man who was in love with someone else. That someone was me.

"Hey, girl." She sounded like the mama from *Friday* with that fake ass greeting.

"Hey to you, too," I said. I could be a fake bitch too.

"Jaslyn, right?"

"Right," I nodded. *This heifer knows who I am,* I thought.

"It's been a long time. I haven't seen you since Tamika and Jawaan's wedding more than a year ago." She squealed as if I had been her best fucking friend at some point. I guess she didn't remember me spotting her on my man's doorstep a few months after that. More than likely, she was just way too smart to acknowledge it.

"I know, right?" I said, returning her squeal.

"It's been a while. What brings you out this way?"

"Just stopped by to talk to Sam. What about you? I didn't know you worked out this way."

"Oh girl, I don't work in this area. I had to see Sam, too. You know since we've been together, we just can't get enough of seeing each other."

"*Together?*" I asked incredulously. "So, I guess that you and Sam are *dating* now?" *Bitch, please!* She had to know that I knew she was lying, but I wasn't ready to tip my hand just yet. *Know when to hold 'em.*

"Girl, the last few weeks have been just wonderful. I really don't know why we didn't stay together all those years ago. I really liked him. It was just silly how we broke up, but we were just kids, you know? But now though, I wouldn't let him go for anything. Our relationship is so special. He's the perfect gentleman..."

What was this dizzy broad talking about? Relationship? I really didn't have time to listen to these fabricated attempts to convince me that Sam would actually give her the time of day. I was tuning her out. I was about to cut her off when she said something that caught my attention, "...when the baby gets here, I'll probably let him name it."

Did she just say what I thought she said? Baby? What baby? How does she know about my *baby?* I shook my head and refocused on the conversation. "Excuse me. What did you just say?"

"I said when the baby gets here, I'll probably let him name it?"

I felt like I had a brick sitting in the pit of my stomach, and as usual, a wave of nausea threatened to overtake me.

"What baby? What baby are you talking about?"

108

"My baby. Our baby. Didn't you hear anything I said? Sampson and I are pregnant."

Know when to fold 'em.

I blacked out. I had to in order to preserve my sanity. But that didn't even help because when I came to, I had my hands wrapped securely around Alicia's neck, and Sam was trying to pull me off her. I could feel the pulse of her artery beating against the skin of my hands. My fingers began to ache from the vise-like grip I had on her throat. I was furious. I heard him yelling, "Jaslyn, get off her! Have you lost your mind? What has gotten into you? Get off of her, damn it!"

I let go of her neck. Alicia was crying and hysterical. Her golden skin had turned to a bright crimson where my fingers had been. "I want that crazy bitch arrested. Who in the hell does she think she is to put her hands on me? Sam, you need to call the police right now!"

Then, I realized what I had done. I had gone crazy, absolutely crazy. And then, I started crying. I was going to jail. Again! I had to get my act together...and soon.

"Alicia, it isn't that serious. She barely touched you. Now, stop all that damn hollering. Remember you are at my place of business! Both of you go into my office. Now!"

I followed silently, but still crying, not really knowing how I was going to explain myself. Before I could get it together, Sam slammed the door behind us and started in on us as we sat down.

"Will one of you please tell me what the hell is going on? Why are the two of you at my job acting like you've lost your damn minds!?" He handed me a Kleenex from his desk, as he demanded an explanation.

"I...I... I came to see you. Then I saw her."

"Is that why you choked her? Because you were jealous? Come on Jazz, you only have yourself to blame. I mean really...how long did you expect me to wait?"

I stood there with my mouth agape. I was stunned at the audacity of his arrogance. *Did he really think that I would stoop to choking someone because of jealousy?* He had to know there was more to the situation.

Alicia spoke before I could respond to his accusations.

"Sam, why are you even talking to her? Damn it! She choked me. I'm the mother of your child, and she choked me! You need to call the police on her immediately!"

"Is that true, Sam? Is she pregnant? Is it yours?"

I looked up, and the truth lay in his eyes. Transparent in every way. He dropped his head and nodded.

Know when to walk away.

Plan A, my choice to be child free, was clearly the better option at this point. I got up to go home, but when I opened the door, the security guard was waiting on me. And he had company. Somebody had called 911.

The police officer stood looming in the doorway. He looked at Sam and asked, "Sir, Is there a problem?"

Alicia pointed at me and shouted, "She attacked me!"

"Is this true, sir?"

"It wasn't that bad. Really," Sam replied in an attempt to defend me.

"Yes, it was, Sam! Dammit, she choked me!"

"Ma'am, would you like to press charges?"

"Definitely!"

The officer turned to me and said, "Ma'am, could you follow me, please?" the Dallas police officer asked. He was so polite it felt like he was escorting me to a table at my favorite restaurant, not the county jail.

I was remanded to Lew Sterrett Jail in downtown Dallas for assault and battery. My friends bailed me out. Again.

A few weeks later, I plead guilty to the charges. During my sentencing, the judge was pissed. With my history with my college boyfriend and my job as a therapist, she didn't understand why I was behaving like a lunatic.

"Ms. Davenport, you clearly have some things you need to deal with. In your profession, you should know that it is unacceptable to put your hands-on people. And, I see you have a history of assaulting people. It says here that you were placed on probation for assaulting a…Nathan Embry and vandalizing his car when you were a college student. What is it that makes you abuse people?" How could I tell the judge that I had to "set it off" at my ex-boyfriend's job because I now had proof positive that he had been cheating on me and had been lying to me all along?

"I should put you under the jail for what you've done. How can you call yourself a counselor when here you are engaging in the very behavior you try to warn others against?"

It didn't matter because she didn't even wait for me to answer. I was so embarrassed. She was chastising me like a child in front of my entire family. Even Sampson was there. I guess he came to support his "baby's mama" who was clearly waiting for them to throw the book at me.

"I just don't understand what was going through your mind. I really don't think *you* know what was going through your head either." I was about to tell Judge Mablean's ass to raise up off me, but she did have my life in her hands, so unfortunately, I had to take the verbal spanking like a child.

"Do you realize you choked a woman? A pregnant woman at that! You'd best be grateful that you weren't charged with attempted murder!"

Judge Judy clearly had a flair for the dramatic. I wanted to say *Come on, now. It really wasn't that bad.* But instead of rolling my eyes like I wanted to, I said, "Yes ma'am. You're right, ma'am. Thank you." I felt like a slave on the auction block. But still, I was glad she kept talking because that meant her mind was drifting further away from giving me twenty to life. I was glad…that is until she mentioned being lenient on me. Then, I just wanted her to shut up.

"Considering the fact, Ms. Davenport, that you haven't had any further criminal incidents since the assault you plead guilty to in college, I'm going to be very careful in how I sentence you. Your attorney tells me that you're pregnant. Is that true?" I felt like Florida Evans. *Damn! Damn! Damn! Why did she have to mention that unfortunate situation? In front of Sam?* If I lied, I would go to jail.

I turned around. I saw the question in Sam's eyes. *Are you?* They were asking, but would telling the truth convict me in his heart? Maybe not. As I faced the judge again, I thought, *just because I was pregnant didn't mean it*

was his baby. So, I confessed, "Yes, ma'am. I'm pregnant."
I thought *That wasn't so bad,* but then the nosy heifer
kept on asking those damnable questions.

"It says here in the pre-sentencing report that
you're almost three months along. Is that right?" Damn,
she was getting on my nerves! All he would have to do
now was do the math. I looked around. By now, Sam had
his eyes closed. I knew he was over there adding it all up
and replaying in his head the conversation we had the
morning after he slept at my house. I knew that he was
going to remember that I said that we didn't sleep
together. I knew he was going to remember being
naked, and I knew that he was going to know that I lied.
He opened his eyes, and that's exactly what I saw. He
looked straight at me. *You liar!* he screamed
telepathically. And I was terrified. Terrified of what he
knew. *Shit!*

"Ms. Davenport? Is that correct?"

I turned back toward the bench. "Yes, ma'am." I
sealed my fate; I had definitely just created a whole new
set of problems.

"Ms. Davenport, because you are admitting to
your mistakes, your standing in your community, the fact
that you have remained out of trouble for the last ten
years, and because you are pregnant, I am going to grant
you some leniency. Hell, the hormones from the
pregnancy alone will make any woman crazy. Therefore,
I am sentencing you to eighteen months deferred
adjudication. Your history in dealing with patients in the
court system should tell you that means you will be
serving your sentence on the street, and upon
completion of your conviction, your sentence will be
expunged and removed from your record. But there are

certain conditions you have to meet. First, you must report to a probation officer once a month; you must complete 150 hours of community service, complete the anger management course offered by the county, and pay a $3000 fine. If you fail to meet these conditions, Ms. Davenport, please know that you will serve the rest of your sentence in the state penitentiary. Do you understand?"

*The pen?*Hell yeah, I understood.

"Yes, your Honor." I heard what she was saying, and I was grateful that I didn't have to spend the next ten years sporting prison blues. *Or was it white? Or orange? Whatever*...I was grateful, but I couldn't focus on any of it. All I could think about was the fact Sam knew I was pregnant. The light sentence did nothing to alleviate the panic festering in my heart. I was about to lose my life. I was about to lose my love. Sam's love. If it wasn't already gone, I realized in that moment what a fuck-up I was.

"Finally, Ms. Davenport," Judge Hatchett continued, "You should be grateful, grateful that you could afford to hire one of the best attorneys in Dallas County, grateful that you have such wonderful friends who called and wrote letters to speak on your behalf and beg for your mercy. One of which...what's the name?" she said, flipping through a stack of papers. As she found the desired document, she exclaimed, "Oh yeah, that's it, Sampson Tate, who went to college with my son, and called in a personal favor from him to ask for my leniency. Your sentence is still within the rules of the law, mind you, but instead of ruining your life, his testimony made me see why I should give you another chance. So, Ms. Davenport, be grateful that you are a very loved and very lucky person. Please make use of this time and deal with your issues so your child won't grow up dealing with the same kind of drama." *Now she was sounding like Judge Mathis.* "Have a good day!" With the bang of her gavel, I was once again a convicted criminal.

Still, the only thing going through my mind was Sam. Sampson Tate. What a beautiful man. He spoke on my behalf. Even though I had embarrassed the hell out of him by acting a damn fool at his office, he was still looking out for me. I turned around to thank him, but he was gone. Alicia was gone, too. What was I going to do? What was he going to do?

But my problems were far from over. Leave of absence is what my boss called it. I needed to take a few months off to get my head together. I held off telling her about my arrest until the last minute. I wanted to wait and see what my sentence would be before I ruined my career. Honestly, I thought about not saying anything at all. But I knew one way or another, the white folks in the front office would find out about my tendency for violence when placed in romantic situations and use it as an excuse to fire me. I reasoned that if I confessed myself, I'd have a better chance of keeping my job. *Leave of absence.* When she told me, my boss looked at me with those condemning eyes. You know the look people in management give to people with my skin tone when they begin to feel like you really are Black and not the savior of the race they thought you were. *I knew the real you would eventually come out. You really are just like all the others.* I should have been shocked, but I wasn't. Not about that. What floored me was when she told me I needed to enroll in the Employee Assistance Program

115

and complete three weeks' worth of therapy. Non-negotiable. If I didn't do it, not only was I a convicted criminal, I would be unemployed. *Know when to run.*

Chapter 13
Sampson
So You're Having My Baby

After the trial, I decided to pay Jaslyn a visit. I was pissed. Although I wasn't sure, it seemed that she had been keeping secrets. If Solomon was right, then we really had slept together, and I was about to be a father. I tried to give her the benefit of the doubt. There had to be a very plausible explanation as to why she was pregnant and hadn't mentioned it to me that I was the father. This *could* be another man's baby. I might be assuming too much. Thinking too highly of myself and about the significance I held in her life. It was just a coincidence that she got pregnant around the same time I spent the night at her house. I took a few days to cool off and think things through, but the more I thought about it, the more I was certain that she had lied. So, I decided that it was time to talk.

I called her house. She answered. "Hello."

"Jaslyn." No formalities were necessary, she knew who it was and what I wanted.

"Yes."

"I'll be over there in thirty minutes." I hung up the phone.

It was Thursday evening, and it was already beginning to get dark. I sat in my truck for a few moments, praying for myself and about whatever life-changing information that I was about to hear. I got out of the truck and said another quick prayer before I rang the doorbell. She didn't answer, so I rang it again. I waited a few moments, still no answer. I started knocking. I didn't want to linger too long. She lived in a subdivision near the University of Texas at Arlington, and from my experience, the residents tended to call the police a little too quickly when they saw a Black man standing on the lawn. She took too long to answer, so I started banging on the door. I needed answers.

"Jaslyn, open the door, I know you're home," I yelled. She opened the door and looked at me. She walked to the sofa and sat down facing the fireplace with her back to me. As I followed behind her, I remembered the day she ended our relationship. We argued because she thought I was cheating on her. I begged her to listen to me. I apologized, and we made love, but then, she broke up with me. *Today,* I thought, *would be a different story but just as hurtful.*

I closed the door then approached her from behind. I noticed that the radio was on, and she started singing. Luther Vandross. *A House Is Not a Home* for God's sake. *Why on earth is she sitting in the middle of the living room wailing like she lost her best friend,* I thought. *Okay, what the hell's going on? She knew I was on my way; I know this is not some childish attempt to avoid me. I seriously don't have time for this shit!* She was singing. Loud and off-key. No wonder she didn't hear me knocking; between the music and her mouth, a bomb could have exploded, and she wouldn't have noticed. She had a horrible voice, but her passion and enthusiasm were endearing. If I weren't so pissed at her, I would have grabbed her and kissed her. Truthfully, I wanted to shake her. If what the judge said was true, I couldn't touch her without catching a case. Besides, I had other plans on my agenda.

I stood behind the sofa and looked down on her as she sang. She was clad in a white cotton tank-top and gray shorts. Her feet, wrapped in socks, were crossed at the ankle and sat on the coffee table. Her hands were clasped across her stomach, and it was there that I noticed the small protrusion through the thin material of her shirt. It was round and firm. It didn't even look like a baby yet, more like a lump, but it was round enough for me to know that she had lied to me. I was ready for the truth. Only Jaslyn could give me that. And she would do just that. Today. No matter how bad she didn't want to.

I tapped her on the shoulder. She jumped up and turned to look at me.

"Is that my baby?" Fuck all that other stuff. I needed to know.

"W...w...what?" she stuttered.

"You heard me. Is that my baby?"

"What makes you think that I'm having *your* baby?

She wanted to be sarcastic. Well, I could too. I sneered as I said, "I'm not so sure that when I left your house a few months ago that we didn't do more than argue. If we did do more than that, then that could very well be *my* baby, couldn't it? Which means, Jaslyn, that you lied to me, and we really did have sex. So, tell me, is that *my* baby? And don't lie! I have a right to know!" I was starting to get loud. My chest was heaving, and I had to control my breathing.

She couldn't look me in my eyes. A dead give-away for someone who was always so direct. She turned away from me and sat back on the couch.

"Get out, Sampson."

Her calmness irritated me.

"No!" I snapped. "The last time we didn't talk things out, you ruined our relationship. I'm not going to let you ruin that baby's life because you're too afraid of telling me the truth. Now talk!"

She took a deep breath. "Look, just leave, okay? Please, leave. You don't want to know the truth."

"Yes, I do." I walked around to the front of the sofa and sat next to her. I leaned forward to force her to look at me. She tried to turn away from me, but I gently placed my fingers on her chin and guided her face so her eyes could meet mine.

"Yes, Jaslyn, I do. I want to know the truth. I need to know. Now please, tell me what is going on." Yelling wasn't working. Maybe, the "sensitive brotha" approach would.

Tears began to roll slowly down her face. She sniffed, wiped her cheeks, then nodded her head. She knows that I hate it when she cries, but I wasn't about to let her off the hook that easily. I asked, "I need to hear you say it. Is that my baby?"

"Yes." The word escaped her lips as a puff of air, almost inaudible. But the message was loud and clear—I was going to be a father.

Fury consumed me. "Then why the fuck didn't you tell me? You let me find out in a fucking courtroom? Were you going to tell me at all? Huh? What were you going to do, Jaslyn? Were you even planning on having the baby? Have an abortion and not tell me? That's it, isn't it? You were going to kill my baby!"

She put her face in her hands and began to cry.

"Stop. And explain to me what the hell you were thinking?"

She shook her head, "I don't know."

120

"No, Jaslyn! That's not good enough. I need answers, and I want them now. Why would you keep something like this from me?"

"Sam, please," she pleaded. "I promise. I'll tell you everything, but I just can't do it right now. You won't believe me. Please, just give me some time. I promise I'll explain everything."

"Are you going to have an abortion? Are you trying to kill my baby without me knowing or without me telling you how I feel?"

"No, Sam. The truth of the matter is that I'm tired, and I don't feel like talking about this right now."

"You don't feel like talking! Are you crazy?" I shouted and jumped up off the couch. "You have got to be losing your mind!"

"Yeah, Sam, I am. I am slowly losing my mind. I choked a girl. I went to jail... back to jail really. I was damn near fired from my job, and they will probably put me on Prozac when I start therapy. So yeah, I have just about gone crazy. All because I'm in love with you." She shook her head and started crying again.

What? In love with me? I skipped over all of the crazy talk and went right to the part that affected my heart. She continued, "I knew when I talked to you it would be like this. I don't want to fight with you, so can you please just wait? Let's wait until you calm down, until I calm down, and you've figured out if this is what you really want."

"No! We need to talk now. Tell me Jaslyn, what would make you lie to me about something like this?"

"Look...," she sighed took a long pause and finally said, "you were drunk, so I lied about having sex with you. That wasn't one of the proudest moments of

121

my life, alright? If I'd had my way, you would have never known that we had sex at all, never mind a baby. Do you know how embarrassed I was? And I had already lied about sleeping with you, so when I found out I was pregnant, I didn't know what to do. Then, when I decided to tell you…well, that's when I found out about your relationship with Alicia."

"Relationship? Alicia and I aren't in a relationship. Why would you think something like that?"

"Well, isn't she having your baby?"

"Yeah, but we're not in a relationship." I threw up my hands in exasperation. "You're having my baby too and look at us."

"That was *so* mean. By the way, what does that say about you?"

"Not much. Not much at all." I took a deep breath.

"Well, I was just going by what she told me."

"Is that why you choked her?"

"I suppose…yes…I don't know. I was upset that's all I can tell you."

"Alicia, lied. We were working on a business deal, and in a moment of weakness, much to my chagrin, I slept with her. And unfortunately, I didn't protect myself…which reminds me, I need to get tested, among other things. The only reason I didn't tell you at the office is that you've been stringing me along for so long…it was like I had something to prove. Quite frankly, I wanted to hurt you."

"It worked."

"Jaslyn, I'm sorry about that, and I know I shouldn't have done you like that in front of her. But I owe you the truth about her. I know you don't believe me, but until one night a few weeks ago, and I mean only one night, there hasn't been anything between me and Alicia. I at least owe you that much. But I'm confused…we didn't use a condom? Or did it break?"

"Did you use one with Alicia?"

"You already know the answer to that. And this ain't about Alicia. It's about you and me. I'm not trying to be funny, alright? I'm usually pretty careful about things like that."

"Did you use a *condom* with Alicia?"

"Stop with that bullshit." She already knew the answer, so why did I need to confirm?

"Exactly!" She knew that I was deflecting but answered me anyway. "No, we didn't use a condom, and I guess I missed taking my pill. I didn't do this on purpose. Does that answer your question?"

"Sure. It's just that I can't believe this is happening to me."

"Look, I'm not trying to trap you."

"I know," I said, but I could feel the cage door closing on my life.

"I don't have to have this baby if you don't want me to. You already have one baby on the way. I'm sure you don't need, or *want*, two."

She had just given me a "get-out-of-jail-free" card. Would I use it? I didn't know what I wanted to do, so I told her the truth. "I don't know what I want; I need a few days to think things over."

"Well, you don't have a lot of time. If you wait too long, you won't leave me with too many options. I just may have to make this decision on my own, and although I don't want to, I am willing to raise this baby alone.

Stunned was an understatement for what I was feeling. I never thought that I would be in this situation. *About to be a daddy. A baby's daddy! With two baby mommas! What happened to my life? I can do better than this,* I thought. My first instinct was to yell, "It's not mine! They're not mine!" but I knew better.

I felt like Atlas with the weight of the world on my shoulders. I wasn't ready to be a father. Hell, I'd never even owned a pet. Not even a dog. You know every kid in the hood had a dog. Killer or Duke or King. Not me. Nothing in my life had prepared me for this moment. Nothing. Not my job, my friends, or my family; especially not my family. I never knew my father. Uncle Junior was around, but he definitely wasn't the type of father I wanted to be. And what would I tell my child about his history? His grandmother was a crack whore, and his grandpa was probably some trick passing through looking for $10 head. I wasn't proud of it, so why should my kid be? No, I definitely wasn't ready to be a daddy!

A few days later, Malik and I were in the kitchen drinking a cup of coffee when I blurted out, "I need you to find my mama." It was Sunday morning, and we were getting ready to leave for church. Solomon was already gone, and Jawaan left before dawn. I could talk to Malik in confidence. I didn't want anyone to know what was going on, not until I could sort it out for myself. Part of figuring out what I needed and wanted to do had to start at the beginning—my mama.

He almost choked when he heard my request. He swallowed hard and then wiped the excess liquid from his mouth and chin with a paper towel. He looked at me hard as if he were trying to figure out if he heard me correctly.

"What?" he finally asked.

"You heard me. I'll pay you whatever you want, but I need you to find Sylvia and fast."

"Why now? Why so fast? You couldn't pay me to find that no-count daddy of mine. I don't give a damn if he never comes back...sorry bastard." Not long after my mother left, Malik's father bailed on him and his family. Mr. Wallace used to work for Orandis's father, but he was fired for coming to work intoxicated. Afterwards, he left his wife and five kids to fend for themselves. Malik hasn't been the same since, especially since Mrs. Turner had to have sex with half the city in order to provide for her family. She tried to hide it, but Malik was the oldest and knew exactly what was going on. Mentioning my mother brought a blast from the past that he desperately wanted to forget. Therefore, he was understandably perturbed by my sudden decision to find my mother.

"Jaslyn's pregnant."

"What?"

"Alicia is too."

"What? Damn nigga, you got drama like that?"

"Yeah man. Crazy, ain't it? I can't raise a family, and I don't know shit about my own."

"You do have a point. But why do you want me to find her? Don't you think it would be better to hire a private investigator?"

"No, I want you to do it. You know the law, plus you're from the streets, and that's where she is. You'll get the job done quickly and discreetly."

"Alright, you got it. But you might not like what you find out. What if she's dead or something?"

"I'm prepared for whatever, but I need to know. I can't move forward with my life until I clear that up.

"You sure?"

"Definitely. Oh, and Malik," I paused for effect, "This is between you and me, okay?"

"You never even had to say it." He slapped me on the back, and we headed off to church.

Three days later, I had my answer. I was at home in my office flipping through some reports when Malik came in and closed the door.

"I've got that information you wanted," he whispered.

I whispered back, "My mother?"

"Yeah. Are you sure you want to know?" he asked in a hush.

"Yes," I whispered in return and then thought about it. "Why the hell are we whispering? Just tell me."

"My bad. Just didn't know how to approach you. Well..."

"Well, what? Is she alive or not?"

"No, Sam, she's not."

I was hit with a brick in my chest. My mother, the only connection to my father, was dead.

My throat, dry and tight, finally opened up to ask, "Do you know what happened to her?"

"She was murdered."

I sat back in my chair as if the breath in my chest was totally gone. I couldn't even ask, but Malik proceeded to tell me what he knew.

"She was in prison in Gatesville for about fifteen years. Mostly, she had a bunch of petty crimes like theft and shoplifting, but she went to prison in Gatesville for attempted murder for trying to kill her boyfriend."

"Are you serious?"

"Yep. He used to beat her, and one night, things went too far, and she stabbed him. When she came home on parole, she went back to him. Of course, they started arguing again, and this time, he killed her. He shot her and then shot himself."

"How did you find her?"

"First, I called this chick I know that works at the phone company. It took a bit of bribing, a promise of dinner and a movie, but she agreed to help me. I asked her to pull up the last phone record she had on your mom. She gave me an address and number." Malik pulled a small piece of paper from his slacks. It was folded in half and was kind of torn around the edges. He handed it to me. I looked at the information and blinked. My breath was frozen in my chest. I tried hard to exhale, but I couldn't get my lungs to cooperate.

"The address is off of Riverside Drive, near Belzise Terrace. I went over there yesterday. There were about ten people sitting on the front porch. You know how it goes in the hood, man. First, they thought I was there to score some dope; then they thought I was there to sell insurance. A brother shows up looking halfway decent, and I'm either buying or selling," he laughed and shook his head. "I finally got somebody to tell me something."

I listened intently as Malik explained how he found my mother. I was confused. *How could my mother live not even fifteen minutes away from Aunt Tootie and not come see me and Solomon? Ever! And now she's dead,* I thought. I didn't understand.

"After I convinced everyone that I wasn't the cops, I showed her picture to this young dude sitting on the porch. He looked at the picture, and it took him a minute because the picture was so old; then he finally recognized her. I told them I was an attorney and that her sister had died and that we were looking for her, so she could be present when we read the will." I raised my eyes in shock. "Hey, I had to say something, and it worked. He said that Sylvia had been his father's girlfriend. Said they would get high together, and they both were in and out of jail. I asked to speak to Sylvia or to his dad, and that's when he told me what happened to her. Dude even asked me if he could get the money since his daddy was dead too? Niggas."

"Thanks, man."

"No problem. You alright?"

"I thought she might be dead, but...it's still hard to digest."

"I know. What are you going to do?"

"I don't know. I'm stumped. My mother is dead, and I don't know who my father is. That was the whole point."

"I think you should go by the house. Darrell— that's the guy I talked to—he lives with his dad's mother. They all lived there. Maybe she knows more than the son does."

"Good idea."

"Are you going to tell Solomon?"

"I don't know...no...not yet."

"Do you want me to go to the house with you?"

"No, that's okay. I appreciate it though. I need to do this on my own, but how much do I owe you?"

"Man, you don't owe me anything. I'd do it again if I had to."

"Thanks again."

"It's cool, man. I'll holla at you later on."

Malik walked out of my office and left me to myself. I picked up the phone and called the number on the piece of paper that Malik had given me. I hung up before anyone could answer because what would I really say on the phone that I couldn't say in person. Instead, I grabbed my car keys and headed for the door.

I got to the house just before dusk. I pulled up to the curb and sat in the car before I got out because I wasn't sure how these young dudes would react to me pulling up to them in a luxury vehicle just before nightfall. It could be dangerous, but I needed answers. There were about five guys sitting on the porch, and they all seemed to be taking orders from one guy in particular. Probably Darrell.

When I finally got out of the car, an older woman came outside to tell everyone it was time to go home. Everyone left, except the kid who was giving orders. He stood in front of his grandmother as he saw me approaching.

"You here about Sylvia?" No greeting. He was ready to protect his grandmother.

"Yes. How do you know?"

"Because you are the second dude to come over here looking all slick. Insurance man ain't rolling in a ride that clean. Your ride don't have no rims, so you not pushing weight, and you ain't a customer. But a dude like you only comes on this side of town if they want something. It's gotta be Sylvia."

His grandmother finally intervened. She had a friendly naгve look like Mary on *227*, yet I could tell that she commanded respect because of the way the guys on the porch scurried away at her bidding. She was tough, but I knew that if I was going to get answers about my mother, she was my best bet.

"Good evening, Miss?"

"That's Mrs. McGraw, son."

"No kidding? You look too young to be married."

She chuckled as she said, "Aren't you the charmer? I'm a widow. You must want something and with flattery like that, you can have whatever you want." It never failed. I haven't met a woman yet that doesn't love a little attention. "What do you want?" she asked.

"Like the young man said, I want to ask you about Sylvia, my mother."

"Mother?"

"Yes, my mother...Sylvia Tate...and my father."

"Oh, I see."

"I haven't seen my mother in over twenty years, and I just learned that she was killed by your son. I have some questions."

"I'm not sure if I can help you."

"Please, Mrs. McGraw. Just a few minutes of your time would be extremely helpful."

"Alright. Come on in. Darrell, watch this man's car. What's your name?"

"Sampson." I looked around nervously because I knew the neighborhood.

"Don't worry. Darrell won't let anything happen to your car. Not as long as you are my guest."

"Thank you! I promise I won't take long. I just need some answers."

"It's fine. Come in and take a seat."

As we walked in Mrs. McGraw's front door, I hesitated, not sure if I wanted to go in. I knew once I opened that door there was no closing it; and now that I was on the cusp of having a few answers to my lifelong drama, I didn't know if I wanted them. I finally resolved to face the demons, or demon, that had been plaguing me all my life.

I followed her into her tiny living room. It was cramped with a sofa, loveseat, recliner, and a table with two small chairs. The table was laden with so much stuff that I could barely distinguish one thing from the next— paper cups, prescription bottles, ashtrays, a newspaper, a can of air freshener, and Kleenex boxes spread like a spider web from one end of the table to the next. I didn't know what to do or where to sit, so I just stood by the door until she pointed to the sofa. I grabbed the corner next to the window and a pile of clothes which I hoped were clean. The only light in the room came from a lamp that stood close to a pair of thick curtains covering the window that were thick and dusty.

Mrs. McGraw posted up in the recliner in front of her floor model television. She resumed her focus on Alex Trebek and the *Jeopardy* contestants. Her tan housecoat was threadbare, and I could barely distinguish her frail body from the brown material of her chair.

"I suppose you want to know why my son killed your mother." she said. Her voice was frail and gravelly which I assumed was a direct result of the pack of menthol cigarettes on the table.

I cringed in anticipation of the story she was about to share; I wanted this information, but it would still hurt. "Yes ma'am. Can you tell me what happened? My mam..." It felt odd, the urge to still call Sylvia "Mama," but I caught myself before it fully fell from my lips. "She never told me who my father was. Was your son my father?"

She looked at me hard, and then she turned her head. I just looked at her, confused by her reaction.

"My son, Eddie, that was his name, he loved your mother. I loved her, too. She was like a daughter to me. I knew she was strung out, but I didn't judge her because my son had his struggles, too. She was a good woman, and I was hoping when she got out of prison that she would help my son get clean. Instead, she started using again."

"Did she tell you why she left us...me and my brother?"

She kept her head turned for a few more minutes. An eternity passed in my heart as I waited for her to answer my questions. She finally looked at me, coughed a few times. Finally, I broke the silence.

"My Aunt Tootie...she raised us...me and Solomon. That's my brother." It seemed like I was saying the same things over and over again. I was nervous and stuttering because I wanted Mrs. McGraw to know as much as possible so she would tell me all that she could. "Aunt Tootie...my aunt...is dead...and I wanted to see my mother to tell her that because I figured that she might want to know that her sister died."

She closed her eyes and drew in another faint, gravelly breath. "She was a good mother to you boys."

" *What?* " I couldn't believe she had the audacity to say Sylvia was a good mother. "My mother was an addict. How do you figure that makes her a good mother?"

"You loved her, didn't you?"

"Yes, but..."

"But nothing. Kids don't love their parents if they are not doing a good job."

"Solomon and I were kids! What else could we do but love her? She was the adult. She should have known better. But instead, she left us alone to get drugs. Dropping us off at Aunt Tootie's at all hours of the night. Different men running in and out of the house every day of the week. Me catching her in the bathroom with a needle in her arm! I really don't think she would get mother of the year."

Mrs. McGraw laughed. "Sylvia said that you were the one with the smart mouth. Even as a kid."

"Well, I didn't get it from her because she wasn't around."

"Why you mad? You look like you turned out alright. You seem good to me."

I shook my head in astonishment and mumbled, "I don't even know what I came here for…"

"I don't either." This old lady was a trip.

That did it. I was pissed. "For starters, why don't you answer my initial question and tell me why she left? Just because she was on drugs didn't mean she had to leave. She could have stayed with us and got clean. And why don't you tell me who my daddy is since you seem to know everything else about me.

"You wanna know the truth?"

"Naw, lie to me. I'm here, ain't I?"

"Sylvia said she left you because your daddy broke her heart."

"You mean to tell me she left us because of some trick? Come on, you don't expect me to believe that, do you?"

"Hmph! She might have done a lot of things but trickin' ain't one of them. Rob, steal, con, selling food stamps, boosting, whatever. You name it, she probably did it. Everything that is but trickin'. She never sold no ass to get high. A woman gotta have some standards, and that was her's."

"Okay, so why didn't she know who our father was?"

"Who says she didn't?"

"Did she?" I was floored. All this time, she knew who my father was and never told me.

"Yeah, she knew.

"Like I told you, she never sold her body to get high. The men you saw her with...they got high and ran hustles together. That's it. As far as your father, you saw him every day. You lived with him."

I blinked. "Wait...what?"

"Junior Wilson is your daddy."

"All this cigarette smoke has you delirious because now you're talking crazy. I knew coming here was a mistake. I'm not listening to this nonsense. Shit, I have business I need to handle. What can I say? It was nice meeting you, Mrs. McGraw. Ummm...other than that...goodbye." I got up to walk out the door, but she stopped me.

"Don't leave now. You wanted answers, so you'll get them because your mother wanted you to have them. I can't believe your aunt didn't tell you any of this, but it's the truth. Junior *is* your father. He never knew it, but Tootie sure as hell did. Sit back down and listen. You need to understand that your mother wasn't the evil person you think she was." I sat back on the couch, but I was ready to run out of the door.

"Sylvia told me that she and Junior used to mess around before he started fooling with Tootie. She was in love, but he wasn't. He started seeing Tootie behind her back. Sylvia confronted Junior in front of her sister, but he lied to her and told Tootie that they were just friends. Your aunt believed him and married him anyway, and Junior kept creeping over to see Sylvia. He would start a fight with Tootie just to leave the house. Eventually, your mama got pregnant with you, and when Tootie asked Sylvia who your daddy was, she told the truth. Tootie didn't leave, and Sylvia kept fooling with Junior because if Tootie didn't care, why should she? By the time your brother came along, they all knew Tootie couldn't have kids. When he started having all those other kids by different women and they still stayed together, Sylvia knew he wasn't going anywhere, so she never told him.

"Eventually, other men started coming around. Guys with money, cars, gifts, *and* even more drugs, including my son. She became a full-fledged drug addict. All those men broke her heart. The more they hurt her, the more she got high. I think looking at you and Solomon everyday just made things too hard for her. She couldn't face you, and she couldn't face herself. When you saw her in that bathroom that day, with that needle in her arm, she didn't even care. All she cared about was getting high. But then Tootie came in, and she was ashamed. So, Sylvia lied and said she was going to rehab. Your aunt wanted y'all to stay with her while Sylvia was gone. Said it was better for you to be with family, and at least be near Junior. So, she left y'all with her."

I was glued in my spot. Sitting there listening to this woman, this stranger, tell me that my uncle was really my father. *What kinda Maury Povich shit is this?*

I finally asked, "How do you know all of this?"

"We were talking one day...a long time ago, and she just told me. She said she wanted someone to know the whole story just in case you came around asking one day." She sighed and then continued, "You didn't need her. If she had stayed in your life, you wouldn't have been shit. But look at you. You're successful. And your brother, Solomon, that's his name, right? He's a preacher."

"How do you know all of this? I've never met you, yet you seem to know a lot about me and my brother."

Mrs. McGraw got up from her chair and walked to a room in the back of the house. She came back a few minutes later with a shoebox in her hand. She sat back down in the recliner and handed it to me.

"Go on. Take a look." She forced it in my hands. I just stared down at the box afraid of what I was about to see. Finally, I opened the top, and the first thing I saw was a photo of me, Aunt Tootie, Uncle Junior and Solomon. It was my graduation day from college. I kept digging through the box. It was like a small museum of my life. There were at least a hundred photos of me and Solomon at home, church, and school—high school graduation, prom, baseball games, and church programs. My heart stopped and the words struggled to escape my lips.

"How? I don't understand...who..."

"Your Aunt. She made sure that Sylvia knew how you were doing. She visited at least once or twice or year to let her know how you guys were doing and check on her. That was still her sister. Tootie always tried to convince her to come home, and Sylvia always promised to come as soon as she got her stuff together. And she would try, but it never lasted for long. So, you see, she did the best thing she could for you. Told you she was a good mother."

I just looked at her.

"Goodbye, Mrs. McGraw," I said as I stood up and walked out the door. I headed toward my car and called Malik.

"How'd it go, playboy? How you feeling?"

"Like my daddy should have pulled out early."

Chapter 14
Jaslyn
Girl Talk

"What's up, chick?"

Shellie was always a clown. I could never have a serious conversation with her without at least one good laugh. She and Lisa both knew that I was pregnant, but they didn't know that I had gone to jail again. I was just too embarrassed to call them, so I called Melissa, and she bailed me out. My sisters and my mama were with me in court, which was bad enough, but now, my job was in jeopardy if I didn't complete the terms of my probation. I needed Shellie and Lisa to help me figure this mess out, so I was calling for an emergency "girl talk" session. "Just come over," I begged. "I need your advice. Lisa is already on her way over."

"What did Sampson do now?

"Nothing, fool! I got arrested."

"What! For what?

"I choked Alicia."

"Are you serious?" The phone did little to hide her disbelief as I envisioned the look of shock on her face.

"Quite. And I'm on the verge of losing my job and my license."

"I'm on my way...with wine! And tequila...Hot chocolate for you though."

I chuckled and said, "Just come on," before hanging up the phone.

When I found out that I was pregnant, I was ashamed. I didn't want to tell anyone because I didn't want to be judged, but I eventually told my family and that included Shellie and Lisa. There was no sense in hiding it; I was grown, so I quickly got over the shame and shock of being an overage, single mother and shared my blessing.

I wasn't sure what Sampson wanted to do. He was furious with me, and I wasn't looking forward to sitting down and hashing this thing out. The bottom line was that I lied to him, and he was not pleased. I thought that I was finally "getting over him" if that's what you called it. Getting to the point where his presence didn't bother me. The point where when people said his name, my stomach didn't do flip-flops, and I didn't panic when I thought I would see him. But I just didn't want to have serious, emotionally draining conversations. I was about to be a mom. Someone's parent. That's what I needed to focus on, yet how could I do that? My life seemed to be unraveling at lightning speed.

Sam was my soulmate, of that I was sure, but I was playing games and focusing on trivial bullshit. I was starting to see that my opportunity to be with the love of my life was gone, but I had found a new love. My baby. My child. I needed to put the pieces of my life back together at least for that purpose. Clearly, I was a mess. My child would not be. My friends would help me. They always had, and they always would.

The doorbell rang as I sat in the living room musing over the state of my existence. I opened the door, and my two best friends arrived at the same time. I hugged each of them and walked them to the couch. Shellie, as promised, brought the wine, tequila, and hot chocolate from Starbucks. She didn't wait to get started either. She was talking as she walked through the front door.

"Girl, what the hell happened?"

Lisa chimed in as she followed behind her, "Yeah, sis, what's going on?"

"Man, I don't know. I just lost it."

"*Why?*" They both exclaimed simultaneously. I grabbed a wine glass for Lisa and a shot glass for Shellie. I wanted to join them, but the hot chocolate had to suffice. Shellie and Lisa poured their drinks as we reclined on the couch, and I relayed all the details of my incident with Alicia and Sam including how he recently showed up at my apartment. I waited for their reactions. Lisa was quiet, but Shellie had questions.

"Sooo...she's pregnant too?"

"Yes. That's what she's saying," Lisa replied.

Shellie responded with, "Whoa!

"Right."

After the initial shock, Shellie asked, "So, why did you choke her instead of whooping Sampson's ass?"

"I don't know...it was the way she told me, I guess. She was bragging...I don't know it...she just irritates the hell out of me. She was the reason we broke up in the first place. She's been throwing herself at him since he and I got together. It's like she never gave us a chance. *She* is the reason we're not together to this day, and here she is in my face talking about how she's pregnant, too. I just couldn't take it."

"So, you let her take your man and your dignity?"

"Damn, Shellie, why do you have to be so mean?"

"I'm not mean; I'm just extra truthful." She laughed.

"Lisa, you've been awfully quiet. What are you thinking?" I asked.

"Mainly, I'm listening. Just trying to figure out how you keep your job. I'm not worried about your relationship with Sampson as much as I am that."

"Well, I still have it for now. I am on an unpaid leave of absence, and I have to participate in counseling. Once I do that, I can return to work."

"Isn't that a trip? The counselor in counseling..." Shellie mused.

Lisa and I nodded in agreement.

Lisa refocused with, "Are you prepared for two months without a check? If not, you know I got you."

"Yeah, me too, Jazz."

"I'm good. I will have to hit up my savings, but I will be ok. Thanks though."

"Either your savings or early child support from yo' baby daddy."

I screamed, "Shellie! You know I would never do that."

"I know. And you are stupid, too. Too nice. Make that bastard pay."

I shook my head, "No. I'm sure he and I can work that out."

Lisa finally asked, "What makes you so sure? Did he ever tell you what he wants to do?"

"Not yet. He said he needed time to think. I know Sam. He will do the right thing especially because he never knew his father."

She continued, "What do you want to do?"

"In the beginning, I thought about not having it, but like I told you before, I talked to my granny, and she changed my mind."

"You'll keep the baby even if Sam doesn't want to?"

"Yes, even if he doesn't want it."

"Alright, sis, we got you." Lisa was always the rock of our friendship.

"Have you heard from him at all?" Shellie asked.

"He texts and calls every day to check on me. By the way, I told him that I still loved him."

They said in unison, "Good!"

"Why'd you say that?"

"Because you need to stop using Alicia as an excuse. Yes, she did whatever, but sis, you are playing this "hard-to-get-walls-up" role is getting old. Shit, If I was Sampson, I would have cut you loose a long time ago. Dude is still trying though. The least you can do is tell him how you really feel...*finally.*"Shellie said.

"True," Lisa agreed.

"Give the man another chance, Jaslyn. This is the perfect reason to put your pride aside, "she said and patted my stomach.

I slapped her hand and added," I know, but now Alicia is pregnant, too. How can I trust him?"

Shellie offered, "Let's be fair, you guys weren't together. And you learn to trust each other one day at a time."

I nodded my head. Then, Lisa looked at me, and her eyes lit up, "Jaslyn, two months off might not be such a bad idea. Hell, we can all take off. Let's all take a vacation. I could surely use one, and I'm sure Shellie could, too. Am I right?"

Shellie took her third shot of tequila and sang, "Let's do it! Where are we going, Lisa?"

"I'm not sure yet. I'll make all the plans."

I wanted to go, but I knew the time wasn't right. "Y'all, I'm good as far as my bills, but I can't take a trip. I don't have any money coming in. I'm sorry, but I can't go."

"Don't worry about it, Jazz. This trip is on me and Shellie. Right, Shell?"

"Bitch, I didn't say I was paying for a trip."

I jerked my head in Shellie's direction. "Wait. Didn't you just say you had my back?"

"Yeah, but I meant like $20 or $30 on a bill."

"I hate you," I said laughing.

Shellie took another shot and said, "Naw, sis. Don't worry. We got you. You need to get away from this foolishness and chill. Get your head together then come back and work things out with yo' baby daddy."

"Ugh! Please stop saying that."

"What? Baby Daddy?"

"Yes."

"HA! But that's what he is."

Lisa spoke up, "Stop it, fool!" She shook her head, then added, "Jaslyn, you should appeal your leave with pay as well. Have you ever been in trouble before?"

"Never. Lisa, I was just so happy they didn't fire me, and that I only have to do community service instead of jail time, I didn't think about appealing, but I will. Thanks...thank you both. Everything is just so crazy right now; I can't even think straight." A tear rolled down my eye, and before I knew it, I had my head in my hands, and I was in a full-blown cry. They both embraced me at the same time. Shellie took a tissue off the coffee table and wiped my tears as Lisa said, "Don't cry, Jaslyn, and don't worry. You messed up, Sis, but God's got you covered. Believe that."

Then Shellie added, "Now suck that shit up. We got work to do!" Then, we all fell out laughing.

Chapter 15
Sampson
Like Father, Like Son

I pulled up to the house that I grew up in feeling anxious. I sat in the car for a few minutes to get my thoughts together. Uncle Junior was standing on the wooden porch waiting for me. I called him earlier to tell him I was coming over. With one hand he covered his eyes to block out the sun, and he clutched his cane for support with the other hand. He moved his hand from over his eyes and waved at me, and I nodded in acknowledgment to let him know that I was about to get out of the car. Before I opened the door, I took a deep breath to steady my nerves and prepare myself for the conversation that was about to change my life.

I looked over at the house. Streaks of gray peeked through the blue and white paint revealing the wood beneath. The yard was small—one tree with broken limbs and leaves the color of mud, dirt lined the sidewalk leading to the porch, and the bushes had died a long time ago. For a brief moment, I felt bad for not coming to help him with the chores.

After a few moments, I got out of the car and walked up to the steps of the porch. It creaked from my weight as I stepped to shake his hand.

"What's up, Uncle Junior?"

He pulled me in for a hug. "Nothing much, nephew. What's up with you?"

I was taken aback; I was overwhelmed. The hug, and then the name.

He called me "nephew," something he had called me as long as I had known him. I never had a problem

147

with it before, but now, it made me cringe. I couldn't imagine him calling me "son." But that's exactly who I was, Junior Wilson's son. I tried to imagine saying my new name. *Sampson Wilson.* I rolled it around in my mind; it didn't sound right. The rhythm of the words didn't complement each other. Besides the fact that I had "son" at the end of each name, when you put the two together, it made no sense. Ironically, the only thing that made sense was that I had to tell my uncle that I knew he was cheating on my aunt with my mother, and he was my biological father.

Uncle Junior pulled away from me to sit down in the only chair on the porch. He rested his cane in between his legs and asked, "What brings you over? Something must be up?"

I sat on the steps of the porch and turned to the side to stare up at him before I asked a question of my own. "What makes you say that?"

"Well, you ain't been over since the funeral?"

"I call and check on you every week, Uncle Junior."

"I know, but you ain't been over here. It makes a difference."

I sighed and looked down at the porch. A few months had passed since the funeral, and I still couldn't make myself go by the house. Even though my uncle was a jerk, I would call him every week to make sure everything was okay or to see if he needed anything. If he needed money or something, I sent it by Solomon. It was just too hard to be in the place that my aunt loved so much and not see her. Even now, as I sat on the porch, I wanted to get up and walk in the kitchen to see what she was cooking for dinner. The urge was so strong that I found myself moving to do it, but a small voice inside told me to stop, that she wasn't going to be there.

"Son, I know it's hard for you to come by here."

Son? Does he know, I thought. I was definitely paranoid.

"I'm not mad at you, but I know something must be going on for you to come over here." He laughed and added, "I thought that the only time I would ever see you again was at church on Sundays."

"Naw, that's not the only time you'll see me. I'll start coming back over but not for a while after this. I just can't make myself do it right now. The only reason I came over today was to tell you something."

"I knew it was something. What's going on?"

"I found Sylvia."

"You did. Well, where the hell is she? Does she know about Camille?"

"She's dead. She was shot by her boyfriend," I said and relayed the details about my search, finding Mrs. McGraw, and the specifics about her murder stopping short of revealing that I had learned the identity of my father.

"Good Lord!"

"I know this sounds harsh, but frankly, I wish I never found her."

"Why you say that?" It was obvious he had no clue what I was about to tell him. That made it harder to do, but instead of beating around the bush, I jumped right in.

"Did you sleep with my mother? Are you our dad?" I could feel my brows touching as I struggled with this new knowledge.

"Hold up now, Sampson. You're going too fast. Father? You and Solomon's daddy?"

"Mrs. McGraw told me that you are my dad. That you slept with your wife's sister. My aunt and my mother. Surely you weren't that lowdown and dirty?"

He leaned back in his chair and took a deep breath. His lack of an immediate answer told me all that I needed to know.

"And she said that Aunt Tootie knew about it. It's true, isn't it?

"Hold on now. I need time to think."

"About what?! You've had more than thirty years to think. All I want is an answer, and I need it from you."

"Calm down, now, just calm down."

"You of all people should know how long I have been wanting to know who my real father is, and the whole time you've been staring me in my face. I can't believe this shit. And to think that you knew all along and lied to me and my brother. Why lie about that? Why be a part of our lives at all if you didn't want us to know that you were our dad?"

"What made you find your mother? What made you ask after all these years?"

I took a deep sigh, "Because I'm going to be a dad, Uncle Junior. I'm going to have kids of my own, and I wanted to fully know who I was so I can be a good dad to my kids."

"You're having a kid?"

"Kids. Two kids by two different women." I shook my head because I still couldn't believe it. "Seems like the apple didn't fall too far from the tree because I took after you anyway."

He dropped his head in what I guess was shame. "Sampson, I didn't know. I didn't know, son. I suspected, but I didn't know. You know I was drinking a lot back then. I was young and stupid. Too stupid and too scared to ask. I was afraid to bring up the subject with Camille because I knew it would just remind her that I had been fooling around with your mom. Camille...your Aunt Tootie always said she didn't know and didn't care who y'all daddy was. She was just happy to have you, so I accepted the role of uncle to make her happy and keep the peace. Please believe that I didn't know."

"Well, she *did* know, and for years she told Sylvia about me and Solomon, our graduations, awards, pictures. Year after year. And no one thought it might be a good idea to tell me and Solomon the truth? I just can't believe this."

"Where is Solomon? Why didn't he come with you?"

"I haven't told him yet. I'm trying to figure out how."

Uncle Junior shook his head, "I see."

"What am I supposed to do? How am I supposed to feel? How do I tell Solomon? What am I going to do now?"

"All I can say is that I'm sorry, so..."

"Don't." I stopped him before the word fell from his lips.

"I'm sorry. We will get through this together." With that, he picked up his cane and walked into the house.

Chapter 16
Jaslyn
Let's Talk About Sex

After Shellie and Lisa left my house, I finished my hot chocolate and climbed into bed. I was glad that my friends came over to help me sort through my bullshit, but I was still ruminating over my situation. My spirit was heavy. I realized that Sampson hadn't called or texted that day, and I became worried, so I flipped open my cell phone and called him instead of waiting. He answered with, "What's up, Jazz?"

"Nothing. What's up with you? I thought you might still be mad at me."

Sampson drew in a long, labored breath but responded, "Just chillin' for now, and I'm not mad. I was just upset that you didn't trust me enough to tell me the truth from the beginning...and how I found out. It was a lot. We're good though. I still have to figure some things out."

It was obvious that something was wrong; however, getting him to admit it seemed like it was going to be difficult. Things weren't like I wanted them to be, but the fact that he was talking to me at all gave me hope. So, instead of ignoring his obvious attempt at avoiding whatever was bothering him, I still wanted to try to get him to talk about what was wrong.

"You sure about that?" I asked.

"Yeah..." he dragged. "Why?"

"You just sound kinda...I don't know...like you haven't been chillin' at all. More stressed than anything."

"Well, I'm always stressed. I do have three grown men living with me, but everything is everything, so I'm

153

chillin'. What's up with you? How's the baby? When do you have your next doctor's appointment?"

"So far, the baby is fine. I have my next appointment in a couple of weeks. Do you want to go with me?"

"Yes. You just let me know when, a'ight?"

"*A'ight?* Sam, what is wrong with you?"

"Nothing. Damn, I told you that already."

His irritation with me almost deterred me from asking the next question, but I continued, so I could figure out what I was dealing with. "Have you been *drinking?*"

"I've had a few. Why? You say that like there's something wrong with me having a drink every now and then."

"I didn't say that there was anything wrong with it. It's just that it's not like you to drink during the week."

"Well, maybe it's about time I started doing some things differently. The way things are going, I need to make some changes in my life."

"Alright, come on now. Talk to me. You sound like you had a hard day."

"Stop talking to me like I'm a kid." he snapped.

"First off, I'm not trying to talk to you like you're a kid. I'm worried about you."

"Well, I've had a bad day, and I'm *trying* not to think about it. But you keep bringing it up, so it's getting kinda hard to let it go," he barked at me.

I'd had just about enough of his attitude, and my patience with him was quickly wearing down. *I do have problems of my own,* I thought.

"Let that be the last time you yell at me, alright?"

154

"Did you call me just to nag the hell out of me?"

"Shit, my bad. I was just trying to make you feel better. That's the only reason I asked."

He got quiet and didn't say anything. I took a soothing breath and tried to turn the conversation back to a positive tone.

"Hey, if you need to talk, I'm here."

"I know. But not right now. I'm just not ready. Feel me?"

"Yeah, I got you, but do you think that drinking is going to solve whatever is wrong?"

He yelled, "Who said I was drinking to solve anything? My god, can't a man come home and have a drink or two!"

"I told you to stop yelling at me! I'll slam this phone down in your face."

"Okay, okay, I'm sorry." I heard him sigh. Then he added, "I'm sorry, Jaslyn. You know I didn't mean to yell at you. Let's forget that we even had this conversation, okay?"

"Sampson, I'm worried about you and the drinking."

"Jaslyn, I had a really long day, and I'm tired. It was just a little something to calm my nerves. That's all. Now, can we *please* talk about something else?"

"You promise?"

"I promise. That's all."

"Okay."

"Good. Now can we talk about something else besides my problems?"

"Sure, that's fine with me. What's on your mind? What do you feel like talking about?"

"Sex."

"*Sex?*"

"Yeah, talk dirty to me!" I swear he had to be grinning through the phone.

"Boy, you are crazy. You must be out of your mind?"

"Not crazy, just horny as hell."

"Whatever. You know how to solve that problem."

"I know, but you won't give me none, so indulge a brother, and let's pretend."

"What about Alicia? I'm sure she's on standby, right?"

"I'm sure she is, but not for me. Stop tripping. I already told you how that went down."

"No, you really didn't."

"I told you that Alicia and I had a one-night stand that got out of control…"

"No details please."

"Oh, don't worry, I'm not offering. I just want to reassure you that there is nothing happening like that, but we said that we weren't going to talk about our problems tonight, remember? You said you just wanted to make me feel better."

"I do want to make you feel better."

"Okay then, talk dirty to me."

"That's so nasty."

"Let's hope so…What you got on?"

"Sam."

"Sam what?"

"Stop playing!"

"I'm not playing. What are you wearing?"

"You don't want to go there, now do you?"

"Oh yes, I do. What are you wearing, girl?" He asked.

"Alright then...nothing."

I heard liquid spew from his lips with force, then he said, "For real?"

"For real."

"Damn, girl! Slow it down a little. You can't tell me you're completely naked and expect me not to react. Tease a brother."

"Okay...Let's start over."

"What...are you wearing?"

"A red robe. It's satin and tied in the front."

"Is that all?"

"Nope."

"What else do you have on? Is there something under the robe?"

"A red lace bra...it barely covers my nipples...and they're swollen."

"Swollen?"

"Yes, swollen and tender. Just thinking about you and your lips...sucking them...makes me hot and moist. So yes, they are swollen—waiting for you to taste them. But that's not all."

"It's not?"

"No. I also have on a matching red lace thong."

"You have on a red thong?"

"Yes, and I'm waiting for you to come and bite them off me. I've been thinking about you all day. I put on your favorite shoes...the red stilettos that lace up the front, and I'm standing in the mirror thinking about how much I want you...but can't have you..."

"You *can* have me."

"No...I can't, and it's killing me. I got the Prince CD on repeat...I want you to touch me...so I close my eyes...and begin to touch my breasts just like you do.

157

My thumbs graze my nipples and at the slightest touch...I scream a little...imagining how your hot, moist mouth feels surrounding them..."

"Damn..."

"I let my hand slide down my torso and untie my robe. I open the robe and let my hands slide down my thighs. They slip inside the lace of my panties and find that special place you call home.

"I open my eyes. I'm in the mirror, but I don't see me...I see you...looking at me like you used to. I found that spot for you, and I rub it like you used to. I start slow, but it feels so good...I can't control it...a little faster and a little harder. My fingers slip a little deeper, and the juices warm my fingers. I take them out and...put them in my mouth...allow my lips to taste them as you would.

"I put them back in that special place and begin again...and oh my...it feels even better this time. My body's warmer, hotter. My hands move faster, and faster... Sam...Oh my God...Oh..."

I dropped the phone, but I could hear him screaming my name.

"Jaslyn! Jaslyn! Shit, Jaslyn, what you doin', girl? Let me do it! Jaslyn!"

I had taken myself to that place. The place he wanted to be...the place I *wanted* him to be. I just couldn't let him right now. We had too much to work on. We needed to rebuild the trust between us before we crossed that threshold again. But for now, this was exactly what I needed.

After my body was completely satisfied, I was able to focus on his voice.

"...pick up the damn phone, girl!"

I grabbed the receiver.

"Huh...I'm sorry...Oh my God. I'm so embarrassed. But damn, I needed that."

"Fuck being embarrassed! You need it, and I need it too. Let me make love to you. Please, Jaslyn. I'm going to your next doctor's appointment."

"It ain't the doctor, Sam. It's me."

"Why won't you let me make love to you?"

"You don't want to make love, Sam. You want to have sex. There's a big difference. I'm not going to force myself into a relationship with you, but I'm not going to play myself either."

"How would you be playing yourself?"

"By having sex with you knowing that it's not leading to anything. Until we can figure out where we stand, phone sex will have to do. Are you mad at me?"

"I'm angrier with myself more than anything. I know I asked for it, but I didn't know it was going to have that much of an effect on me...or you for that matter. I guess I'll go to the bathroom and play a little game with myself that I haven't played since I was a teenager!"

"Well, I'm going to take a shower and head to bed. Talk to you tomorrow?"

"Yeah, okay," he snapped and slammed the phone down in my face.

Thirty minutes later, he was standing outside at my door with takeout. I let him in. I guess I wasn't as strong as I thought.

The next day, I woke up, and Sam was lying next to me, staring at me. "Good morning," he said.

I got out of bed and headed to the bathroom to put on my robe. After the fried rice and egg rolls, Sam and I finished what we started on the phone. My clothes were on the floor, and I still wasn't comfortable with my protruding stomach which worked out in my favor because I always enjoyed when Sam, or any man, made love to me from behind. I brushed my teeth and came back and said, "Good morning."

"You had to do all of that before you spoke to me?"

"Morning breath. I don't want to scare you away, at least not yet. By the way, we need to talk."

"Yes. We do."

"Do you want to go first or me?"

"Ladies always first."

"I want to apologize for lying to you about us having sex...and not telling you sooner about being pregnant. I was scared, and I had already told you nothing happened and...well, it doesn't matter why I did it. You deserved to know the truth, and I kept it from you."

"Agreed. I accept. I'm still mad about it, but I'm ready to move on."

"Thank you. I also want you to know that I really want your support, but if you aren't ready to be a dad, and you don't want to be involved, I understand."

"What type of nigga do you think I am? Do you honestly think that I would abandon my children?"

"No, I don't think that."

"Then why would you even come at me like that?"

"I don't know. I'm just trying to give you the option."

"Stop." He grabbed my hand, looked me in my eyes, and said, "Ain't no other option for me. The only option I have is to be a father. A good one. So, miss me with the bullshit. Now, are you finished?"

"Not quite."

"Okay, what else you gotta tell me?" He chuckled.

"I love you, but I understand if you don't feel the same way anymore; although the night we had sex, you told me that you did. If you just said it in the moment, if it was a mistake, that's cool. I want you to know how I feel, and I want to know where you stand so I can move on. Like, I won't keep sleeping with you if you don't feel the same way. I won't put myself through that." My words seemed to spill out in one breath. "Now...I'm done."

He was silent for a moment, still holding my hand but no longer looking at me, instead focused on an invisible dot in the ceiling. "You said quite a lot."

"I know. I meant every word."

"Hmm. Since we're apologizing, let me offer mine. I'm sorry for snapping at you yesterday. When I found that you were pregnant, I tripped out. You and Alicia at the same time. It's a lot to digest, and I panicked."

I got nervous because I didn't know where he was going with the conversation.

"I started thinking about my family and the fact that I was abandoned by my mother, and I never knew my father. I started wondering what type of father could I be if I never even knew mine. So, I decided to find my parents, and yesterday was the day I found them." I could feel my eyes grow an inch or wider as he continued. "My mother, I learned, was murdered by an ex-boyfriend, and just when I felt like that I would never be able to find my father, I learned that my Uncle Junior is actually my dad."

"Oh my God, Sampson. How is that possible?" I couldn't hide my shock.

161

"I don't want to get into all the details, but he had an affair with my mother. It seems that my aunt knew about it. Neither she nor my mother told Uncle Junior that Solomon and I were his kids. So, you see, yesterday was hard for a brother. It's still hard. I felt like I was about to lose my mind, but Jaslyn, in that moment, you felt like a place of peace. And as far as loving you, I never stopped, but you need more than love to make a relationship work, especially the second time around." My heart sank. *Was this all for nothing?* I thought. "I don't know if I can give you what you need right now. You don't trust me, that's clear. I can't trust you to communicate with me. So until we can communicate and rebuild the trust between us, I don't know if a relationship will work. If sex is off the table, I understand, but I need to be honest because I don't want to lie to you; I don't want to hurt you again."

"Too late."

"Jazz..."

"No, Sam, it's okay. I wanted the truth. I needed to know, so I can move on."

"You didn't let me finish."

"Well, I think you've said it all."

"No, I haven't. I need to say that I'm willing to try.

"Really?" I could feel a breath of relief escape my lips because I had been holding air that I needed to release.

"Yes, really, but don't lie to me again. Ever. That's a deal-breaker."

I managed to say, "Fair enough," but I was grateful to know that he was willing to work on our relationship. However, I needed him to know that I still struggled with a few things, namely Alicia. So, I decided to be straightforward. "If we are going to talk about deal–breakers, then you need to get Alicia together. No more of this 'she just popped up' and 'we just had sex' shit that seems to keep happening. A woman can only do what you allow."

He closed his eyes for a moment to think about what I had said. He opened the eyes that I loved, light brown, golden almost, and I knew in that moment how deeply I loved him.

He smiled and said, "Understood. "Now give me a kiss," and he pulled my face down to his.

Part Two
Family Affairs

Chapter 17
Sampson
Doctor's Orders

Jaslyn and I had been dating for a few months. She was about seven months pregnant, and I should have been in a hurry to make things more permanent with her, but we wanted to make sure that we had a strong foundation. We were good, but Alicia...Alicia was different. I kept communication with her to a minimum. We only discussed the baby. I tried to attend appointments with her, but she was controlling everything. She called me one day and asked me to meet her at the doctor's office that afternoon because she was having some complications. She said something about gestational diabetes and something serious with her blood pressure. I had promised Jaslyn that we would meet for dinner; I knew I should have probably cancelled, but I also knew that Jaslyn would be pissed. However, my first responsibility was to my children.

I had a plan. I could be there for Alicia and leave in enough time to meet Jaslyn. If I was on time, I would make it to the hospital by three that afternoon and leave by five. I could still meet Jaslyn for dinner by seven. I was pushing it, but I couldn't let Jaslyn down. We were just getting to a place where we were getting along, and we were starting to trust each other again. It was a fragile place, and I knew that even the slightest misstep could destroy it, especially when doing anything with Alicia. If I allowed anything to destroy our connection, I would have to start all over again trying to rebuild the relationship, and I just didn't think I had it in me. I was hopeful that one day we could figure out how to get back to where we used to be, better than we used to be, but that would surely take some work.

As I left my office for the day, I instructed my secretary to call Jaslyn and move our plans back to 7:30 PM, giving myself some wiggle room. I told her to make reservations at a popular soul food restaurant near downtown Fort Worth. She loved the food, atmosphere, and music. I knew she would be excited because her favorite local band would be playing.

I arrived at the doctor's office about twenty minutes late because I had a meeting that ran over, and just my luck, I got caught in traffic. I told the receptionist who I was and why I was there. She had a nurse come from the back and escort me to the examination room where Alicia and the doctor were already engaged in conversation. I walked through the door and Alicia greeted me with, "So you decided to show up?" What could I say? I just nodded my head and took a seat next to her.

"Sam, this is my doctor and soror, Lynn Morris. Lynn, this is Sampson Tate. I believe I've explained him to you."

Explain? What was I? An Algebra problem? I knew then that this was going to be a long visit. I didn't want to argue, so I ignored the comment and stood up to shake her hand and say hello properly. "Nice to meet you."

"Hello, Sam. It's nice to finally meet you as well," she said with a dry smirk removing any doubt that she knew about our situation. I was embarrassed.

I sat back down as Dr. Morris explained that Alicia was now considered high-risk, and she was going to place her on bed rest. What that meant, I wasn't sure. I needed to learn so I could figure out how I could support her. I took a deep breath, my eyes closed in contemplation of what came next.

One of the nurses stuck her head in the room for Dr. Morris's attention. "If you'll excuse me," she pleaded and left the room before I could say anything.

I had so many questions, but I didn't know where to begin. I knew she wouldn't be able to go back to work until she delivered the baby. She was about seven months along now. She wouldn't return to work for at least three months considering bed rest and maternity leave. I was nervous. I wasn't excited about having to deal with Alicia at all, but I wanted my baby, healthy and whole. So, I was going to help as much as I could, but I needed answers. When Dr. Morris walked out, I started in on Alicia trying to get them.

"How did this happen?"

"What do you mean '*how did this happen*'? What are you saying?" Alicia's voice rose in anger. I wasn't accusing her of anything...but, yet I was. I was confused. She was such a manipulative and deceitful person that I wouldn't have believed her had I not been there to hear it for myself. I wanted to understand what she, we, were facing. At the same time, I wanted to make sure she wasn't lying to me, trying to get me further involved in her life than I needed to be just because she could. However, this is where we were, trying to navigate a pregnancy together, all because I couldn't keep my dick in my pants.

"I'm not accusing you of anything. I just want to understand what is happening. How does someone get or how did you get this thing...preeclampsia? And gestational diabetes?" I could feel my brows furrow, and my head started hurting so I started rubbing my temples.

Just as I finished my question, Dr. Morris walked back into the room. "Ah, Mr. Tate, that's a good question. Let me try to explain. Let's start with pre-eclampsia. It's a condition women can get during pregnancy that is characterized by high blood pressure. Although it is treatable, it is very serious. If left untreated, it can be serious for both the mom and the baby. Take a look at Alicia's feet. See how swollen they look? "

I nodded.

"That is one of the symptoms of preeclampsia. Her blood pressure levels were elevated. Her systolic reading is normally around 135 and her diastolic reading is normally around sixty-five. At yesterday's appointment, her blood pressure was 165 over 90. We gave her a urine test. It's standard practice at least once during the pregnancy. Her ketone levels were high, and that combined with the elevated blood pressure helps me determine the diagnosis for preeclampsia."

I could feel the pupils in my eyes grow larger as Dr. Morris continued explaining.

"It can cause swelling, headaches, and epigastric pain. That's pain in the abdomen near the ribcage. Worst-case scenarios include seizures and strokes with possible fatalities for the mom and baby if we don't get her blood pressure under control."

I was shocked. I thought Alicia was trying to manipulate me, but she was actually dealing with some serious shit. I still had a bunch of questions, but I didn't know where to begin. Just as I began to wrap my head around pre-eclampsia, Dr. Morris started explaining Alicia's second condition.

"So, Mr. Tate, Mom has two conditions going on. I've covered the first, preeclampsia. Do you have any questions?

"Yes...No." Dr. Morris raised an eyebrow, so I added, "Not right now. I'll let you finish explaining first.

"Well, her second condition is called gestational diabetes which is a form of diabetes a mom can develop during pregnancy when the body can't break down blood sugar because there isn't enough insulin. Normal blood sugar should be less than 180. Yesterday, Alicia's last reading was 205. Because of Alicia's pre-eclampsia and elevated blood sugar, we ran a second test. Today her blood sugar level is 210. Because of the two elevated readings, I must diagnose Alicia with gestational diabetes and begin treatment right away."

"Treatment? What type of treatment? Like, what does all this mean?" Man, I needed a drink and fast. I didn't fully understand what this lady was telling me, but it sounded serious, and I was worried that something would happen to my kid.

"As a black female, it is important that we take Alicia's treatment plan seriously. Both conditions are treatable, but if left untreated, they can cause serious problems."

"What type of problems? I mean you told me about the complications from preeclampsia, but what about this...this...gestational diabetes?"

"Well, like regular diabetes, it can affect how the organs function, and it can also cause high blood sugar in the fetus. In addition, Alicia could develop heart disease or diabetes later in life, but don't panic. We just

171

need to monitor her closely and implement a good treatment plan."

"So, what's the plan, Doctor, because I am freaking out."

"I discussed this with Alicia before you arrived. I'll let her explain to see if she was paying attention. She's a pretty stubborn patient."

"Oh girl! You know I was listening."

"Can you just tell me, please?" I was starting to get frustrated.

She looked at me and rolled her eyes before she said, "She's going to prescribe me blood pressure medication. I have to adhere to a healthy diet, and light exercise, which includes the bed rest that she mentioned earlier."

I looked at the doctor, horrified. "So, she's going to be in bed all day?"

"Not exactly. More than anything, she needs to stop working. She's my friend, and I know that she is quite ambitious and works a lot. But for now, she needs to slow down, at least until she delivers. However, I still want her to walk or do some form of light exercise every day. We need to get her blood pressure under control, but diet and exercise can help prevent too much weight gain which would exacerbate gestational diabetes. It's just good, commonsense science.

"Alicia is approximately twenty-eight weeks. She needs to get to forty. We have a while to go. We want to make sure both mom and baby go home together. Now, I've given you the worst-case scenarios because it seems that you don't believe her, but Mr. Tate, you need to listen to Alicia. She is the mom, and she will know before anyone else if something is not right. If she follows orders, everything should go as planned and there shouldn't be any problems with mom, baby, or the delivery. So, *Dad*—she put emphasis on dad— "we need your help making sure that she takes her meds and follows orders. It's crunch time. You feel me?"

"I feel you, Doc." During the entire visit, Dr. Morris was extremely professional, so the code switch at the end took me by surprise. However, I appreciated the candor.

I knew that she was Alicia's sorority sister, but her demeanor allowed me to forget for a moment until she followed up with, "As a Black OB-GYN, the prenatal health of black women is especially important to me. Too many of us die because no one listens to us. I'm listening, though, because not only is Alicia a black woman, she is also my friend." With that, she stood up and shook my hand.

"Alicia, pick up those meds today, and no more working. Not even from home."

I knew this was serious because Alicia remained quiet for almost the entire visit. She simply nodded and said, "I hear you."

"*And* you need to limit anything that causes you stress. I'm serious," Dr. Morris explained as she looked directly at me.

Alicia answered with, "I know, and I hear you. No stress. I'll get the meds today."

"Good. I'll talk to you later, soror. Goodbye, Mr. Tate." She gave me a slight side-eye as she left the room.

I was speechless for a moment. All I could muster up to say was, "You good?"

Alicia sounded optimistic. "I just need to wrap up a few loose ends at work, and then, I'll be all set."

"But you heard what she just said."

"I did, but, Sam, I can't just leave things undone. This is my career."

"But the baby..."

"The baby will be fine. I'll be fine...this is my health too, you know? Just in case you forgot." She sounded offended. "I just need to finish a few more things and close this deal. Then I'll be done."

"Can't you do that from home or turn things over to an assistant or colleague?"

"You know I'm not handing my work off to anyone, especially not with my name on it. I will have done all the work for someone else to get the credit?" she asked. "Hell no! I'll try to work from home, but I'll need to be in the office for a few weeks."

"I'll give you one week."

"*Give me?* Sampson, you are not my father or my boss." She raised her eyebrows in defiance.

I ignored the dig. "You have one week to wrap up things at work, Alicia. After that, you need to start working from home."

"I'm an adult. I don't appreciate you trying to treat me like a child," her tone was calm, but she was clearly pissed.

"Then you need to be responsible and follow the orders that your friend gave you. This isn't about you anymore. When it comes to my kid, I'll do what I need to do to protect him. What's your friend's name, Dr. Lynn Morris? I'm sure that I can get her number. I'm not above snitching."

"You know what they used to say in Stop Six? Snitches get stitches."

"Hell, I'm shocked you know that. You and your mom didn't really fellowship with us common folk."

"I don't deny it," she smirked.

"Whatever. Anyway, you heard what I said. One week, Alicia. I mean it."

"Fine."

"What else do you need me to do?"

"Nothing. I'm good." She was stoic in her response. In that way, she and Jaslyn were alike, stubborn and unyielding when challenged.

"Alicia, Come on!"

"Listen, I don't want any problems out of your ghetto baby mama because you are trying to help me."

"Jaslyn is far from ghetto."

"She choked me!"

"Stop exaggerating. She barely touched you."

"Whatever. I don't want any more issues."

"I don't either. I'm going to be there for both of my children. You and Jaslyn will need to learn to get along. So, what else do you need?"

"I'm serious. I don't need anything. I know where we stand."

"Oh...okay." That was the first time she didn't try to use a situation to her advantage in order to get closer to me. I was super shocked. "Do you need a ride home?"

"No, I drove."

"At least let me pick up your medicine."

"Fine. Bring it by my house this evening. I gotta go. I'll talk to you later." And then, she got up and left.

I sat there with my thoughts. I had promised her that I would pick up her medicine, but I also promised Jaslyn we would get dinner. I had already delayed dinner plans, and I couldn't renege on picking up Alicia's blood pressure medicine, not after I just gave her such a hard time about being responsible and how I wanted to support her. I needed to figure out how to balance it all and quickly.

Chapter 18
Sampson
Promises, Promises

It was six-thirty when I got home. I had one hour before I was supposed to meet Jaslyn for dinner, but I needed to get Alicia's medicine, drop it off, and pick Jaslyn up for our date all by seven-thirty. I was pushing it. I went home to take a shower and change. Solomon was home. I guess he could tell something was up because when I walked through the front door he immediately inquired, "What's wrong with you?"

"Nothing. "

"Stop lying. It's all over your face. Talk to me. What's going on?

"I'm in a rush, and I don't have time to go into details, but I had to meet Alicia at the hospital today. Her doctor explained that she has issues with her blood pressure and something called gestational diabetes. She was placed on bed rest."

"Whoa! That sounds serious. You good?"

"Not really, but I will be. I have a date with Jaslyn tonight, so hopefully, that will put me in a good mood."

"Jaslyn? You need to fix your face then, bro. She's not trying to hear about your problems with Alicia."

"Don't I know it."

"How is she doing?"

"She's doing great as far as the baby is concerned. Her career is another story. She's on leave from work, and the case with Alicia doesn't help."

I changed from my suit into jeans, loafers, and a sweater faster than Clark Kent transformed into Superman. I grabbed my keys and said a quick goodbye to Solomon, and I was out of the door. Between a slow pharmacy and DFW traffic, I called Jaslyn to tell her that I would be late. She asked me why, and I took a deep sigh and admitted, "Alicia is having some issues, and I need to drop her medicine off tonight." There was a pregnant pause and finally silence. She had hung up the phone. I knew I had fucked up, and traffic was so bad that I didn't make it to her house until nine o'clock. She was deservedly pissed.

When she opened the door for me, she didn't utter one word. She just stepped to the side and let me in. I walked to the couch, and she came and sat beside me with her arms folded. We were both facing forward, eyes glued to the television. I couldn't look at her; I knew that I had disappointed her.

"Jaslyn, I'm sorry."

That was all that I could get out. Her nose was flared, and she was visibly gritting her teeth.

"I'm not going to do this with you again!" she spat. "You need to figure your shit out! Either you want me or you don't. If you don't, I'm fine with that, but what you not gone do is keep going back and forth between me and Alicia. If this is the way things are going to be, we can just end things now. You promised me that you would handle her, but here she is again! So, I'm asking you now, what do you want to do?"

"I already told you that I want to make this work. Why do you keep asking that?"

"*This*"—she waved her hands in a circle— "is just too complicated. You have two women pregnant at the same time! Do you realize how many stereotypes we are fulfilling? I never wanted to be...I never *want* to be anybody's baby mama.

"Then be my girlfriend."

Jaslyn looked at me as if I were crazy. I continued, "I'm serious. I want you to be my girlfriend...again! Whatever we have to do to make this thing work, I am willing to do. Are you?"

"I don't know. Alicia certainly won't make this easy for either of us, and you can't keep breaking promises and missing dates."

"Give me a chance. Trust me."

Jaslyn took a deep breath and closed her eyes. She stayed that way for a moment, sitting still with her thoughts. I was nervous, not sure what she was thinking. Eventually, she responded with only, "We'll see," and it hit me like a ball in the chest. I was crushed.

"Wow!"

She shrugged her shoulders; I guess she wasn't sure how to respond to the disappointment and the blow to my ego.

"Don't do that?"

"What?"

"Deflect. You're not being straight up. Just giving me nonchalant responses that don't require anything. It's pissing me off. Why don't you say how you really feel?

"Who says that I'm not?" She was working hard to remain calm. Jaslyn never wanted to risk putting her true emotions on display. She suppressed them until she had an emotional eruption. I knew that was the last thing she wanted; she always tried to remain detached and unphased. I could only assume that was the only way to make sure she wasn't hurt again. So instead of telling me the truth, what she said was, "You talk a good game. Right now, you are saying all of the right things, but all that doesn't mean anything. What are you really willing to do to be with me? I need to see it. So, don't just talk about it, do it!"

"What do you want? You want me to kiss your ass?"

"If that's what it takes."

"I'm not going to kiss your ass, Jaslyn!"

"So now the real you comes out," she laughed. "I don't want you to kiss my ass, Sampson. The truth of the matter is, I don't know how much I can trust you. You see every time we try to get together, you end up fucking Alicia, and it's always after you have professed all of these feelings you have for me. "

I wiped my brow, a silent acknowledgment that she was right, but still unyielding, I confessed, "I'm not going to beg you to be with me. I'm not. I've said all I had to say, and I have done all that I can." But still, I pleaded, "I don't understand what you want from me."

She finally exploded, frustrated with my lack of understanding. "I want you to be honest with me! I want you to be loyal to me! I want you to not cheat on me! Is that too much to ask? For you to be faithful? To me! I want you to keep your word and to not break my heart!" She continued with tears streaming down her face, "Every time I look at you, I'm reminded that you have a child with another woman. I don't care that we were not together. I don't care! It hurts to know that. You have obligations and responsibilities as a father that just might make being with me too hard for you! And eventually, you will quit on me. You will leave me because being a father is and should be the most important thing to you. I won't set myself up to be hurt.

"You want me to deny my child?" I was mortified that she would ask me to do something like that. "Please,

Jaslyn, don't ask me to do that. You know I won't turn my back on my kid." I was struggling with dread and sadness.

"Of course not, Sampson. That's not what I mean or want. It's just hard for me knowing that my child and I don't have you to ourselves. I...we have to share you, and frankly, I don't want to. A family like the one we are trying to create is hard. We all have to work together, and I cannot work with Alicia. I can't. I don't like her, and I don't think I have the capacity to overcome that even for the children. That's a lifetime of drama. I don't want that. It has already ruined my career. So, we'll see what happens. We will see."

"Damn it, Jaslyn!" I blew out a puff of air to sigh. She was absolutely right. Absolutely. In her eyes, I didn't have a good track record. I knew it, but I couldn't admit that to her. All I could say or do was to agree. "All right. We'll see." And then, I got up from the couch and paced away from her.

Just like any man, I had an ego, and she had just bruised it. It was easier to walk away than to admit culpability in a very messy situation. *You're right, and I'm wrong*, I thought. The words wouldn't form on my lips, yet they resonated in my mind. I couldn't do it. I just gave up. I wouldn't fight with her anymore.

Then again, I didn't really know if I had what it would take to make a relationship with Jaslyn work. I just knew what I wanted, and what I wanted was her so I was going to try. It's stupid to love each other and not be together. Stupid. But, I didn't verbalize what I was thinking to her. She was a beautiful woman. Through this whole ordeal, she fought me, but she had been there for me too. She knew that my friends were having issues.

181

After I found out about my mom and Uncle Junior, she was the first person I told after Malik. She didn't judge me or them.

We were friends once, I missed that. I missed being in her arms. I missed her laughter. Even after all this time, I still missed her.

Jawaan called me in the middle of our argument and my musings. I answered the call and turned to walk to the hallway, "What's up, man?"

He got straight to the point, "The investigator called me. They are making a decision on my case tomorrow."

It had been a few months since Jawaan reported the incident, and as he predicted, he was placed on administrative leave. Instead of going to work, he had been reporting to the administration building every day, and he was told not to speak to anybody on campus, not even the principal and especially not to any students. The investigation was dragging on and he was becoming increasingly frustrated with the process.

"Are you okay?"

"I'm not sure. I can't talk to my principal, so I feel like I'm in the dark. I really don't know what's going on."

"Really? Even though you reported it?"

"Yes..." Jawaan sighed in frustration.

"Listen, man, let me get you an attorney. I'll text you the number."

"That's okay. My attorney has been handling everything."

"Well, what did she say?"

"I mean she agreed with the investigator that is standard. So, you know, I just have to go through the process until the investigation is complete. She thinks it should go in my favor, but she also said you can never be sure. She assured me that she will make sure I get due process." I heard him chuckle, but I knew he was afraid.

"Are you sure you don't want me to hire a lawyer for you? I would feel better if you did. Don't worry about money, man, you know I got you. Those education unions are a joke."

He sighed, "True, but I won't accept your money. It's too much. I'm already freeloading on your couch. That would be asking too much."

"Jawaan, you are just as much my brother as Solomon. If I got it, you got it."

"I appreciate it, I really do. Let me see how this goes down. If things don't work out, I will definitely take you up on the offer."

"We're family," I said. Then I asked, "Tamika?" It was all I needed to say.

"I didn't tell her that I've been reporting to admin."

"Why not?"

"I don't know. Embarrassed, I guess...we started talking a few weeks ago, and I just haven't found the words..." His voice had an ache to it."

"How is she?"

"Cold. Aloof. Sad. Confused. Furious...all of that."

"How are you?"

"I'm good."

I didn't believe him, "Really? This is me, nigga."

"I'll be ok. I just need this to be over."

"I'm here for you, bro."

"I know. Thanks."

We hung up the phone. I took my hand to wipe my face in frustration. My friend, my brother, was hurting, and I couldn't help him. I couldn't fix it. I wanted to scream; I almost did until I remembered that Jaslyn was still waiting.

I walked back into the room, and before I could speak, she asked, "Jawaan?"

I nodded.

"It's bad, isn't it?"

I nodded again. It was the only response I could muster.

"Look, we don't have to finish this discussion today. You are worried about your friend. Just be there for him or go have a drink to relieve some stress. I get it," she said with a shrug, clearly much calmer than she was a few minutes ago, but her voice warmed my heart. I knew then that this time I wasn't going to let her get away.

I left Jaslyn's house with a goal, but not a plan. The goal: make her my wife. I just didn't know how I would convince her, so although I was encouraged, I was still anxious and confused. I believed in the old adage, "A goal without a plan is just a dream waiting to happen." So not knowing how I would get her to my side of things bothered me. I was tired of dreaming.

It seemed like I had no control over my life—my love life, my home life, this situation with Jaslyn, and I still hadn't told Solomon about Uncle Junior. How did all of our lives get this messed up? Out of all of our friends, Malik's life had the best outlook, which was sad considering he had the worst attitude.

I figured it was just our time to go through the fire, and we would have to face the fire together. My only hope was that by God's grace we would all come out on top.

***

The next day, Jawaan called me after his meeting with the investigator. The news—he had been fired.

He had just left the administration building and was on his way to his house to pack some more clothes. He knew that he was in this for the long haul, so he wanted to be prepared. His plan was to call Tamika and tell her the news when she got off from work. I persuaded him to tell her in person when she got home and to meet me for an early lunch to strategize on how to handle the fallout. I wanted to help save my friend's marriage, reputation, and career. He was innocent, but the accusation was enough to destroy even the strongest person.

We met for sandwiches at a local deli shop in Dallas. Jawaan walked up to me and shook my hand, and I pulled him in for a brotherly hug. We didn't say anything, just released each other after a moment, turned, and walked into the shop. As we stood in line to place our orders, he was quiet. We waited in line for about ten minutes before we placed our orders. He placed his order, I placed mine, we took our seats and waited for our orders to be brought to us. No words passed between us for at least fifteen minutes. I could see his anxiety; he kept rubbing his knees like they were hurting and trying to massage the pain away. I understood why he wasn't saying anything, but I was puzzled that I was speechless, too. It felt awkward not talking to him, not being able to offer a word of encouragement. I guess subconsciously I knew he needed the space to process.

As we sat in silence waiting for our food, I looked around the room. The deli was small and quaint with an

East Coast feel to it. To people who grew up in Fort Worth, Dallas restaurants always tried to be the New York City of Texas. It was popular so it was always busy, and the service was always a bit shaky. The restaurant was dark with cherry wood furniture and decorated with lots of photos of the owner with local celebrities and college athletes. There were flat-screen TVs all around broadcasting twenty-four-hour sports networks and two old-school arcade games.

"I expected it to happen"—he finally spoke—"based on other people who had been called down. The union rep sorta told me the same thing when we talked. I knew it was coming, but I hoped it wouldn't. It's still hard, you know?

I looked at him and affirmed, "Yes, I know."

"It's embarrassing. To be blamed for something you didn't do, to have your life's work questioned. My reputation is garbage now. How do I bounce back from this? I will never be able to teach again. Then what am I supposed to do? Tamika will really divorce..."

I interrupted him, "You are going to get your job back, and Tamika is *not* going to divorce you! Not happening."

"In education, you are guilty until proven innocent. It is my word against a student's, and they always believe the student." Then he whispered, "I'm fucked!" Then, he did something I had never seen him do. He put his head in his hands and wept. I didn't know what to do or say.

When he stopped, I asked, "Have you told your parents?"

Through his sniffles, I heard him, "Not yet, but I need to just in case it hits the news. I was going to call them after I called Tamika."

"No phone calls, man. We are going to tell your dad today, in person."

"What?"

"Yes. No parent wants to hear news like this over the phone, so after we finish here, we will head to Fort Worth to tell your dad. Call Tamika and let her know you will be coming by this evening to talk to her and tell her as soon as you get home what you are facing with the district. She at least knows part of the story. Your parents don't know any of it. Besides, I need his advice too."

"You? What's going on with you?"

As our food arrived, I realized that with all that Jawaan had been going through, I didn't tell him about finding my father, learning my mother was dead, or about my current status with Jaslyn. Even though he lived with me, both of our lives were so chaotic that most days we only saw each other in passing so we communicated most of the time by phone. We hadn't had time to just sit down and talk. We had some catching up to do while we ate.

Chapter 19
Jaslyn
My Worst Enemy

When Sampson left my house, I was still angry, but I didn't know if my anger was justified. How could I be mad at a man for wanting to be a supportive parent? But I was. In my mind, I pictured a future filled with broken promises and letdowns, so I just couldn't help myself. It was a natural reflex to push him away. My guard went up, yet I wanted to scream, "Yes, Sampson, I want us to work!" But the words stopped at the edge of my lips and instead formed the strange sound that echoed, "We'll see." I felt defeated. I was beating myself up because I was my own worst enemy.

As I thought back over my past relationships, I realized that I was the common denominator. Every man I dated was different; they all had different issues—Kyle was a player; Nathan was gay, and Lorenzo had baby mama drama. And then of course, there was Sampson and Alicia. Never mind the various dates I went on after we dated. One dude threatened to put me out of his car on the way to the movies and make me walk. Another guy took me to dinner, and when he went to the restroom, he never returned. I only realized that he was gone once the waiter appeared with the check. I was there for thirty minutes waiting for him, and then I realized, "This nigga done left me with the bill!"

After Sampson and I broke up, I didn't want to be in a relationship. I just wanted to do me, so I did. I traveled, I explored, I partied, I read, and I dated. I dated a lot! Some great, some not so great. Handsome, ugly, fat, and fine. I dated as much as I could. After a while, most of them would want a commitment, but I was emotionally unavailable. I wanted to be unavailable though. It was my protection; I was in control, and I loved it. I don't regret those missed connections though. The only source of regret and pain I have ever felt is never having fully seen what Sampson and I could have been.

With Sampson, I was vulnerable, but I felt free. I was able to risk exposing my heart to him. I had never really felt that way completely with another man, and I never wanted to feel that way with anyone else. Yet, here I am, wanting to feel the same way with the same man. Except this time would be foolish because he had already shown me who he was.

I say all of that to say this—it wasn't them; it was me. I was the common denominator. It was something that I was doing that led me to choose men that were just not right for me, including Sampson.

All men change you, for better or for worse. They change who you are and how you relate to people. It was easy to make excuses for them. As a woman, I rationalized bad behavior from men when I saw them react or respond a certain way. I blamed it on them having fragile egos, needing to be in charge, or coming from broken homes. At the end of the day, people choose who they want to be in life; they choose how they want to respond. Even if they want to be positive, cooperative, compassionate, or patient, they can also choose to be assholes. People also choose who they want in their lives. So, if a man wanted to be with me, he made a conscious, rational decision to do so. It was his choice. If he treated me like a queen, it was his choice. If he ignored me, it was his choice. If he cheated on me, it was his choice. Like most women, I had the power to choose what I allowed, and I had allowed too much from men for too long. Sampson was suffering the consequences of all those that came before him. I had to give it to him though; he was saying all the right things to regain my trust, but if I gave him another chance and he broke my trust again, where did that leave me? I would have rather lived with the regret of not knowing rather than choosing to take the risk of being hurt by him again.

I waited a few days before I called him to finish our conversation about the status of our relationship. I was in a space where I felt needy and clingy, but I needed answers. I didn't want to argue, but this is how the conversation started; I knew that it was going to end the same way. It didn't matter at this point. I needed some type of resolution. More than anything, I wanted him to clearly define what we meant to each other. When he picked up the phone, I didn't dress up the call with pleasantries. I dove right in.

"Sampson, do you love me?"

"What?"

"You heard me. Do you love me?"

"What the hell? Where the hell did that come from?"

"I just want to know."

"What the hell do you think I have been doing? I asked you to be my girlfriend. You're the one who won't commit and wanna ask me if I love you? Miss me with that bullshit."

"Just because you want me to be your girlfriend doesn't mean that you love me. Why won't you answer the question? Yes or no, it's real simple."

"Because you are playing games and I'm tired of it. Like I said, miss me with that crap."

"Okay then, fine. Forget it. But let me say this...since we have been back in each other's lives, you've had sex with me, had a baby with me, and now, you want me to be your girlfriend. The one thing you haven't done is tell me that you love me...at least not while you were sober. How do you expect me to commit to you, and I don't even know if you really love me?"

"Is that what this is all about? Three words?"

"Yep. Three words."

"You have got to be kidding me. Really? After all I've said, after all I've done, you still aren't sure that I love you? Are you fucking serious?"

He was fuming. "Jaslyn, people say those words all the time, and they mean nothing. They say it just because it sounds good or just to get what they want. They say those words to make someone feel good, and so *they* won't feel bad. They are just words! I prefer to show people how I feel about them and not just sling empty words around. I want to provide for you. I want to protect you. I want to pray for you and with you. All of that...that should tell you how I feel about you. Me saying three words shouldn't all of a sudden convince you that I have feelings for you."

I wasn't deterred by his aggravation. "I get all of that, but those three words...they are important to me! It's what you do *and* say, they both matter. I need to hear them, so I will know that what you are doing for me is a direct reflection of how you feel about me. Let me make it plain..."

He interrupted, "Don't talk to me like I'm stupid, Jaslyn." I had clearly struck a nerve.

"I'm not trying to talk to you like you're stupid. I just want you to actually get where I'm coming from."

"I get it. Now, can we just move on?"

"Not until I've said what I need to say. If you don't want me talking to you like you're stupid, then don't treat me like a child."

I heard him mumble, "This shit is childish."

I took a deep breath before I continued because if I reacted how I really wanted to, then this wasn't going to end well. "I'm going to ignore that because...because I just will. Bottom line, I want to know that you provide and protect me because you have professed your love for me. If you love me, you will not only show me, but you will say it. But don't worry, since you obviously don't want to say it, I won't force you to. However, I'm not going to sit around and wait to hear it either."

I stopped for a moment to catch my breath, and then I added, "You can have feelings for someone, Sampson, and not love them. Telling me you have feelings for me is not the same as telling me that you love me. Just be honest with me. How do you feel about ME? How do you feel about Alicia?"

He blew up, "How much more honest can I be?! Alicia means nothing to me!"

"She obviously means something because you keep sleeping with her!"

"I slept with her ONE TIME! I have told you repeatedly that it was a mistake...you know what, I'm not going to keep going around and around about this. You want to know how I'm feeling? I'm feeling confused because the real question is not whether or not I love you. The real question is why do I still want to be with you?"

My jaw dropped. *That hurt!* I wanted to know how he felt, and he was about to tell me.

"You don't trust me! We are always fighting, and you lied to me!"

"Don't keep throwing that up in my face!" I was frustrated and embarrassed, and I didn't want to be reminded that I had been dishonest.

"But you did! I remember asking you specifically if we slept together, and what did you say?"

I was almost speechless but managed to counter with, "Don't try to blame me for your actions, Sam. We are both grown. It's not my fault you can't handle your liquor."

"Whatever, Jazz. Like I said, I should be asking myself why I am trying so hard. I'm fighting hard to make this work between us, but you seem to be sabotaging it. On purpose. You have to want to let your guard down, I can't force you to do it. And honestly, this shit is getting old. What more do you want me to do?"

I blurted, "Apologize!"

This was almost like a chess match because that seemed to catch him off guard. "For what? I didn't do anything."

"Are you freaking kidding me right now?"

"I'm so serious."

"Sampson, you never apologized for cheating on me."

"I don't know how to make this any clearer. I did not cheat on you. I told you that. It's been so long; I barely remember. When you showed up at my house, I was putting Alicia out, and she threw herself at me. I would not cheat on you because I knew then that I wanted to marry you."

"Marry me?"

"Yes, Jaslyn. Marry you. I knew it after the first dance at Jawaan and Tamika's barbecue. You remember that?"

"Yes, I do."

"You were just...refreshing, and that is what I needed in my life. Someone who could be real and honest and vulnerable. Someone who could have fun. You made sense to me. I knew before I ever made love to you that I wanted you in my life forever. I did not, and still don't, want Alicia Matthews. I haven't wanted Alicia since the eighth grade. Don't you get it? It's you that I want to be with. If you don't believe me, ask Alicia. Better yet, get Tamika to ask her. They both like to gossip, and she has no reason to lie to her. It's been so long she will probably tell the truth without even thinking about it."

"Still?"

"Still what?"

"Want to marry me?"

"Yes...yes, I do; although, for the life of me I don't know why."

I felt like a fool. I didn't know what to say. I could barely breathe. I was confused and excited at the same time. He never cheated on me. But how could I believe that?

Sampson interrupted the silence between us with these words, "I didn't cheat on you, but I am sorry for the pain I've caused you, for giving up and not insisting that you listen to me. All of this pain, all of this drama could have been avoided if I had just manned up and made you listen to me back then. But I gave up. I just didn't have the energy to fight for it. That was the biggest mistake of my life. You are a good woman, Jaslyn. Beautiful and genuine. I want you in my life, and I promise you this, if you give us another chance, I will never give up on us again.

"I need time to think," was all I could manage to say.

He blew out his breath in exasperation and said, "Fine." Then he hung up the phone.

A few days later, I called someone that I hadn't talked to in a long time, my cousin, Tamika. When we were little, we were very close, but as we got older, we kind of grew apart. Then a few years ago, she got married. She invited me to the wedding, and that's where I met Sam; she married his best friend. They introduced us, and the rest is history.

Tamika was a real-life drama queen, but she always kept it real. If you wanted the truth, straight, no chaser, then she was your girl. I needed that right now. I was in a sticky situation with Sam, and I needed a reality check. Tamika was just the person to give it to me. Sam reassured me that nothing happened, and nothing was going on between him and Alicia, but my insecurities continued to feed my doubts. If there was anything going on, Tamika would know, and if she didn't, she would find out and tell me. Of that, I was sure. Anything she told me would help put my mind at ease or finally move on.

I knew she was having some issues with her husband, Jawaan, but she would talk to me without letting her own personal situation cloud her judgment. So, I picked up the phone and dialed her number. I held my breath waiting for her to answer. When she finally picked up the phone, I was relieved. I felt like a pot about ready to boil over. I didn't wait for her to even say hello. "Tamika, I need to talk to you."

"Well, hello to you too. Who is this?"

"This is Jaslyn. Are you busy?"

"Oh, hey girl! I'm not busy. What's up?"

"I need your advice."

"Okay. What is it? Talk to me, girl. You know I'm the Oprah Winfrey of the ghetto! What's going on?"

"For someone with a college education, you have no sense!"

"None at all. Now, what's up? Talk to me!"

"Well...I'm pregnant."

"It's about time. Congratulations! Who's the baby daddy?"

"Please don't call him that. I hate that phrase."

"Whatever. Are you married to him?"

"No, you know I'm not married to anybody right now."

"Then he's your baby daddy. Don't be ashamed," she cackled. "Who is it?"

"Sampson."

"Sampson who?"

"Sampson Tate."

"Jawaan's best friend?"

"Yes, Tamika. You know who I'm talking about." I hoped that she felt my eye roll through the phone.

"Girl, shut up! Jawaan didn't tell me anything. When did y'all hook up again? I thought that relationship was over and done with."

"It is."

"What? Don't leave me hanging. Fill me in on the details."

I relayed all the details of what had transpired between Sam, Alicia and myself so far. Not surprisingly, she was astonished.

"Girl, that's a hot mess."

"Don't I know it."

"I wouldn't let it worry me though."

"Now that surprises me. I was quite sure you would tell me to tuck tail and run."

"For what? He's not trying to run game on you, and he isn't doing half of the shit to you that he could do. Sounds to me like he is just trying to do the right thing by everybody."

"How can you say that?"

"Look, Jaslyn, let me explain something to you. Men are very simple. They are either players, or they're not. Sam is not a player. He's just an honest dude that's looking for an honest chick. So far you haven't been very honest with him or yourself. That's what broke y'all up the first time. You know damn well he could give two cents about Alicia Matthews. But you were so scared of how you were feeling, you used that situation as an excuse to ruin the relationship. You have a second chance now, don't fuck it up. You won't get a third."

"How can you be so sure that he still feels the same way I do."

"Because I have a degree in Niggaology."

"What the hell is that?"

"That means that I have seen and been through too much not to know when a nigga is trying to play me or trying to play one of my girls. Baby daddy drama...girl, that ain't shit. Before Jawaan and I got married, I went out with a dude once, and he stole my watch. I let him spend the whole weekend with me. I paid for our tickets to the movies. I paid for dinner. I even got that nigga's car fixed. I let him fuck me real good before he left, so I was all good. Little did I know that his sticky finger ass stole the watch my grandmother gave me for my birthday. Now, what is his punk ass gone do with a gold bangle watch for a woman."

Before I could stop laughing, she added, "He probably pawned it...crackhead."

"You are stupid!"

"I'm for real. Not to mention the shit I'm going through with Jawaan right now."

I could hear the sadness and stress in her voice as she trailed off.

"Tamika, I am so sorry. I didn't mean to burden you with my problems. That was so insensitive of me. Please forgive me."

"Girl, don't worry about that. We're family. I'm here for you anytime."

"How is everything with you and Jawaan?"

"You know, Jaslyn, I believe him. I know he didn't do anything with that girl. I know my man, you know. I'm just teaching him a lesson for allowing himself to get in that kind of position where she could even accuse him of such nonsense. That's the only reason I won't let him come home yet. But I will eventually. I'm getting horny."

I shook my head. "Girl, you are a mess. Thanks, Tamika."

"Don't even worry about it. Trust me and hang in there. Sam is not trying to get in your pocketbook, and he's not trying to play games with you. So, he's alright in my book. The shit you're going through, half of it you brought on yourself. If he acknowledges his wrong in it and is willing to make up for it, then you guys can work through anything."

After I spoke with Tamika, I made my first appointment for therapy. I was using the Employee Assistance Program, so I was skeptical about the quality of care that I was going to get. I really wanted a black female, and after some research, I found a black woman near Arlington named Hope Jackson.

Her office was a one-story brick home that she had renovated for her practice. It was warm and comfortable, and the decor was an ode to blackness– African masks, artwork, and posters of old Black Hollywood. I felt comfortable in the space, but her questions were a bit more disarming.

"So, Jaslyn, what brings you here today?"

It was my first session, and I felt different being on the other side of the seat. I was used to asking the questions, and they were usually about what a client needed. I was a social worker which meant that I helped my clients find resources, and I helped them to solve problems. My job was to help them get on their feet after they left an abusive relationship. I didn't even know how to begin to answer the question, so I blurted out the first thing that came to my mind, "I was court-ordered. I thought you knew that."

"I do, but that is not the reason that you are here."

"What do you mean?"

"The court order is a consequence of your behavior. I want you to think about the behaviors that brought you to this place. Brought you to..." She looked at some notes in a file, "a place where you assaulted a woman."

"Oh that."

"Yes. That."

"Well, I guess I was upset. I was...just...I really just blacked out. I was angry."

"Angry about what?"

I didn't like talking about myself. It felt awkward, and her questions felt intrusive. I sat there for a minute and looked around to occupy my mind, but she was patient. She didn't move on from the question. She had a shelf full of books, so I looked away from her to focus on the books instead of her peering eyes. That was easier than talking to and looking at her.

"It's okay, Jaslyn, I'm here to help. I see that you are a counselor at a women's shelter. You know my job is to help you. I'm not here to attack you or judge you."

"I know that, but it feels that way. I'm not used to being in this seat; I'm used to asking the questions...well, at least providing the support and guidance. I don't like how this feels."

"This won't be easy; I can't lie. It will get worse before it gets better, but if you stick with the process and see it through, it will get better. Okay?"

"Okay."

"So, let's start over. What brings you here today?"

I thought about my answer. I thought about being angry and hurt when Alicia told me that she was pregnant. However, I also thought back years ago when I caught my college boyfriend, Nathan, cheating on me. I thought about my reaction to him, how I cursed him out and vandalized his car. I thought about Kyle, my high school boyfriend, and how hurt I was when he broke up with me to go back to his ex-girlfriend. I thought about how I didn't trust Lorenzo with his baby mama. All

Lorenzo wanted was to treat me with honor and respect. Like Sampson, he wanted to love me, but all I did was mistreat him and sabotage the relationship. More than anything, I thought about how much I missed my dad. After he left my mom, our relationship just wasn't the same, and I could never figure out how to bridge the gap. It felt like an ocean stood between us, and I didn't know how to swim. I didn't want to learn either.

"I guess, more than anything, I am disappointed...in the men who claim they love me. They have all disappointed me so much in some way, and frankly, I'm disappointed in myself for my reactions because of it." My face felt hot from the tears that had been stored up from years of frustrating disappointment and lowered expectations.

She handed me a tissue and said, "Let's talk about it."

Chapter 20
Sampson
Moving On

On our next date, Jaslyn asked me to attend therapy with her. I was taken aback initially, so my first response was to ask, "What the hell!? What kind of date is that?"

"It's what I want and need. I need to know that you are fully committed and willing to do the work to help make *us* work." How could I refuse?

She set up the appointment with her therapist, and we went on a Thursday after work. Her therapist was a black woman named Hope Jackson. Her office was a red brick house that was located in a small suburb near Arlington called Pantego. She greeted us at the door.

"Welcome back, Jaslyn! My receptionist is off for the day, but come on in, and I will take care of you."

Jaslyn reached out to hug her. "It's good to see you, Hope. I'm sorry about the late appointment, but it was the only time that worked for both of us."

She turned to look at me with a big, bright smile. "You must be Sampson." She already knew my name. I started to wonder how bad this was going to be.

"I am. Nice to meet you."

"Come in and let's get started." She reminded me of Jill Scott; she was earthy and voluptuous. Full of grace and class along with a hint of hood. She escorted us to a room that was separated by French doors. The space was all brown wood and furnished with two leather sofas, two chairs, and an ottoman. To contrast the dark brown, Hope had included red and yellow pillows and African American artwork. It was a comfortable space. It even

203

smelled good, like sandalwood. I relaxed a little bit when we sat down on a sofa across from her.

"Sampson, do you know why you were asked to come today?"

"Well, not really...well kind of. Jaslyn told me that she wanted to know that I was committed to making our relationship work."

"Are you?"

Now, I had an attitude. "I'm here, ain't I?"

"Don't worry. I'm not here to attack you. My job is simply to help my client to get to a place where she is able to deal with her problems in a healthy way. She expressed to me that you are a part of her life, and she wants to resolve some issues with you in order for you guys to move forward."

"Okay."

"Jaslyn, are you okay if I start with Sampson first today."

"Go right ahead."

"Sampson, in your opinion, what do you think you and Jaslyn should work on?"

I thought about it before I answered.

I looked at Jaslyn as she focused on Hope. She wouldn't look at me which concerned me. "Well, I don't want to keep bringing up the past. We are in a good place right now, and I don't want us to go backward."

"Ahh...I see. There's a saying that says, 'Those who don't deal with their past are destined to repeat it.' Would you agree with that?"

"I guess, but..."

"Do you think that you and Jaslyn have fully dealt with your past issues?"

"I thought so. I explained to her what happened between me and Alicia. Then and now. It was nothing. I don't understand why this is still an issue."

Jaslyn finally spoke up. "Yes, you explained, but you never apologized."

"Apologize for what? What did I do now?" I could feel my neck getting hot, but Hope tried to intervene.

"Jaslyn, what do you think Sampson should be apologizing for?"

"It is hard to explain...but Sam really hurt me."

"But *how*, Jazz?" I was confused. "I already apologized for hurting you, and we have already talked about that so can you please just let it go. Damn!"

"I know that you said nothing happened between you and Alicia the first time...you know when I caught you together, and I wanted to believe you. Then you and I reconnect, and, you know, now I'm pregnant. But she's pregnant too. So, how am I supposed to believe you when you say that nothing happened, when I saw you together, and when you slept with her the second time. This girl keeps coming around, and it's like you're not doing anything to stop her. I was hurt and disappointed that I couldn't trust you like I thought that I could."

"Wow." I felt like Jaslyn took her fist and punched me in the gut. "Are you saying that you still don't trust me?'

"Well...yes...kind of...but let me explain. When you left, I closed off a part of my heart. I don't hate men; I don't hate you. I never have. I'm not bitter. I just can't or couldn't allow myself to feel what I felt for you for anyone else. It's too risky, and I'm afraid of getting hurt again so I shut down. It wasn't even intentional. It was just...necessary...instinctual...for me to close off my heart to you and anyone who had the potential to hurt me."

"But I didn't leave. You sent me away."

"The main thing is that I felt I couldn't trust you. So, in my mind, you left."

"But I never left you. You left me. I wanted us to work, but you shut me out and didn't listen to what I had to say at all."

"Sampson, you hurt me. I didn't know what to do other than leave. Leaving was easy and safe, and now, we have this between us. How can I trust you not to hurt me again?"

"I don't want to rehash this *again*. I feel like we are going in circles, but I need you to understand that I never cheated on you. I don't care what it looked like or appeared to be; I was not cheating on you."

"What about now? Alicia is pregnant now."

"Yes, she is. That's my fault. But Jazz, we were not together, you were barely talking to me. Alicia and I...it wasn't even a booty call. I don't know what to call it...we just fucked. Once! That's it. Unfortunately, because of it, we have a baby on the way. You and I have a baby on the way, too. It's crazy and stupid, but it is what it is." I paused and waited for her to respond. She just sat there staring at me, with tears rimming the edge of her eyes. She was hurting. I knew it, but she didn't voice it.

I asked her, "Why don't you trust me? I told you before that I don't have any feelings for Alicia. I hate to say it like this, but she was a *jump-off.*"

"Don't call her that."

"I agree. Poor choice of words. But that's the only way to get you to understand what happened between

206

us. We weren't dating; we weren't in a relationship. It just happened. One time. I regret it, but I can't change it. It meant nothing."

"This baby might change that. It *will* change that."

"It's not what I wanted, but I can't take it back." I wanted Hope to intervene again, so I paused to look at her, but she was listening and taking notes.

"I know you can't."

"What do you want me to do?"

"I don't know if there is anything you *can* do."

"We're over then?"

"No, I'm not saying that. I'm just telling you how I feel and telling you what I have discovered about myself, why I react the way that I do. I am just processing. I've done it in my sessions with Hope, but I need to do it with you too because if I don't, I won't be able to truly get over any of it."

Hope finally interjected. "Sampson, it might feel natural to want to do something, to fix a problem so that Jaslyn will feel better." She hit the nail on the head because that is exactly what I wanted to do. "Sometimes, time and communication are the only things to help rebuild trust. Did you know that she was feeling this way?"

"I didn't know that she was still feeling this way because we talked about this before. Then, she was angry, I guess; I didn't know that I disappointed her. We were not together when I slept with Alicia, so it feels unfair for her to judge me."

"Jaslyn, do you want to explain your disappointment?"

"I guess what I mean by that is of all the men that I've dated, of all the men that I've loved, you were the best. I just knew that my relationship with you would help make all of the hurt I felt in the past worth it. But then, you hurt me, too. I know you didn't mean to do it; however, that doesn't change the fact that you put yourself in a position for this girl to seduce you. My heart just couldn't take another letdown. The disappointment I felt was because you let me down just like Nathan, Kyle, and my dad."

I remembered the names of Jaslyn's ex-boyfriends, and I wanted to get mad because she was judging me based on how some other dudes had treated her. Before I blew up at her, I took a moment to breathe, and I heard Hope say, "Remember, Sampson, she's not judging you or blaming you. Listen to what she is saying. Jaslyn is asking you to acknowledge how she feels. To consider how your behavior contributed to her experience."

I nodded my head as I thought about how to respond. "So, you're telling me that it's not just me that you are disappointed in, but I contributed to the disappointment you have felt over the years?"

"Kind of...yes. But Sampson, I also let myself down. I shut you out. I didn't listen. I was hurt, angry, and scared about what appeared to be going on. I should have listened. I should have gotten out of the car and asked what was going on. And later, when we reconnected, I should have told you the truth, that we slept together. I should have told you that I was pregnant. More than anything, I should have had a conversation with my dad and told him how much his leaving us hurt me. It is so much. Most of it doesn't have anything to do with you, but I need you to know it and understand it. My disappointment led to me being afraid, angry, dishonest, and violent. I'm working through it though. If you love me like you say you do, then you've got to be patient and ride this out as I figure it all out."

Before I knew it, I reached out to grab her hand. I squeezed it as I said, "I got you. I got you. And I'm sorry for hurting you and disappointing you. Give me a chance to show you that I am a man of my word. I will protect you and honor you. And I promise you, I will try my damnedest to never hurt you again. I want us to be together. Can we at least try for the sake of our child?"

"Yes."

"Thank you."

"I want to go slow...let's date again. I want us to date again."

"What do you mean?"

"I mean that we are really great at sex, but the other things that make a relationship work, we kinda suck. So, I mean let's try to be friends first and lovers second. Okay?"

"Whatever you want. I just know that I want us to work."

"I want that, too."

"I don't...I haven't said it often, but I do love you, Jaslyn."

"Whatever, nigga."

I smiled. "I do." She shook her head in disbelief, but I continued, "Again, I'm sorry for hurting you. More than anything, I am sorry for disappointing you."

She looked at me, "Are you really?"

"Yes, I said as I took my thumbs and wiped her teardrops from the corners of her eyes." It was never my intention to hurt you. I only wanted to love you, but I was naive. I allowed myself to be placed in a bad position. I won't do that again."

"Okay."

"Do you believe me?"

"I believe you will try."

"That's enough for me."

"Sampson, is there anything else that you would like to add?" Hope asked me.

"No. I just want her to know that I meant what I said because honestly, I really don't want to talk about this shit again." We all laughed.

The following weekend, Jaslyn and I went on our next date. It was my turn to pick, so I decided to go to church. Since Aunt Tootie died, I had gone every Sunday. Jaslyn admitted that it had been a minute, and Jesus had probably forgotten her name. She wasn't excited about going. Black church service tended to go on for hours. However, Jaslyn was also hesitant because she was an unwed mother, so she was sure one of the ushers was going to make her go down in front of the church to confess her sins and ask for forgiveness. What can I say? Church Folk. But she knew that it was important to me. I also told her that Solomon was preaching, so she agreed to go. After the service, we decided to go to brunch with Solomon and my friends. Malik, Jawaan, and Tamika all came to church that Sunday to support Solomon. We always made it a point to go when he was preaching. He encouraged us to come other times, too, but Malik and Jawaan told him, "Baby steps."

The restaurant was located near downtown Fort Worth on West 7th Street. It was about a fifteen-minute drive from our church in Stop Six, so it was the perfect location. As we waited to be seated, Solomon embraced Jaslyn like she was the sister he never had. "Jaslyn, it's good to see you."

"It's good to see you too, Solomon. Hi, Jawaan. Hello, Malik." Tamika, of course, had to add her own spin on the situation.

"Heifer, you can't speak to me?"

"Hey, girl! I'm sorry. You know how we do."

"I was about to say. Now, shit, we are family! You can't be nicer to them than you are to me."

"You know I know better than that." The hostess notified us that our table was ready, and she walked us to our seats which were adjacent to the bar. I decided to go order a drink as Jaslyn moved to sit with Tamika. They seemed to be engrossed in a "how's-life-been-treating-you" conversation, laughing and catching up about God knows what. Malik and Solomon sat at the table with the girls, while Jawaan and I had a drink at the bar and took the opportunity to check in with each other.

I sat down next to him and dove right in. "I see that you and Tamika are on good terms now."

"Yeah, man! I'm relieved."

"Really?!" I was shocked.

"I thought I was going to lose her."

"Wow. I remember when being with Tamika was the furthest thing from your mind. Couldn't pay you to settle down with her.'

Jawaan laughed, "I was a kid, man. Hell, we used to breakdance too. People change, and I grew up. I know what's important to me, and my wife is one of those things."

I nodded my head as I said, "That's what's up. How's the job situation?"

"The district reinstated me."

"That's great! How did that happen?"

"Well, my attorney suggested we appeal the district's decision to fire me. Of course, I agreed. She started fighting right away. She petitioned to get the witness statements, and when she started reviewing the statements, several of Jackie's friends stated that she made the whole thing up. She told them she was going to do it because she had a crush on me. My attorney met with the investigators again and pointed out that her witnesses verified that Jackie made up the whole thing. The administration decided to call her back in, and they presented her with the statements, and she admitted it."

"Are you serious?"

"As a heart attack! It seems as if the investigators didn't originally present those statements to my attorney. They were trying to cover the district and firing me seemed to be the easiest thing to do. My attorney told them to give me my job back or we would sue."

"That's great, man!"

"My lawyer also made the district clear my personnel file. The district agreed and told me that I could go back to work."

"What happened to the girl? Does she receive any type of punishment?"

"I'm not sure. I didn't even ask. They will probably give her some type of suspension, and hopefully, some counseling. I don't know and don't care. I'm just glad that it's over."

"Are you crazy? Man, that girl almost ruined your life!"

"No, I'm not crazy; I'm blessed. And I'm grateful. Sometimes, the best thing to do is just move on. What good will it do me if I try to bury that girl? It will just make me bitter. The truth came out; my name is clear, and I have my wife back. I'm good."

"So, what's next?"

"I'm transferring."

"Really? Why?"

"I'm good, but I'm not stupid. Being at the same school with the girl that accused me of an inappropriate relationship will be hella awkward, so it's time for a fresh start. I don't want to be at the same school with her, so I asked to be placed at another campus until the end of the school year. I'll apply for another job in the summer in a district that is closer to home. A coaching buddy told me about an assistant athletic director position. I think I'm going to apply. If I get it, it will allow me to leave the classroom and make more money."

"I'm happy for you, bro."

"Thanks, man. Enough about me. What's up with you and your girl?" He nodded at Jaslyn.

"Man, it's been challenging, but we are good. We are on the right track. Actually, we went to therapy."

"Interesting. How did that go?"

"I wasn't feeling it at first, but we were able to clear up a few things. It seems to be having a positive effect on our communication and her mood. I've been thinking of setting up my own session, you know, and talk about this shit with Uncle Junior."

"Oh yeah. You definitely need to work through that shit. How is Solomon taking it?"

"I haven't told him yet?"

"Dude! Why not?"

"I don't know. I just can't seem to find the words to tell him."

"You better figure that shit out."

"I know. I need to tell him about Uncle Junior, and I need to figure out a way to propose to Jaslyn."

"Nigga, you've been to one therapy session, and now, you wanna get married!? I can't believe you."

"I've been thinking about it anyway. Even though we struggle, and it's challenging and hard, there isn't anyone else that I'd rather be with. If love is going to be hard, I'd rather it be hard with her. Not anyone else. She's it, man. She's the one."

"If that's the case, then congratulations! Have you told Malik and Solomon?"

"Not yet, but I will.

"Well, don't tell Tamika until you are ready for Jaslyn to know. I love my wife, but the girl has a mouth like an old refrigerator...she can't keep nothing!"

"Yep. Tamika, the Mouth of the South! On that note, let's get back to the table before she begins to wonder what's taking us so long." I slapped him on the back and got up to head back to the table.

When I got home that evening, I told Malik that I wanted to get married. "I'm going to propose to Jaslyn."

"Are you serious?!" Malik was shocked. "I wouldn't do it."

"Why not?"

He sucked his teeth before he responded, "Why would you? She has given you no reason to believe that she would say yes. And after all of the shit that she's put you through, you wanna propose? It's like you are begging for drama. You're an idiot!"

I laughed because at least he was honest. Malik was right; I was an idiot. I really wanted Jaslyn and I to live together before we even considered marriage because I thought that would satisfy her until all the drama with Alicia was over. When I asked her to live with me though, she wasn't having it. She looked at me with a straight face and said, "I've tried shacking; it doesn't work for me." She didn't say it, but I knew that meant she wanted to get married. I thought it over and realized I wanted Jaslyn in my life forever.

When she had the nerve to ask me if I loved her, I was furious. I have loved that woman since the first day I met her at Jawaan and Tamika's wedding. Even during our separation, I continued to love her. I lost her before, but I wasn't doing it again.

I needed to give Jaslyn a reason to believe in me and trust me again. So far, I had been like every other man in her life, a disappointment. When it came to my love life, it was time for me to get my shit together and step up to the plate. I would get Alicia straight and take care of my baby, but it was time to move and make things official. It was time to put a ring on it.

"Man, are you sure?" Malik asked just before he took a drag on a joint.

"Yes. Yes, I am sure. I need to show her that I am in this for the long haul. I'm going to see my attorney in a few hours."

He raised his eyebrows, "For what? A prenup, I hope." He shook his head and took another drag. "Jaslyn is a great girl. Great woman! She hates me, but I think she is top-notch. However, your history with her...let's just say it leaves a lot to be desired. Not exactly a fairy tale, know what I mean? I wouldn't put my money on this marriage making it."

"Damn! You just gone dog us out like that?"

"Hey, I'm just calling it like I see it."

"Whatever, nigga. Mind the business that pays you."

"True. I'm working on it."

Malik had a good point, but I believed that Jaslyn and I would make it. Until then, there was some business that I needed to take care of. I walked out of the room to make a call that was long overdue.

Alicia and I needed to have a conversation about custody and child support, but I didn't know where to start. I knew I wanted to be a part of my child's life and provide support, but it was clear to me that I needed to set boundaries. So, I decided to consult an attorney. I didn't want to ask my business attorney for a referral because I didn't want him in my personal business. I didn't need him asking questions, at least not in this situation. Too many questions might lead to me having to explain how I became a father in the first place, and I wasn't ready for those conversations yet. Some things should just be kept private.

I asked Malik if he knew someone that could help me, and he gave me the number of "this honey he had been seeing since my days on the force," as he put it. Her name was Pamela Franks, and she was an expert in family law. I called to set up an appointment; her office was in downtown Fort Worth. She had an opening the following afternoon, so I had my secretary clear my calendar.

Her secretary greeted me the next day when I walked into her office. "Good afternoon, Mr. Tate," she sang before I could even close the door behind me. "Ms. Franks will be with you in a moment. Just have a seat. Would you like some water or something while you wait?"

"I don't want anything. I'm fine, thank you." I smiled at the elderly black woman seated behind the front desk. I wasn't surprised that she knew who I was without introducing myself. I tell my secretary that it is her business to know each and every client when they walk through the door. There should be no surprises, and everyone should be made to feel that they are the only client that matters. The more they know who is entering the door, the better prepared they are to help me provide great service. Her secretary's professionalism gave me confidence that I had come to the right office.

I took a seat in a leather chair directly across from her desk as she picked up the phone and dialed. "Mr. Tate is here for his appointment," she announced. After a brief pause, she said, "Yes, ma'am," and then she placed the phone on the receiver. "Ms. Franks asked me to apologize. She is finishing a conference call. She will be just a few more minutes."

"It's not a problem. I cleared my schedule for the rest of the afternoon, so I have time."

After sitting for five minutes, the door behind the secretary's desk opened. A petite Caucasian woman stepped out. Short, red hair framed her ruddy cheekbones, and her brown suit was tailored to fit her small frame. I was shocked. Malik never mentioned her race. It didn't matter or bother me, but his love for black

217

women was no secret, and given the relationship he described, I assumed she would be Black. But I didn't care. I just needed some good legal advice. I made a mental note that Malik and I needed to talk later.

Ms. Franks walked up to me with her hand extended to shake mine, "Good afternoon, Mr. Tate. I apologize for keeping you waiting." She smiled as I stood up to shake her hand. She had a friendly disposition, relaxed and confident. As I stood over her, she looked up, directly into my eye, a clear indication that she wasn't intimidated by my height nor my color.

"No problem. I just appreciate you for seeing me on such short notice."

"Malik said that you were in a bind and needed help. That's why I'm here. Let's move into my office so we can chat, and you can tell me what it is you need my help with." She turned, and I followed behind her.

We entered her office which was decorated in blues and browns. Her degrees were posted on the wall behind her desk—undergrad from Texas Christian University and a law degree from Southern Methodist University. Rival schools but two of the best in Texas. Her office was really two spaces in one, and we sat at a small conference table across from her desk.

"Okay, Mr. Tate. Tell me what's going on?"

"I'm kind of embarrassed."

"Please don't be. Nothing you tell me will shock me, and of course, everything is confidential. I've been in this business a long time, and nothing surprises me anymore."

"I don't know where to start."

"Start from the beginning."

218

I paused, took a breath, and then blurted, "I have two women pregnant at the same time." I was so ashamed to say it. I'm sure that if it were possible for a black man, my skin would be beet red.

She chuckled a bit. "Okay. Go on, Mr. Tate."

"Well..." I hesitated, still ashamed and worried that I was being judged for being another black man with baby mama drama and who didn't want to take care of his kids.

"Go on. I promise it won't bother or surprise me, and it doesn't leave this office."

"Well, as I said, I have two women pregnant at the same time. One of them I love, and the other woman I can't stand to look at."

"Are they fighting?"

"No, not really...well maybe."

"Well, are they, or aren't they?"

"Only because they haven't interacted much, and one of them has a restraining order against the other one."

"Restraining order? Why is there a restraining order? I'm getting confused. Let's start by giving me their names and some background as to what is going on."

"Jaslyn Davenport and Alicia Matthews. I'm in love with Jaslyn. Our relationship has had its share of drama, and it's mainly because of Alicia. Jaslyn and I dated a while back. I would say we were falling in love. One night, Alicia shows up to seduce me. She kissed me actually, but nothing was going on. Jaslyn arrived as I was pulling away from the kiss, and...it just looked bad. She assumed the worst and broke up with me. We reconnected several months ago, slept together. I also

219

reconnected with Alicia and slept with her, too. You know, just because...anyway. Alicia came to my office and told me she was pregnant. Jaslyn showed up too, Alicia told her that she was pregnant before I could, and before I knew it, Jaslyn choked Alicia. Kind of...tried to...anyway, Alicia pressed charges. I went to the hearing to support her and speak on her behalf. That's when I learned that she was pregnant, too. I'm just...I don't know. It's a mess, and I don't know how to fix it."

"I can't lie, Mr. Tate. That is a lot to digest at one time." She put her pen to her mouth as she contemplated her next question, "So, you're in love with Jaslyn, and you have no relationship with Alicia."

"I hate her actually."

"Hate is a strong word, Mr. Tate. How is that going to affect your relationship with your children? What are your plans to provide for them?"

"That's why I need your help. Jaslyn and I have been working through our issues. Working on forgiving, communicating, and learning to trust each other. She is not a violent person, not most times. She's just hurt by what she thinks that I have done to hurt her. Even still, I want to marry her...I'm going to marry her. As far as Alicia goes, I want to be there for my child and provide. I want to help raise him, so I want joint custody. But I want nothing to do with her."

"Have you discussed this with Ms. Matthews?"

"No ma'am, and frankly, Alicia is manipulative, so I prefer to limit my conversations with her. I would rather have things clearly outlined by the courts because I can't trust her. I was told that I could volunteer for child support. How does that work?

"Are you sure that it is your baby?"

"As far as I know, yes, it's my baby. Why would you ask me a question like that?"

"Mr. Tate, if that child is not your baby, and you start to pay child support, you will only have a limited time to prove that you are not the father without penalty. If you wait too long, the courts will require you to be financially responsible for the child even though it may be proven ten years later that you are not the biological father."

"Are you serious? How is that possible?"

"The state does not want any child to be fatherless. Therefore, if you choose to pay child support, and make no attempts to determine paternity within a given timeframe, you will be legally responsible until the child turns eighteen.

"Wow. I'm just...I don't know what to do. I don't want to come across like an asshole, but I don't want to take care of another man's responsibility. What do you recommend, Ms. Franks? Can I ask for a paternity test now?"

"No."

"Why the hell not?"

"It is too early to determine paternity. You have to wait until the child is born. Conducting a test of that nature on an unborn child would put the fetus at serious risk, so you have to wait."

"I have to test early, but I have to wait, too. I'm confused. How can I do what is right for the child and me? I don't want to be a jerk about this, but I don't want this woman thinking that she can take advantage of me either."

"Well, we can petition the court for a paternity test to be conducted as soon as the baby is born. We can at least start that process now, and once the baby is here, we get the test. If the results prove that you are the father, then our next move will be to petition the courts for voluntary child support and visitation."

"What happens if I am not the father?"

She sighed. "If it is determined that you are not the father, then you are free from any further obligation to the mother or the child."

"When do we start?"

"Before we proceed, what about the other mother, Jaslyn? How do you want to proceed with her? Are you sure that you are the father of her child?"

"Yes, I'm sure. Like I said before, I'm going to marry her."

"Until you are married, you can also petition for child support and visitation just to be on the safe side."

"No, thanks. I appreciate the advice, but I'm sure. We will be married sooner rather than later." I stood to leave. "Thank you for your time, Ms. Franks. I'll be in touch." She nodded her head, and I turned to leave.

Alicia called as I walked to my car. When I saw her name on the caller ID, I cringed but answered anyway.

"What's up?" I kept the conversation dry. I knew that I should be kind and respectful, but I really didn't like Alicia. Every time that I had any type of contact with her, she caused me nothing but problems. I should have learned my lesson in the eighth grade when she dumped me. *Now, I'm about to pay child support to this broad?* I thought. I was linked for a lifetime because fatherhood didn't end at eighteen, and I was determined that my kid would know that he was loved and supported despite the strained relationship I had with his mother. Naw, forget strained...I just didn't like her ass. Out of respect for my kid, I answered the phone.

She took a breath like she was offended, but I said it again. "What's up?"

"Excuse me?"

"What do you want, Alicia?"

"I was calling to tell you that we are having a son."

I was stunned into silence because during Jaslyn's last doctor's visit, we learned that she was having a son. Two boys. I felt pressure rising in my chest. I was proud and petrified. Alicia interrupted my thoughts with, "I also wanted to talk to you about the logistics of delivery."

"That's a few months away, so why do we need to talk about that right now?"

"We still need to plan for it especially since you have other obligations."

"Okay. I'll have my secretary call you to schedule a meeting. There are a couple of things we need to talk about."

"*Secretary?* And what else do we need to talk about?"

I hesitated because I knew that she would not be pleased with what I was about to say, but it was more important now that I knew I was having a son to make sure that my rights were protected. So, I bit the bullet and dropped, "Let's start with paternity, and then, custody and child support."

"Paternity! Are you fucking kidding me!? I can't believe that you are doing this right now!" Alicia screamed through the phone.

I knew this reaction was coming, and I knew that I seemed cruel. But I had to do it. Many a dude had spent a lifetime paying for a child that wasn't his. I wouldn't be one of them.

"Alicia, calm down. It's standard procedure."

"Standard for who? A deadbeat dad?"

"Quite the opposite, actually. It's standard for a man who wants to be a responsible father."

"Sampson, I haven't even had the baby yet, and you are already questioning the paternity!? How are you trying to be a responsible father if you are saying this baby is not yours?"

"That's not what I'm saying, Alicia."

"If you want a paternity test, then that means that you don't believe you are the father!"

"No, what I am saying is that I want to make *sure* before we go any further. Once I am sure, then we can proceed."

"Proceed? Negro, do you hear yourself?! You sound like you are conducting a business transaction!"

"Well, aren't we? This is basically the final step to the business you started when you began trying to seduce me."

"You asshole!" She hung the phone up in my face.

Well, that went well.

Chapter 21
Jaslyn
Bees with Honey

I was pushing seven months when my sisters and friends threw me a baby shower. This wasn't just any old shower. This was more like a party for grown folks, and the baby was thrown in for good measure. It was a good combination of classy meets country; they decided to have a picnic at the park. When they planned the shower, I was originally on board, but I didn't consider that it would be July in Texas. Between the almost-one-hundred-degree heat, sweltering sun, and mosquitoes on steroids, I wasn't really having a good time. Maybe if I wasn't carrying extra weight, my ankles weren't swollen, and if I didn't have to breathe for two people, this would have been bearable, but I was struggling. I almost left, but everyone else seemed to be having a good time, so I just chilled under the pavilion next to the chest with the cold beverages.

I looked around the park at the party. It was a sight to see. This felt more like a family reunion. The blue balloons and table filled with diapers, onesies, gift bags, stroller, and diaper bags, and yellow and blue baby items were the biggest indication that this was a baby shower. This was an occasion for the adults to fellowship and have fun. With Malik serving as the DJ, Francine and Melissa holding it down at the card table, Shellie leading everyone in all the latest line dances, this felt like the night when Sampson and I had our first dance at Tamika and Jawaan's house. It seemed like such a long time ago. One dance, almost two years ago, led to a lifetime connection. Sampson and I were now connected for at least the next eighteen years, raising a son together in a world that wasn't necessarily ready to welcome and love him like his parents.

I was deep in my thoughts when Solomon walked over and started talking to me. "What's on your mind?"

"Just thinking about being a mom."

"Ahh...I see."

"Thinking about raising a black son. Like, what do I tell him about girls? Really, you know, helping him understand that '*no means no.*' How do I start the conversation about hearing a white person call him a nigger for the first time? How soon should I start '*the talk*'? You know the talk about interacting with the police, letting him know that it is better to fight in court than die in the street? How can I talk to my son about stuff like this when I can't even get along with his brother's mother?"

I felt the tears roll down my face. Solomon looked at me with the deepest compassion. He grabbed a napkin from the table and handed it to me so I could dry my tears.

He placed a firm but gentle hand on my shoulder and remarked softly, "Such heavy thoughts on such a joyous day. You should be celebrating."

"I have celebrated enough. We have been out here for over three hours. It's hot, and I am ready to go home. I don't know why I agreed to having a baby shower outside in the middle of July!" I shook my head and folded the tissue, "Thanks by the way...thanks for the tissue."

"You're welcome." Solomon took a deep sigh and then sat down next to me. "Jaslyn, I don't have an answer to those questions. And they are definitely things that you have to think about, but I do know one thing."

"What is that?"

"You won't be able to figure those answers out today. So just chill and enjoy the party, and if you are ready to leave, say so. Sam won't have a problem with you leaving." We both looked out at Sam sitting in a lawn chair next to Jawaan, Chicago, and a few more dudes laughing and drinking cold beers. Solomon added, "As a matter of fact, no one will be mad if you leave. You and I both know that this shower...no this...*party* will go on all night no matter what. That's just what we do." I chuckled as he said, "Go home, sis."

"I will."

"And another thing...getting along with Alicia."

"Yes, what about it?"

"Can I be honest with you?"

"Sure." I was curious."

"Stop focusing so much on her negative behavior. You need to do what's right no matter what. Not only for your peace of mind but for your son. He will know that you love his brother by how you treat his mother. Take it from me, kids learn more from what you do than what you say. At least Sampson and I did."

"You make a good point, but she makes it so hard."

"It doesn't matter what she does. You do what's right? Can I tell you something?"

"You mean there is more?"

"Yes, there is more. When we were in college, I always admired you. You were beautiful, smart, and popular, and you always carried yourself with such dignity and grace. You were just a cool, dope ass chick. Until my frat brother cheated on you."

"Ahh...Nathan. You knew about that?

"The whole chapter knew. We knew he was a jerk, and we all wondered what you saw in him. Then, word got around that you busted him cheating and went to jail behind it. I was stunned. Now, I'm not saying you shouldn't have been hurt and angry, but he was the one that was wrong, not you. But you went to jail, not him. Crazy, right?"

"Go on."

"Well, it's the same with Alicia. She's the one out here scheming to get with my brother, but your actions are getting *you* in trouble. That makes no sense. You are better than this."

"You're right."

My eyes teared up, but Solomon said, "Don't cry. I'm not trying to make you upset. I just want to be honest with you because I want you to win, sis. You're the woman that I want for my brother."

"But why?"

"Like I said, you're one cool ass, dope ass chick. He deserves that."

"Wow. Thank you so much."

"You're welcome. Remember, play it cool. You don't have to react how she wants you to react. My Aunt Tootie used to say, 'You get more bees with honey.' So, keep it cool and watch how things turn around. Now, go home before you have a heat stroke."

I hugged him, "Does Sam know that he has such an amazing brother?"

"No! He thinks he's the better brother, but you and I know the truth. He winked, and added, "I'll go get him and tell him to start packing up to get you home."

As Solomon walked away, I was grateful that he was so honest with me. His candidness reaffirmed all of the things that Hope and I had been working on. It was time for me to grow the fuck up.

Chapter 22
Sampson
What Happens in Vegas

Jaslyn and I were working to make our relationship healthy. It was like building from the ground up; it was worth it though. Things were going better than they had in a long time. She was certainly trying to communicate how she was feeling instead of bottling up her emotions. I was trying my best to court her like she wanted. After we had the argument about me canceling on her, I had a standing date on my calendar for date night. We talked every day, and after our therapy session, I knew I wanted to marry her. *Crazy, right?* Counseling showed me that we could get through anything as long as we communicated. I wanted to propose in a special way, and I wanted to get married before my son was born. I was running out of time, so I reached out to Shellie and Lisa to help me come up with a plan. The plan was risky, but I trusted their instincts. After all, they were her best friends.

Jaslyn spent the night with me one evening, and I decided to put the plan into action the next morning. When I woke up, I rolled over to stroke her skin and inhale her scent. *Was I dreaming? Or is she still here,* I thought. I stared at her sleeping softly—the mother of my child.

I almost felt bad for having sex with her while she was pregnant, but the doctor said it was okay, I tried to tear that ass up! Man, I missed making love to her. I'd had sex with plenty of other women, even made love to some, but it was something about being with her.

I looked at her as she breathed deeply. The girl always did sleep hard. Today was no different.

I took my hand and stroked her face. She didn't move, which was good because she always had an attitude in the morning. I wanted to open the blinds, but she loved to sleep in a pitch-black room. The light would only aggravate her, and I didn't want her grumpy countenance to ruin my mood. I wanted her to feel what I was feeling. Contentment. It felt so good to say it, to be it. Content. It's a very underrated emotion, but now that I had found it, I never wanted to leave it. Jaslyn made me feel content. I was happy just being in her presence.

I knew what I had to do. I stroked her face again, and surprisingly, she opened her eyes after one touch.

"Why are you messing with my face?" she grumbled. I laughed. *I told you she would have an attitude.*

"I'm just happy that you're still here. I'm so used to you running away from me."

She yawned and stretched, then threw the covers back. She got out of the bed and walked to the bathroom. She stood at the sink and turned on the faucet. The running water, the only sound in the room. Her naked silhouette, a shadow in the dim room. Even with her protruding stomach, she turned me on.

She brushed her teeth and washed her face. When she returned to bed, she had put on her bathrobe.

"Why'd you put that on? I was enjoying the view." I tried to disrobe her.

"Ha. Ha. You're not funny, Sampson."

"I'm serious. You're sexy. And I love looking at you." I reached for her robe again, but she slapped my hand away.

"Stop it." she snapped.

232

"I'm serious, Jaslyn. Let me look at you. You're beautiful."

"Thanks for the compliment, Sam, but I am far from sexy right now. I do appreciate you trying to make me feel good though."

"I'm not just trying to make you feel good. You are sexy. You're sexy to me."

She stood by the bed and put her hand around the object I had placed on the pillow while she was in the restroom. She picked it up and looked at me. "What's this?"

"A key to the condo?" It was a question because I was nervous about her reaction.

"Why is it on my pillow? It wasn't there just a minute ago."

"It's yours. I want you to live with me."

"We've already talked about this. I lived with someone before, and it didn't work. I don't know…living together…without being married? That's not a good idea."

"Look, Jazz, I know you want to get married, and eventually, I do too, but let's be honest, we've been through a lot. A whole lot more than the average couple, and this is my way of letting you know that I'll always be real with you and do right by you. But I also want us to take our time in the process. If we can live together for a year, or two, without fucking up too badly, then maybe marriage will be our next step. What do you think?"

"Well…I'm glad you're being honest about how you feel, but I'm also scared as shit right now."

"Me too."

"I just started therapy."

"I know…you have a few issues."

233

Jaslyn threw a light punch to my forearm. "Hey!"

I shrugged my shoulders. "The truth is the truth," I said laughing. "Seriously, even with all of your issues, I love you, and I want to be with you."

"Then marry me."

"I've already explained why I'm not marrying you. You know we're not ready to get married yet." I paused, then added, "Before you answer, there is something that I need to tell you. I met with a lawyer."

"About what?"

"Alicia and child support. I want to pay."

"Okay. And?"

"That's it. I want to pay child support, and I want you to know that before we move forward."

She said, "That's the least you can do. Don't let that be all."

"So, you are okay with that?"

"Child support is the bare minimum. I don't like the girl, but that has nothing to do with her kid. I don't expect anything less."

"Cool. Well, I also think that all of us should sit down and discuss how we will raise our kids together."

She twisted her face and said, "Agreed, but I'm not sure how productive that will be. And don't you think we are doing this thing backward?"

"What do you mean?"

"Don't get me wrong. I love you, I really do, and I want to be with you, but this is not the order in which I thought my life would go. You remember that nursery rhyme about the boy and the girl kissing?'

"No."

"It started something like this 'Jenny and Johnny sitting in a tree.' Well, at the end, the song tells what happens after you kiss. '*First* comes love, *then* comes marriage, *then* comes the baby in the baby carriage.' We're doing this all wrong! Love, marriage, then the kids, Sampson. Not baby, live together, then marriage. Hell, we don't even have marriage...that's a maybe...if everything is cool. We've got this all screwed up."

"Well, it's not like that, Jazz. For that, what can I say but I'm sorry. I surely didn't plan things out this way. And you left out the most important part—we did love each other first. Maybe we didn't know how to show it, but that part we got right. And that's what matters most, that we loved each other first. Now, the baby and the marriage, we might need to work on that part. This ain't a nursery rhyme or a fantasy. What we have is real, as real as it gets. It may not be perfect, but it is *real.* As long as we stay real and true to each other, we can make this work, and that's more than I can say for most folks."

She took a deep breath but remained silent. I could feel her anxiety as she reflected on my offer.

"So, what's up?"

"What's up?"

"Yeah. What's up? Are you going to live with me and be my baby mama?"

She reacted just as I suspected, "I'll live with you, but I'll be damned if I let you call me your baby mama."

I laughed then added, "How about B. M.?"

"What? Am I gone be B.M. #1 and Alicia B.M. #2? Hell no!"

I laughed even harder.

"Sam, that shit ain't funny. Stop playing! I'm not going to be anybody's *baby mama.*"

She calmed down, and I turned my laughter down to a smile.

"When do I move in?"

"Shellie and Lisa are already packing your stuff."

"What?"

"I knew you'd say yes." I grinned the grin of a lottery winner.

"You did, huh? Well, I changed my mind."

"Too late." I grabbed her and kissed her. She shrieked, "Stop it!" and we fell back against the bed.

The plan was for me to take Jaslyn to Vegas for a mini-vacation and celebrate us moving in together. I told her that this would give Solomon and Malik time to move out. To her, it made sense. However, when we got to Vegas, I would propose and marry her on the same day. We would spend a few days there for our honeymoon. Everyone knew the plan and would be there for the wedding. The only person that didn't know was Jazz. It was a good old-fashioned, surprise elopement.

I didn't delay the plan. We arrived at the hotel suite Thursday night, and after breakfast in bed on Friday morning; I set the plan in motion. I started giving orders.

"Get dressed."

"For what? We have all day."

"Just get dressed. I have a surprise for you." I had arranged for a car service to pick us up at the hotel at ten that morning. As Jaslyn showered and dressed, I called to confirm that the car was waiting. I also texted Shellie, Lisa, Malik, and Solomon to make sure they had everything ready and let them know that we were on the way.

Jaslyn came out of the restroom in a sundress and sandals.

"I'm ready."

"Cool. Give me a few minutes." I showered and threw on some jeans, a t–shirt, and a pair of Adidas.

I came out of the bathroom and said, "Let's go."

When we got in the car, I placed a blindfold on her face, making sure that it was secure enough that she couldn't see.

So far, she was following along, but after about a ten-minute drive, she asked, "Where are you taking me?"

She was pissed; Jaslyn is a woman who liked control. She grabbed at the blindfold that I attached to her face; I slapped her hands down.

"Did you just hit me!?"

"I tapped your hand; I need you to follow directions. You only have two rules—do not touch the blindfold and trust me. Do you trust me, Jaslyn?"

"Huh? What? Yes, I trust you...I trust you as far as I can see you, and right now, I can't see you. Now, let me take this damn thing off my face!"

I laughed at her frustration. "No. You have to trust me. Just trust me. I've got everything under control."

"Sampson!"

I didn't respond. I knew if I said anything else we would end up in an argument, and I didn't want to argue. Not on this day. It was too important. Too special.

"Well, will you at least tell me where you are taking me? Please, Sampson?"

"Be patient. We are almost there."

I drove about fifteen more minutes until I arrived at our destination. I pulled up, parked the car, turned off the ignition, opened my car door to get out, and walked around to the passenger side. I opened her door and unbuckled her seatbelt.

"Lift your hand."

She lifted her hand, and I grabbed it to place it in mine. She grabbed on, holding my hand tightly. Her grip was strong and tense.

"Now, turn toward my voice and put your feet on the ground."

She blew out a gust of air and snapped, "You wouldn't have to guide me if you would just let me take this thing off my eyes."

I leaned in and whispered, "I like guiding you, Jaslyn." I felt the grip of her hand relax around my fingers, and I saw the corners of her mouth turn up. But Jaslyn being Jaslyn refused to say anything, refused to give up full control. It was okay. Eventually, we would be on the same page.

"Just listen to me and we will be there shortly."

I placed my hand under her elbow and guided her to stand. I leaned and whispered again, "I'm going to hook my arms in your arms. Lean into me and walk. And don't complain. Just follow my instructions. The longer you complain, the longer it takes to get to our destination. Do you understand me, Jaslyn?"

She nodded her head and responded, "Yes."

"Now, walk with me and listen to my voice."

We walked toward the building with her stumbling periodically. I guided her up several steps and into the door. We walked down the hall and stopped in front of a small office off the main hallway. "We're here."

She lifted her hand to her face.

"No, Jaslyn. Let me do it. Let me lead you." I stepped behind her to remove the blindfold. I took it off and moved to stand beside her.

She looked at the sign on the door and then looked at me. "Wedding Chapel? Why are we here?" She frowned and turned up her nose in confusion.

I laughed at her reaction. "We are here to get married."

"What? Stop playing."

"I'm serious." I dug my hand into my jeans and pulled out a small blue box with a white ribbon. I got down on one knew and took her hand in mine. "Jaslyn Davenport, will you marry me?"

"Sampson, you are crazy!"

"That may very well be true, but I am serious about marrying you."

"We don't even have a marriage license!"

"Don't worry, that has been taken care of. We just need to sign it and meet Solomon in the chapel so he can perform the ceremony."

"Solomon?"

"Yes, Solomon. If you say yes, we are getting married today."

"Why now? Why today? How?"

"Because I love you." She started crying. "I will explain everything after you answer me because if you say no, does why and how really matter? Now, would you please answer my question? Will you marry me?"

She nodded.

"No. I need to hear you say it. Yes or no? Do you want to spend the rest of your life as my wife?"

"Yes, Sampson, I want to be your wife."

I opened the box and put the ring on her finger. Then, I hopped up and planted a huge kiss on her lips. I looked at her, smiled, used my thumbs to wipe her tears, and pulled her into my arms.

"Thank goodness! My knee was starting to hurt. Girl, I'm an old man now!" She laughed as I shouted, "Let's do this!"

We went inside where everyone was waiting for us, including Jaslyn's sisters.

We met the chapel coordinator in her office, and I reached in my pocket and pulled out my wallet. I took out two driver's licenses and presented them both to the chapel coordinator, and Malik handed her the marriage license.

"How did you..."

"It was a group effort. Malik went to the Clark County Marriage Bureau when he got to Vegas. For a few extra dollars under the table and a copy of your driver's license, they hooked him up."

"Carol?"

"No. That was actually me. I made a copy while you were asleep." I winked.

Jaslyn feigned indignation, "You went in my purse?!"

After we signed the documents, the clerk directed us down the hall toward a small sanctuary where we would get married.

"Wait! I can't get married in jeans!"

"Don't worry." Before we went into the sanctuary, I walked her toward the restroom. Outside stood Shellie and Lisa. She had a Vera Wang bag, and Lisa held onto a Jimmy Choo shoe box. Malik stood next to them with my tuxedo housed in my garment bag and my shoes.

Shellie yelled, "Come on, girl!" Then, she reached to grab her arm and took her into the restroom to help her get changed.

Once we were both dressed, Jaslyn and I were married in that small sanctuary in Vegas! Flashy lights, neon decor, slot machines next to the pulpit, and Elvis as an usher. It was typical Vegas decor but perfect. Fun and spontaneous. We partied with our friends and family the rest of the day. Gambling, partying and club hopping, enjoying the strip and the shows in Vegas with our family and friends.

Chapter 23
Jaslyn
Co-Parenting for Dummies

A few weeks after Sampson and I were married, I started getting extremely emotional. I was eight months along; I was fat, and I was insecure, and I was cranky. I was starting arguments about everything. Sam was forever patient, at least he tried to be. I was still struggling to fully communicate what my true feelings were about the situation with Alicia, and instead of telling him how I felt, I held it all in and became moody. One morning, it all almost exploded in an argument that was entirely my fault.

We were watching a *Law and Order* marathon together, the one with the Black detective—the episodes with Detective Green were my favorite— and I was clearly pouting. Sam tried to ignore me. He was lying on the couch with his head in my lap. I kept fidgeting, squirming, and sighing until he finally acknowledged that something was wrong—passive-aggressive, I know.

"What's wrong with you? Are you okay?"

"I'm fine. I'm just not feeling well; I have a cold."

"Then, you're not fine. You're sick, so you need to go to the hospital. Now!" He had become extra-attentive to my health *and even that* got on my nerves.

"Chill, bro. It's just a cold. Dang!" I was irritated.

"Bro? I've been reduced to '*bro*? What have you been watching on tv?"

"Sorry. It's the kids that I tutor."

He laughed in acknowledgment. "Solomon told me that you asked him if you could tutor the kids at church after school."

"I had to clear it with the probation office, and he got permission from the pastor though." She shook her head, "I never thought I would be working with kids. It's a challenge because as much as I want to be the model professional for them, sometimes I have to get on their level and speak their language. Know what I mean?"

I nodded, "I get it, but you really do sound like a reality show."

"I know, right?" she laughed.

"About this cold...seriously, Jazz, you need to take care of yourself."

"Sam, if it was anything more than a cold, I would go to the doctor. I'm fine. I don't have a fever. I'm resting; I'm drinking plenty of fluids, and I'm taking my cold medicine. I even have my humidifier going. I'm fine!"

"Okay," he hesitated, "But if it doesn't get better in a day or two, promise me that you will go to the doctor."

"Ugh! You doing too much!"

"We have to find you a permanent job because cable TV is lowering your IQ."

"Shut your trap," I said and then sneezed. "I promise that I will go to the doctor if I don't get better in a few days."

"Thank you. Speaking of job, what's the status of your job? Are you still thinking of starting your shelter?"

"I appealed a few weeks back. I am still on leave, but they changed it to paid leave because I had never been in trouble before. The shelter...I'm still going to do it, but I'm going to wait a few years until SJ gets older. That way I can have a steady income for a while."

"SJ? So, you have named my son already?"

"Not quite. I'm stuck on Sampson, Jr. or a name that starts with an S to continue the tradition."

"We are not naming my son Junior. And as far as income, I got you."

"Whatever. My mother taught me that a woman should always have her own money and to never get stuck holding the bag," He shook his head in disbelief as I added, "And I might go to the doctor anyway; I want a C-section. I'm ready to have this baby."

"Stop talking crazy."

"I'm serious. My feet are swollen. My face is swollen. My back hurts, and I can't bend over. I've literally gained thirty pounds! I am so over this process."

"Well, you don't have much longer. Just hang in there."

I changed directions. "When is Alicia due?"

He rose up from my lap to look at me. Lately, I found him in that position often, his head laying in my lap close to my stomach as if he was listening for a heartbeat. I was usually irritated by it, but tonight, I was comforted. I reached up to touch his hair; my fingers playing in his curls.

"You're asking about Alicia. Why?"

"I shrugged, "I don't know...just curious."

"You are never *just curious* about anything, and especially not about Alicia. Talk to me. What's on your mind?"

I took a deep breath, which was already labored from my pregnancy, but the cold was making it even harder to breathe. "Well, if we have our babies at the same time, where will you be? With me or with her? If you choose to be with me, you neglect her baby; and if you choose her, you neglect my baby. You love me, but how does love overcome something like that?"

He didn't say anything at first. He placed his head back in my lap, and there was a long silence between us. Finally, he confessed, "I've been thinking about the same thing. You all are so close together that it's a strong possibility you deliver at the same time. I'm sorry about that, but I can't change the situation. Is this why you want a C-section?"

"Partially, yes. Yes!"

"I don't have an answer for you. Not one that will make you feel better. All I can say is that I love you. You know that, and you know that I will do anything for you. You also know that I am going to do everything to be present and available for both of my children...somehow. So, I hope you are not asking me to choose between them."

"We've already talked about this; you know that is not what I am asking. What I am asking...what I am saying is that I am having a hard time understanding how this is all going to work. My dream for having a baby was that I wanted my man, my husband, to be by my side the entire time when I gave birth. However, I know that at some point your attention is going to be divided between two families. How do we make that work?"

"I have one wife. That's you. I guess I... we...have to figure out how to make two families one. You and Alicia are going to have to get along. You will have to be a great mom to both of my kids. Can you do that? For me?"

"I don't know, Sam; that's asking a lot. I will try. I won't ever mistreat a child, even if I don't like the mother."

"That's all I can ask. I know that we can't expect God to bless situations that he hasn't ordained, and getting two women pregnant at the same time is definitely not of God." He shook his head as he explained, "But I've been praying about this whole situation, asking for His forgiveness and guidance...His wisdom. I don't know how He is going to do it, but I believe that God is going to help me get through this for everybody. He's going to help me to be the father that I never had and be the husband I want to be. That's all I can tell you, Jaslyn. I'm going to try, every day, to be a good husband to you and a great father to my kids. If I have to kill myself running around trying, then that's what I'm going to do. Y'all deserve that."

I started crying. I knew how much being a good father meant to him, especially finding out about Uncle Junior. And honestly, after his response, I felt like shit for even asking. *Petty.* I had to do better.

"Don't cry." If he only knew the real reason I was crying. I felt like an ass.

"It's all good. It's the hormones, nigga."

"Nigga? Wow!!"

We both laughed, and I kissed the top of his head.

"I love you, and I am glad I'm your wife but..."

"But what?"

"But if we are going to make this last, we need to make that move and talk to Alicia?"

"Alicia...how could I forget."

"We all need to be on the same page."

247

"I'm still not sure about that. I know I agreed to talk to her...I'm just not sure it will end well."

"I'm not either, but I know it needs to happen."

"True."

He shook his head and added, "Okay, I'll set it up."

One week later, I walked into Sampson's office building thirty minutes early. His secretary escorted me to a conference room across from his office, and I took a seat facing the glass doors. I wanted to see Alicia when she walked in.

I said a quick prayer to calm my nerves and so I wouldn't have a repeat performance of our last encounter at this office.

I wasn't the only one that wanted to be early that morning because five minutes after I arrived, Alicia walked into the conference room dressed like she was auditioning to be a Black, and pregnant, Audrey Hepburn—black dress, Chanel sunglasses, pearls, and six-inch Manolo Blahnik shoes. I was definitely underdressed. My pregnancy uniform normally consisted of a dressy t-shirt, yoga pants, and sneakers. Today, I had on a comfortable sundress and slip-on sandals because I could no longer reach my feet to tie my shoes. I moaned as I thought, *I hate being pregnant.*

Shocked to see me, Alicia greeted me with, "What are you doing here?"

"Sam didn't tell you that I was going to be here?" He made such a big deal about us meeting that I couldn't imagine that he left out that I would be a part of this discussion.

Before she could respond, Sam walked in behind her and said, "No, I didn't tell her because I knew she wouldn't come."

Alicia was furious. She pointed at me and said, "She is not supposed to be near me!"

"Alicia, can you ignore the restraining order...at least for today? We all need to talk." He walked around the conference table and sat next to me.

She sat down across from me and said, "Whatever. If she gets out of line..."

I cut her off and said, "Here is what I need you to understand. I don't do drama. What happened before...that was a lapse in judgment. That's not me at all. So, whatever you think you are about to do or say, I need you to check that now. I will respect you, and you will respect me. Got it?"

"You are not my mother."

"Nope. Sure not. Not trying to be. I just need you to know that this will be a civilized conversation between the three of us. If not, we can stop now."

"Drop the attitude, Miss Jaslyn, or I walk."

"I don't have an attitude. I'm just firm in what I'm saying. If you walk, that's on you, but know that I am a part of Sampson's life; therefore, I will be a part of your child's life, so we need to come to a good understanding. Got it?"

"Well, now, you are just being nasty. Sampson, are you sure you want to deal with this hood rat?"

I put my hands on the table to stand up, and Sam put his hand on my forearm to stop me.

"Alicia, Jaslyn...I need you both to stop it. Let's all be civil. How about I guide this conversation. One thing is true, all three of us have to deal with each other, and

249

we need to be able to do that respectfully. Period. Jazz, if you don't do drama, then act like it. Alicia, there is no sense in attacking anybody's character so stop it.

"She started it! "Alicia yelled.

I didn't say anything, but pushed back from the table and folded my arms. The sound of my heartbeat was audible as I tried to control my temper before I lost control. I slowed my breathing by inhaling and exhaling, trying hard to focus on the strategies I learned from my therapist, but this bitch was making it hard.

Sam was trying to gain control of the situation but struggling to maintain order. "I don't care. I'm stopping it." He was scolding us because we were behaving like teenagers. It was stupid. "Now, the reason I called this meeting is to clarify a few things. First, when it comes to my children, I will be there for both of them. I don't need you guys to like each other. I just need you to, at least, show each other respect so *we*can set a good example.

"Yes," I mumbled a visible sign that I was pouting.

"Sampson, please don't think that you are going to run my life. This is my life, and I will dictate how and when you see him."

"I figured you would say something like that." He reached into the pocket of his jacket, pulled out an envelope, and handed it to Alicia.

"What's this?"

"A petition for joint custody and a document verifying my voluntary payment of child support."

Alicia's jaw dropped. "You are actually going to go through with this? You're telling me that you really want a paternity test...and *custody?*"

"Yes, I do. I tried talking to explain that to you before, but you didn't want to listen. I only want joint custody. I'm not trying to take your rights away. I just want to make sure that I have mine...if the test proves that the child is mine, of course."

It was Alicia's turn to stand, but instead of being mad at Sam, she pointed at me. "It's you! You're behind all of this!"

Before I could respond, Sam defended me. "This isn't Jaslyn's fault. This was my idea."

"You know what? I knew in middle school that you were a simp! Joint custody, my ass! You're not getting shit!"

"Alicia, what did you expect from me?"

"I expected you to be a man about this shit and marry me! Not get another bitch pregnant!"

"*Bitch?*" I pressed my hands on the table to stand up, but Sam put his hand on my chest so I couldn't move.

"It's okay, Jaslyn. I've got this." Sam kept his hand on my chest for a few moments and looked me in my eyes to reassure me, making sure that I wasn't going to do or say anything, and then he proceeded. I could see in his eyes what he was saying to me, *Trust me.* "I was never going to marry you. You know that and so do I. I'm not going to even go into all of the reasons why. Furthermore, let's chill with the name calling. It's not necessary. I need you to respect my wife."

"*Wife?*"

"Yes, wife. Jaslyn and I are married."

"You know what? You must be the biggest fool on the planet. Good luck with that, and I'll see you in court." With that, she made a grand exit out of the door.

Sampson grabbed my hand, and I blew out a breath that I didn't know I was holding. *So much for getting on the same page.*

Chapter 24
Sampson
No More Drama

"So, you're a married man now. What's it like?"

Malik and I met at my condo for drinks. When he moved out, he and Solomon decided to become roommates. Malik had moved all of his belongings, but Solomon still needed to move a few more things and would be coming later to pack the last of his stuff and leave my key. Malik and I wanted to catch up because we hadn't really talked since the wedding.

"It's challenging, but great, man. I can't complain."

"Even though I helped, I still can't believe it. You even had us move out and everything?"

"It was time for y'all to get your own places anyway. With Jawaan back at home, I just needed to get rid of you and Solomon. You know what's really shocking? You and Solomon being roommates. How is that working?"

"It's actually pretty cool. When I want to see a honey, I just usually meet her at her place. Besides, it's temporary until I can get this business off the ground and making a profit."

"How is that going by the way?"

"Slow."

"What are you going to do for cash in the meantime? I know you don't want to use up all of your retirement and investments."

"Well actually, Pamela offered me some work as a private investigator for her firm. You know, spying on cheating husbands and shit like that."

253

"Pamela? Pamela Franks...my attorney?"

"Yep. She's cool...we're cool. And the pay is nice. Gotta do what I gotta do."

"No doubt."

"Where is Solomon?"

"He's on his way over now to move the rest of his stuff."

"I'm still shocked...you and Jaslyn are married..." Malik shook his head and sighed at the same time.

"I know it's hard to believe especially since we started out so crazy?"

"Actually, you two started out great, and then, it went crazy. Too crazy! You seem to be running harems and shit; a brother can't tell what you got going on these days."

"You jealous, nigga?

He laughed and took a drink of his cognac. "Hell no! As a matter of fact, at least you married Jaslyn and not that thirsty-ass Alicia."

I smiled the smile of a happy man. "It was never going to be Alicia. She was a childhood crush. That's it, that's all. Jaslyn is the only woman for me."

"Well, you seem happy, bro. I'm excited for you."

"Thanks, man."

"What are you going to do about Alicia?"

"I guess I never mentioned that to you, huh? I called Pamela like you told me."

"Yeah? How did it go?"

"She's awesome! By the way, you didn't tell me that she wasn't Black."

"Did I need to?"

"Not at all. It's just that you have always been down for the sistas, I never thought that you were into white women like that."

"I'm still down for the sistas. I'm just an equal opportunity lover."

"Whatever." I laughed.

"So, what's the plan for you and Alicia?"

"I'm going to have a blood test completed when the baby is born. If the baby is mine, Ms. Franks will petition the courts for voluntary child support. I don't want to wait for her to do anything. I need to control this situation; things are already in motion. Jaslyn and I met with Alicia yesterday. She was pissed."

"Are you crazy? Why would you voluntarily allow the government in your pocket? And your business?"

I shook my head. "I am not going to allow Alicia to manipulate me financially or emotionally. This way I protect myself and the relationship that I want to build with my kid. I won't allow her to use time with my son as a bargaining chip when she can't get her way."

"Do you think she would go that far?"

"Hell, you don't? Look at everything she has done already. I can't take that chance. By doing things this way, a judge will decide what is fair and outline all the guidelines surrounding custody and visitation. If she violates the agreement, I will take her back to court and sue her ass for full custody.

"True. You've really thought this whole thing out."

"Yes, I have. I will not let any child of mine go fatherless. My son will know who I am from the very first day he enters the world. I will not abandon him like I was."

255

"How is Jaslyn, your new wife might I add, taking the news?"

"Let's just say she hasn't choked her again. But hey, baby steps."

Malik coughed, almost choking as he swallowed his last drink of cognac. "Good luck with that."

Just then, Solomon walked in. He still had a key. "What's up, y'all?"

"Nothing. What's up with you? Where are you coming from?"

"I just left the church."

"Man, you are always at that damn church. Are you trying to be the pastor or something?" Malik was joking but not joking.

Solomon didn't miss a beat. "Funny you should say that. The pastor is retiring and asked me if I would be interested in the job."

Malik exclaimed, "Are you serious?"

"Yes! You know that I have been preaching there every few weeks. He also asked me to lead the Bible study class on Wednesday nights, so I have been helping him out with that. He asked me to help, but I didn't know this was the reason why."

I was curious what his answer would be. I knew, but I needed him to confirm it. "What did you say?"

"I told him that I would think about it. Y'all, that church is small, and I just got this new job so I can make my half of the rent with Malik. I don't know if I'll have the time to serve the people like I will need to."

"Speaking of rent...give me my key back. You can't just be walking in and out of my house like that anymore. You might scare my wife."

He slapped his leg and said, "Well damn! Here you go." He took the key off the key chain and tossed it at me. "It was about time you and Jaslyn figured your shit out. Where is she anyway?"

"She's shopping with her friends because she wants to redecorate the extra room."

Solomon laughed, "Sounds like she's already taking over, I guess. Why didn't you move in with her? Isn't her house bigger than this condo?"

"It is, but this is closer to my job, and I have more equity than she does. She's going to rent her place out for a while. Eventually, we will get a bigger place that's centrally located. We just compromised. Thanks for the key. And when did you start cussing? You've managed to use damn and shit on the same day."

"Come on, Sam. I am your brother. Cussing? Negro, we grew up in the same house. I cuss sometimes; I just don't do it all the time. Most of the time, it's not necessary, but you and Jaslyn were making me weary."

"Touchĕ. So, when will you make a decision about the church?"

"I still need to pray about it, but I told him that I would let him know by the end of the week. If I accept, the deacons and church leadership will still have to accept."

"Of course, they will accept. You got this, man!"

Malik had to chime in, "Especially if it's left up to the choir. You know the honeys in the alto section love you. And is that girl still stalking you?"

Solomon just shook his head and conceded, "You are a fool, no she is not. She moved on to greener pastures once the pastor asked her if he needed to move her membership. Shit got a little crazy for a minute, I'm glad it's over."

"You never said anything," I said.

"Well, you have your own drama, and once the pastor got things under control, it wasn't worth talking about."

I felt compelled to talk to Solomon about our father, Uncle Junior. "Hey...you got a minute, bro? I really need to talk to you."

"Sure. What's up?"

I looked at Malik, and he knew where this was going. "On that note, I'll leave so you guys can have your family time. Sam, I'll holla at you later, and Solomon, I'll see you at the crib?" He stood up and pulled me into a brotherly hug with one arm and did the same to Solomon before he left.

Solomon sat down across from me. "What type of business is he starting again? He told me, but Malik is such a clown I never know what to believe. I told him as long as he could pay his portion of the bills, he was good."

"He decided to start a security company— bodyguards and private investigations. He did some P.I. work for me, and afterward, he figured he could monetize his law enforcement skills."

"Nice! He should be great at that, but P.I. work? What type of P.I. work did you need?"

"That's what I need to talk to you about."

"Okay, talk. What's up?"

"I wanted to find our mother." And I proceeded to tell my brother about how I learned that our mother was murdered and who our real father was. When I finished the story, his face had lost its color.

"What took you so long to tell me? It's been months!"

"I don't know...I didn't know how. I was trying to figure it out."

"There's nothing to figure out. You just tell me!"

"You're right."

Solomon's eyes were almost the color of blood when he demanded, "And I want to talk to Uncle Junior!"

"When?"

"Now."

"Are you sure?"

"Now!" He fumed.

I pulled out my cell phone to call Uncle Junior to let him know that we were on our way. He only responded with, "He knows, don't he?"

I said yes and hung up the phone, and Solomon and I walked out of the house to have a sit down with our father.

It took about thirty minutes to get there. He left the screen door open for us. We walked into the house from the living room and headed to the kitchen. Uncle Junior was sitting at the kitchen table with his cane leaning against the table. He had a cup of coffee in front of him and a fresh pot was brewing so it would be ready when he finished the first cup.

This was the first time I had been inside of the house since Aunt Tootie's funeral. I looked around and nothing had changed. White cabinets matched the white stove and white refrigerator. The small kitchen table sat in the middle of the kitchen on yellow linoleum floors that needed a good mopping. A porcelain plate with a picture of Black Jesus hung next to the window with yellow curtains over the sink. When I was a kid, I would sit at the table to eat breakfast before going to school, and I would stare at the plate and wonder why Jesus had skin darker than mine but hair wavy and long like a young Ron O'Neal in the blaxploitation movie *Superfly*.

Facing us when we walked in, Uncle Junior asked, "Y'all want something to eat?"

We sat down, one on each side of him. "No, thank you," I said, and Solomon stayed quiet.

"I reckon you want to talk, and this gone take a while, so I'm going to fix me a plate of hash anyway. You both are welcome to have some." I smirked remembering the entrïe of my youth. Potatoes, ground beef, and onions. I think he told me once that he learned how to make it in the army. Aunt Tootie was a master at it, too. It was a quick meal that would stick to your stomach; it was also cheap and went a long way. The memory gave me comfort. It reminded me of the love Aunt Tootie gave me. I missed her, and I wished she was here. I had so many questions that I wanted her to help answer, but Junior was all that I had. "No thanks. I'm not hungry." I was still waiting for Solomon to say something, but he just sat there staring at our uncle, our father, like he was a stranger.

Uncle Junior grabbed his cane and got up from the table with a wobble as evidence that even after all these years; he was never comfortable with his prosthetic leg. As he opened the door to the refrigerator, Solomon stood up and grabbed his shoulder to turn him around. He looked Uncle Junior directly in his eyes. Uncle Junior was frail. His hair was gray and unruly with skin like leather and eyes the color of cloudy glass. He was unsteady like he was nervous and afraid. I didn't know what to say or do. This had to play out. I looked at the pain on Solomon's face, and I feared that he would hurt the only man in our life. Yes, he deserved our ire, but wasn't he a victim, too? However, Solomon's clenched jaw and trembling hands were starting to make me regret this visit. I stood to intervene when Solomon pulled Uncle Junior into the deepest embrace and released a lifetime of tears. I fell back in my chair and did the same.

Chapter 25
Jaslyn
Labor and Delivery

I went over to Alicia's house because after our sit-down with Sampson, I knew we needed to have a one-on-one conversation only two women could have. You know like Betty Wright said, "*Woman to Woman.*" I didn't like how things ended. Sampson called all the shots; she was still mad, and I was too. If we, she and I, didn't bury this hatchet, this drama could go on forever, and sooner or later, we would be at each other's throats again no matter how much Sampson tried to intervene. And to me, that was just stupid. I had already done enough stupid shit to last a lifetime.

Given our situation, we would be dealing with each other for at least eighteen years, and I wasn't trying to live a life of confusion and chaos. I definitely didn't want our kids to experience that. So, I got Alicia's phone number from Tamika and sent her a text to ask if we could meet. I explained that I wanted to talk and apologize. She wasn't eager to talk to me, but she sent me her address and told me that I could stop by that afternoon. I would have preferred to meet at a restaurant, you know, a public place with witnesses, but being that she was on bed rest, I agreed without protest.

I pulled up to the house around 3:30 PM. I'm not sure what triggered it, but the hair on my arms started to stand up. Something didn't feel right about this visit. I sat in the car and got myself together. I looked in the rear-view mirror to check my hair and make-up. I couldn't have "baby mama" catch me slipping. I liked what I saw.

I had a fresh haircut. My red lipstick gave me that pop of color that I loved. I wasn't sure why I had the flutters.

I looked down at my protruding stomach, and SJ gave me a slight kick. He was a little more active than normal, so I figured that was the issue. My child was trying to warn me, "Mommy don't go in there!" However, I knew that I couldn't turn back now. This needed to happen.

I said a quick prayer that God would be present. We were both pregnant, so if she made me mad, I knew I couldn't fight her, especially not with that restraining order still being in place. I really would be in jail, and I would definitely lose my job. I prayed that we could both be respectful to one another just long enough to resolve our differences and get an understanding of how we would handle parenting together. That's it, that's all.

I sat in the car for a few more minutes and took a few deep breaths to calm my nerves and my baby. SJ started moving again, so I gave him a few words of encouragement, too. "Don't worry. Mommy is going to talk to your brother's mom. I know you can tell that Mommy doesn't like her, but that's ok. That won't stop me from loving your brother. We are going to make this work, so just calm down for me, okay?"

After a while, that seemed to work. I got out of the car, walked to the door, and rang the doorbell. A few moments later, Alicia arrived and opened the door. And there I was, staring at the face of the devil incarnate, wanting so desperately to choke her again. I looked at her stomach, stretching the breadth of her pink dress, and I felt the kicks in my stomach begin again. I ignored them, determined that it was time to get down to the business of being a grown-up.

"Hello, Alicia. Thanks for agreeing to meet with me. Can I come in?"

"Sure."

She moved to the side as I entered the foyer of her home. I looked around, and it seemed to be typical Alicia, all glitz and glam. It was beautiful, but all I could think was, "How is she going to raise a kid in this museum?" The high ceiling contained a glass chandelier that illuminated the sunlight. In the center sat a table with a stone base and glass top to house pictures of her, her family, and her friends. There were several pictures of an older woman with gray hair but Alicia's face—her mother. Her hair was long and thick, and the sun from the room highlighted her silver strands. Every frame was silver or glass and added to the bright and airy feeling of the room. The sun was shining through the beveled windows that surrounded the front door. It felt like having direct contact with the sky. I looked around, amazed and impressed. I was unwilling to show it; I was speechless for a minute, and Alicia picked up on it and proceeded to start the conversation that I asked to have.

"So. What do you want to talk about?"

"No pleasantries? No hello? Or how are you doing? Just business, huh? Can we at least sit down?"

"Jaslyn, no disrespect, but I didn't forget that I have a restraining order against you. I'm really not trying to interact with you more than I have to. You said you wanted to talk, and out of respect for our situations I'm willing to do it, but that's it. However, I would really appreciate it if we can make this quick."

"Oh. Okay..." I blinked. "Well, let me get to it then." I really wanted to revert back to the old me and cuss her ass out, but what good would that do? Now was the time for me to exercise some restraint. It wasn't just about me anymore. It was time to do what was best for my family, and like it or not, Alicia was about to be my family.

"First, let me start by apologizing. I am so sorry for what I did to you. It was inappropriate and slightly ghetto. I'm not going to even ask you to understand. Just know that after some time and much-needed therapy sessions, I know that I was wrong."

"Okay."

Okay? I was taken aback. S*urely, she could at least acknowledge my apology!* I regrouped because this visit wasn't about her. It was about all of us. *Do the right thing, Jaslyn!*

"I just wanted to get that off my chest so we can move forward. The meeting that we had with Sampson didn't go as it should have, and I thought maybe if you and I talked, you know, woman-to-woman, more importantly, mom-to-mom, we could really resolve things."

"Like what?"

This bitch.

"Like the fact that we don't like each other. We can't even be in the same room together."

"Honestly, Jaslyn, I barely know you. Why you think I don't like you is beyond me. For whatever reason, you hate me."

She wanted to get down to business. I took my therapist's advice and inhaled deeply before I spoke. "Hate is such a strong word. Irritated, frustrated, annoyed even...those are much better words for how I feel about you."

"But why? What have I ever done to you?"

"Let's not play stupid. At least have enough respect for me to be honest."

She chuckled in annoyance. "Respect? So, I'm supposed to respect the woman who choked me? Wow! Look, I don't have time for this. You wanted to talk, so tell me, Jaslyn, why are you irritated, frustrated, or annoyed with *me*?"

"Ah, I see that you need a history lesson. When I first met you at Tamika's shower and you learned that I was dating Sampson, you tried your hardest to convince me that he was a loser. Now that I think about it, lame is probably a better word for how you described him. Then, I found out a few months later that you were trying your best to seduce him. So much so that Sam and I broke up. Do you not recall that? Do you not see why your presence might vex my spirit just a little bit?"

"Whatever. Is this all you wanted? I'm not going to do this "baby-mama-drama" shit with you. I have more important things to do. Thank you for telling me how you feel, and if that's all, you can leave."

Lord, this girl is really testing me. I added, "You're right. You won't get any drama from me. I have let go of any resentment that I have toward you. It's all in the past. I thought you should know that your son is safe with me. When he is around, I will treat him like my own, and all I am asking is that you do the same so we can move forward as a family."

I saw Alicia grab her stomach and wince as she made clear to me, "I will never allow my son to be around you!".

"Are you okay?" I ignored the insult because it was obvious that she was in pain.

"I'm fine. Why do you think I would ever allow you to be around my child?"

"Okay, I'm looking at our situation like this—we are now a blended family, and I want to make sure that this works. I know you want to be sure that I do right by your child. We might not ever be friends, but we can always be respectful to each other."

"*Blended family?*Bitch, get out!"

My patience was gone. "I told you before that is not my fucking name!"

She spit her words at me, "Get out! Right now, before I call the police!"

"Are you serious?"

"I mean it. Leave right now, or I'm going to have your trifling ass thrown in jail...again! I don't care if you are pregnant. And fuck your apology! You just wanted to rub that shit in my face."

I was trying to be mature, but since she kept coming at me sideways, I decided to give her what she wanted and really rub it in her face, "Like it or not, I'm your son's stepmother. I'll always be around him."

It was then that she bent over as she clutched her stomach even harder, "Get the fuck out!"

She grabbed the table she was standing next to and started crying.

I reached out to grab her by the shoulders. "Alicia!"

Through tears, she pleaded, "Please leave," then fell to her knees.

"Hell no! I'm calling 9-1-1!"

I pulled out my phone and dialed those life-saving digits.

"This is your 9-1-1 operator. What's your emergency?"

"Please send the paramedics! ASAP!"

"What is your location?"

I gave the operator the address.

"What's the nature of your emergency?"

"I think a woman is losing her baby. She's crying and clutching her stomach like she's cramping. She fell to her knees. I know something is wrong."

"Do you see any blood?"

"No."

"That's good. What's her name and how old is she?"

"Her name is Alicia Matthews. Alicia, how old are you?"

"I...I... I can't see. It's blurry."

"She just told me that she can't see. What should I do?"

"Stay with her. I have dispatched the paramedics. They are on the way. What's your name?

I gave the operator my name.

"Thank you, Jaslyn. Please stay on the phone until help arrives. Just reassure her that help is on the way. "

"They are sending an ambulance. It's going to be okay."

She didn't say anything. She stayed on her knees, crying and groaning. I tried to console her as much as I could. "I'll stay with you."

She looked at me and asked, "Who are you?" I knew that things had gone terribly wrong.

"Ma'am, she just said that she doesn't know who I am! When are the paramedics going to get here?" Alicia lived in a nice, swanky neighborhood. It shouldn't have taken long.

"They should be there any minute."

I felt hot tears roll down my face, and I started breathing slowly to stay calm. I didn't like her, but I'd be damned if she lost this baby. I wouldn't wish that on anyone.

I heard the sirens, and my heart rate started to slow just a little bit in anticipation of their arrival. The fire department had a great reputation for arriving first on the scene as well as providing emergency medical services until the paramedics or police arrived. Alicia lived in one of the best neighborhoods in the city, but she was still Black. And in one of the largest cities in the nation, Black people still struggled to receive adequate care from the medical community. White folks and Black folks were still trying to "just get along" but weren't quite there yet.

Two firemen walked in the door with medic bags. Two tall and muscular white men, one with blond hair and the other with black and a mix of gray.

They could see the worry in my eyes.

"Ma'am, can you tell us what is going on?"

I described the incident as they started to work on her, checking her blood pressure and looking into her eyes. I knew they would work on her until the ambulance arrived to further assess Alicia's condition or transport her to the hospital. They started asking Alicia questions.

"Ma'am, can you tell us your name?"

"Matt... Alice..."

They looked at me, "Is that her name?"

"Her name is Alicia Matthews."

They asked her again, "Ma'am, can you tell us your name?"

"Alicia Matt..."

"That's much better. Can you tell the day of the week?"

"It's February." It was a Saturday morning in August, so I was confused.

"Who is the president?"

Alicia managed to reply, "Ronald Reagan." Bush was in his second term; I knew this was bad.

As both firemen looked at me, the paramedics walked in. A white male and a Hispanic female. The fireman asking the questions met the paramedics at the door and described what was going on. Meanwhile, SJ was turning somersaults in my stomach.

The paramedics took over. "Do you know if she is on any medications?"

"Other than prenatal vitamins, I am not sure what she is taking."

The female EMT started asking Alicia the same damn questions the firemen asked her, so at this point, I lost it.

"Damn it! He just asked her the same shit! Can we take her to the hospital already?"

"Ma'am, we are just trying to do our jobs. We need to understand what is going on."

"Well, do it faster! Can one of y'all please tell me what the hell is wrong?"

The firemen had completely handed the situation over to the paramedics and left quietly. "Her blood pressure is extremely high. The blurry vision combined with the memory issues; we think that she might be having a stroke. We are transporting her to the hospital. Will you be riding with her?"

"I guess I should, right?"

"You don't have to, but it would be helpful."

"Then, let's go! Now!"

"Yes, ma'am."

At some point, I had hung up the phone on emergency dispatch, and the male paramedic brought in the gurney while the other tried to help Alicia up off the floor.

"Where are you taking me?"

I reassured her, "It's okay. They are taking you to the hospital." She didn't respond. She just followed their directions. When she was firmly positioned on the gurney, she turned her head away. She had on a dress, so I made sure that her legs and bottom were covered and secure.

They rolled her to the ambulance, and once inside, they started hooking her up to monitors and typing in information on a funny-looking laptop. Things were happening so fast that I couldn't tell who did what. My nerves were shot, mainly because I knew that I wouldn't be able to explain to Sam why I even went to her home, but I had to call him anyway.

I took my phone out and made the call. He didn't answer, so I left a message.

"Sampson, call me ASAP! It's an emergency. I'm with Alicia, and she has to be taken to the hospital. The paramedics said it might be a stroke." Then, I turned to ask, "Where are you taking her?"

"Harris Hospital is the closest, so we'll take her there."

"That's fine."

I remembered that I hadn't hung up the phone. I ended the call with, "Meet us at Harris Hospital."

I hung up the phone and said a prayer, "Lord, please let this girl and her baby be okay."

Chapter 26
Sampson
What the Fuck Happened?

When I got to the hospital, I was livid! I got Jaslyn's message after she had been in the hospital with Alicia for two hours. *Like why the fuck did she even go over there?* I thought. If she would have just let me handle things, then my son wouldn't be in danger. I felt scared, angry, worried, sad, and helpless all at the same time. I felt like I was having a panic attack, but I had to pull it together.

I truly expected Jaslyn to be out front waiting for me to arrive. I pulled up to the hospital valet area to drop off my truck, walked inside of the main entry, and headed to the information desk. The information desk was located in a foyer that contained a waterfall surrounded by green plants, and circular skylights provided an open and airy feel. This didn't seem like a place where my child's life was in jeopardy.

When I approached the information desk, I expected the receptionist to return my worry with an air of somberness and gloom. Instead, she was pleasant and upbeat when she greeted me. I informed her that I was looking for Alicia Matthews, and she pulled up her name on the computer then told me they had taken Alicia to labor and delivery triage. I headed toward the exit and thanked her at the same time. I was damn near running by the time I got to the waiting room, and when I looked around, Jaslyn wasn't there.

I was getting frustrated. I couldn't believe that she would call me to the hospital and leave before I even

275

arrived to tell me what was going on. I wanted to speak with a doctor sooner rather than later. The receptionist had given me Alicia's room information, so I headed to her room hoping that I could at least speak with a nurse. I was panicking, and I wasn't thinking clearly because I walked right by the nurse's station and didn't think to stop and ask any questions.

I opened the door and pushed into the room. Alicia was sleeping and Jaslyn was waiting with her in the only chair that was available. She looked at me with fear and worry, but I couldn't reassure her. I was grateful that she hadn't left like I thought she would, but I was still too worried my damn self, but at least my anger with her dissipated long enough for me to ask, "Where is the doctor?"

"He's running some tests. He said he would be back soon; it's been about thirty minutes."

"What type of tests?"

"Well, they are doing an EKG and a CT scan. Like I told you on the phone, they think she might have had a stroke."

"That's serious!"

"Yes, it is. I didn't know that she had pre-eclampsia and gestational diabetes. You should have told me."

"That is why she was on leave from work. Why didn't you meet me outside? I told you that I was on my way."

"And leave her alone? I wasn't going to leave until you got here or someone from her family showed up. I don't know her family to call anybody. I don't know...someone needed to be here to speak with the doctors."

"That was nice of you." I meant it. I was still mad, yet I would have to deal with that later.

"I called Tamika. She said she would call her mom."

As she finished, Alicia's mother walked into the room. All these years later, she still looked the same. She was Alicia's twin, lean with long silver hair. Her skin was soft with few wrinkles around the corners of her mouth and crow's feet that twinkled at the edge of her eyes. Father Time was catching up to her, but she seemed to be running a pretty good race.

As soon as she entered the room, Alicia's mother announced, "They said that only two people can be in here at a time so one of you has to go."

Jaslyn stood up. "I'll go."

I grabbed Jaslyn's hand before she left. "Are you going to wait for me or are you calling a ride?" My words said one thing, but my eyes told her what I really meant, *I need you, and I need your support.*

"If you want me to, I'll wait."

"Please."

"I'll be in the waiting room."

"Are you sure?"

"Yes, I'll wait. Also, you both need to know that the nurse has checked on her, but when she wakes up, she'll probably be hungry. We've been here for a while, and the doctor should be back soon with her test results."

Alicia's mom grabbed Jazz by the arm, and I knew that all hell was about to break loose. However, she simply turned Jaslyn toward her. "Thank you so much."

Jaslyn nodded her head and patted Mrs. Matthews on the arm. After that, she left the room. I was stunned, but I wouldn't even think about it. I just needed to make sure that my kid was okay.

"Mrs. Matthews, I'll be right back. I just need to get a few more details from Jaslyn."

She took Jaslyn's seat as I vacated the room. I went to the waiting room, and she wasn't there. Knowing that I was upset, I was sure that she had broken her promise to stay. I asked the receptionist from earlier if she had seen her, and she told me that she saw Jaslyn heading to the ladies' room. I took a seat in the back row facing the television, so I could keep my mind occupied until she came out. She walked out about ten minutes later and stood over me.

"You good?" I asked.

"Yeah, I'm good. What's up?"

"You weren't out here. The receptionist told me she saw you heading to the restroom. You were in there for a while. I was concerned."

"Well, my bladder was full." She patted her stomach indicating why and took a seat in the empty chair next to me. When she sat down, I bent over, put my head in my hands, and cried. I wept for dear life. I didn't have any more fight left in me. I didn't have any words. I was devastated and defeated. I felt Jaslyn put her arms around me, and instead of giving me comfort, it just made me cry harder. She hugged me as tight as she could, given that she was sitting next to me.

I heard her say, "Sampson, look at me." I couldn't, but she insisted, "Look at me."

I lifted my head and turned to her. "Everything is going to be alright."

"You don't know that."

"Trust me. Alicia is strong. From the few times that we have interacted, I know that she's persistent and stubborn. That's why she and I bump heads. We are alike in some ways. Your son is strong and tough. He's a fighter."

"How do you know that?"

"Because you are strong and tough. You are a fighter, and if he's anything like his dad, he will be the same way. The doctor was certain that things would be okay."

Alicia's mom walked out, and I wiped my eyes.

"The doctor came back with the results and confirmed that she had a stroke. They are going to admit her so they can monitor her. She's only about thirty-two weeks, so they are going to try to get her stable. If her condition doesn't stabilize, then she will have to have an emergency C-section to make sure the baby survives."

I cringed, "Are you kidding me?"

She sighed. "I just wanted to let you know. The next few hours are critical. Leave me your number, and I will call you if anything changes."

"I'm staying." She looked at me, then gave Jaslyn an awkward side-eye. "She's staying, too. She's my wife." I wasn't sure how much she knew about our situation, but I knew that, unlike her daughter, she didn't like drama.

"Stay right here, and I'll find out where they are taking her."

As Mrs. Matthews walked away, I turned to Jaslyn and pulled her into me. I was mad at her, but I didn't know what I would do without her.

Chapter 27
Jaslyn
Believe Black Women

Alicia had been at the hospital for a few days. She was able to safely deliver the baby by C-section, and they stabilized her condition. Sam told me that she was seeing a great neurologist, and she also had some weakness on the right side of her body, but other than that, she didn't have much physical damage. Against my better judgment, I decided to go back to the hospital to apologize. I knew that Sampson was pissed that I went to see Alicia in the first place, but I also knew that he didn't understand my motives. I tried to explain to him that Alicia and I needed to work out our issues together. I felt that the problem between us was that all of our interactions had been competitive and negative. They were all centered around Sam. Now that we were going to be in each other's lives, we needed to get to know each other and work together to resolve our issues. At least, that is what I hoped would happen.

We were going to be raising children together, and all of my responses to her presence in Sam's life had been violent or petty. I wanted to put aside my difference with Alicia and agree to be mutually respectful for the benefit of our children. Sam said I was just being messy.

My motivation no longer mattered. My visit to Alicia triggered her in the wrong way, and because of it, she was in the hospital. Her baby, my stepson, was premature because of me; I felt awful. I wouldn't wish harm on any mother or her baby.

I wanted to apologize, so I made it up in my mind that I would do just that. I stopped at the hospital gift shop and bought a blue "Welcome Baby Boy" gift basket. It had blankets, bottles, and onesies—things that I knew she would need. I vowed that I wouldn't start trouble. I was there to offer my gift and my apology, and then, I would make a gracious, but hasty, exit and be out.

I walked into her room ready for her mom or some other family member to let me have it. But she was alone. She was awake and shivering. I put the gift on the counter across from her bed and then walked over to her.

"Alicia, are you okay?"

She stared at me, long and hard. "Who...Why are you here?" Physically, Alicia was fine. The sunlight shining through the window made her hair appear to be the color of sand. It was pulled back into a ponytail and made her high cheekbones stand out. She was still beautiful—physically. According to the update that I got from Sampson, the only sign that she'd had a stroke was her struggle to remember some things...small things, and some people.

"Alicia, it's Jaslyn. I came to apologize. Look, that doesn't matter right now. You don't look well. Where is Samuel?"

Her hooded eyes opened at the mention of her son. "My baby...he...he is in NICU for now."

"Right. Sorry. That was so dumb of me. You are shivering. What is going on?" The temperature in the room was fine, so I didn't understand what would make her shake like that.

"I told the nurse earlier. She said that she would call the doctor. It's been almost an hour."

I looked at the digital monitor with her blood pressure, and it was clearly elevated. From what I knew, it was too high. I got nervous and panicked, so I picked up the buzzer and called for assistance.

"May I help you?"

"Yes. I'm in room 592. The patient, Alicia Matthews, needs to see a doctor. Right now, please."

"Okay, ma'am. We will send someone in."

Ten minutes later, a nurse walked into the room. She was medium height with stringy, brown hair and a stomach that told me she drank a six-pack of Miller Hi-Life every night when she watched reruns of Roseanne. She had a ruddy complexion along with a facial expression that seemed to convey a lack of empathy. I wondered how she ended up choosing nursing as a profession. The body language as she entered the room screamed that she was definitely annoyed.

"What's the problem?"

"She needs to see a doctor!"

"What for?"

"She is shivering! Surely, you can see that....and her blood pressure is elevated!"

"I'll drop the temperature, and she needs to give the pain medication time to work."

I was pissed. Did she think I was stupid? She blatantly ignored Alicia's condition and my request for help. "The temperature is just fine! And what the hell does pain medication have to do with her blood pressure? She told me she asked to see a doctor an hour ago. She just had a baby and a stroke! How long is she supposed to wait for someone to help her?"

"The doctor is busy."

"Bi..." Then I caught myself. I couldn't afford to go back to jail. "Too busy to see a patient with pre-eclampsia and gestational diabetes, who just delivered her baby prematurely due to complications from both? Make that make sense to me." She didn't say anything, but the red on her neck was rising to her face like a needle on a thermometer. "Right. I didn't think you could. Look, ma'am...call the doctor. Now. If the first doctor isn't available, call another. Keep calling until you get someone up here to help her. If you don't and something happens to her, then I will have my husband sue you and this hospital so fast and so hard that your grandkids grandkids will be eating from the soup line."

Her face was fully red, and her nostrils were flaring. She wanted to cuss me out, but she knew better. Instead, she stormed out of the room, and four minutes later a doctor walked in. Tall with dark brown hair, he reeked of arrogance as he peered over his glasses at me and then at Alicia.

"I was told you needed to see a doctor. What's the issue?"

I repeated to him what I said to the nurse as he reviewed her chart.

"I understand you are concerned, but we just have to give the medication time to work."

"What about her blood pressure?"

"Her regular doctor prescribed her some good medication. It just needs time to come down after delivery. Don't worry. She'll be fine."

He wasn't rude, but he wasn't fully listening either. "But it's been a whole day!"

"We will check on her again tomorrow." He walked out before I could ask him anything else. I take it back...he was an asshole.

I turned to Alicia. "Where is your mom?"

"She went home to change."

"Have you talked to Sam today?" He was at the hospital until late last night. He planned to come back today, but he needed to wrap up a few things at work first.

"Not since this morning." She closed her eyes as if she was going back to sleep.

"I'm calling him; I don't trust these people."

"Thank you."

I pulled out my cell phone and dialed my husband's number. He answered on the first ring.

"Hey, Jazz. What's up?"

"I'm at the hospital with Alicia. She needs to see a doctor, but they aren't listening to her or me, so you need to get up here. Now!"

"Wait...what? What are you doing there? I thought I told you not to..."

"Look! We don't have time to argue. Just listen to me! The girl is shivering, and her blood pressure is 210/105. That's not good!"

"I know her Ob-Gyn's name. They are friends. I'll look up the number and call her. I don't know her mother's number though."

"You need to do better. From here on out, get her emergency contact info. She's the mother of your child." I blew out a sigh and added, "You call her doctor. I'll get her mom's number from her phone, or I'll call Tamika to see if she can contact her mom."

I hung up, and I grabbed Alicia's cell from the table next to her bed. "Alicia, what's the passcode, so I can call your mom?" She was shivering like she was having a seizure, and I couldn't understand what she was saying. I had to think quickly. Roseanne's ass was about to help me whether she wanted to or not. However, when I got to the nurse's station, she wasn't around. Instead, there was a Black nurse there, and sadly, I felt relieved. Somehow, in my spirit, I knew that she would hear me out more than the other nurse. She was short, about my height with thick, curly hair that she wore in a ponytail. I looked at her name tag that was pinned to her blue scrubs. Tonya. I was praying that Tonya would hear me, and Alicia would get the help that she needed.

"Hi, Tonya! I need your help."

"Hello! How can I help you?" I could already tell that she cared. It was a voice that held compassion and grace. I was so anxious for help that all my words spilled out at once. "I'm here visiting a friend, and she's shivering and the blood pressure on the monitor looks really high. I spoke with the nurse and the doctor, but they both told me just to wait but she's not getting any better and I'm not her family, so I don't have her mom's number, but she needs to see someone right away." Then I took a breath. Tonya didn't bat an eyelash.

"What's the patient's name and room number?"

"Alicia Matthews and she's in room 592."

"Okay, let me see how I can help." Nurse Tonya walked with me to the room, and the compassion she showed me seemed to magnify when she talked to Alicia. "Okay, mom, how are you doing?"

"Not good." She looked at Alicia's charts and printouts. I didn't know what she was looking at, yet I felt that she was taking it seriously. She looked at me and said give me just a few minutes. She left and came back with two other people, and shortly after, another doctor walked through the door. He asked me to step outside, and just as I was about to say no, Sampson and Alicia's mother walked into the room at the same time. I breathed a sigh of relief, but I grabbed Sampson and her mother and walked out of the room to tell them what was going on.

I didn't know if we would ever get along, but at that moment, I did for her what I would want someone to do for me—listen.

Chapter 28
Sampson
Weird-Ass Family

All of the pressure that I was feeling almost overwhelmed me, but I refused to give in to the fear that I was going to fail my children because my father had failed me and my brother. Instead, I tried to focus on intentionality and what I wanted most for my sons—I wanted them to be happy, to feel protected, and to know that their needs would be met. More than anything, I wanted them to feel loved. Nothing in the world would stop me from making sure my sons felt that from me, their father. That was heavy on my mind every day since Alicia gave birth a few days ago, and Jaslyn was now close to giving birth.

It had been a few days since everything happened with Alicia, and my heart was full yet heavy. I had never thought about being a father until it was time to be a father. Now, it was all that was on my mind. A few days had passed since Jaslyn's visit to the hospital, and I was sitting on the side of the bed with my head in my hands thinking about all of it. I was getting ready to go back to the hospital to see my son and check on his mother. Everything seemed so trivial now that he was here. The arguments, the child support, the paternity test—none of it mattered anymore. All that mattered was him, and the son that would arrive soon. I breathed a heavy sigh, realizing the burden that I now carried raising black men.

When the phone rang, I looked at the caller ID then answered, "Good morning, Mrs. Matthews."

"Good morning, Sampson. How are you?"

"I'm doing well. How are you? How is Alicia this morning?"

"I'm fine. Alicia is fine. They sent her home yesterday evening after you left. Of course, the baby is still here, but Alicia is out of the woods and home resting. I also wanted to say thank you for speaking up for my daughter."

"I appreciate your gratitude, Mrs. Matthews, but actually it was my wife, Jaslyn, who spoke up for her."

"Please extend my thanks to her. It doesn't matter who it was; I appreciate it, and had she not been there, I don't know if my daughter would be alive."

"Well, you're welcome, and I will definitely let her know that you said thank you and you appreciate what she did."

"I do. By the way, I found out some interesting information about Alicia's attending nurse. One of my church members has a daughter that works at the hospital as patient care tech. She called me and told me that her daughter heard a rumor that the nurse hadn't actually given her any pain medication or her blood pressure medicine."

"Are you serious?"

"Yes, and according to the rumor mill, Alicia isn't the only person this has happened to. I contacted my attorney, and he advised me that we should request the medical records. However, it might take a few days for the hospital to release the information, if they release it at all. You know they will try hard to avoid accepting responsibility for this. Honestly, I'm just glad that her doctor and the nurse Jaslyn talked to caught the issue in time. Alicia will be fine, but I'm going to make sure that my attorney follows through so that there is a thorough investigation of that nurse, so this doesn't happen to anyone else."

"Wow! Is there anything I can do to help?" Jaslyn walked in the room and sat on the bed next to me as I was finishing my call with Mrs. Matthews.

"You can file the complaint with me. Will you stop by the hospital today?" My son was still in NICU, and I didn't miss a visit. Today would be no different.

"Jaslyn and I are getting ready to head that way."

"We can talk when you get here. When is she due by the way?"

"Any day now."

"Perfect. It's a busy time for you." She laughed and added, "I'll let you go so you can be on your way. Thanks again for the flowers that you sent Alicia and for your support. I wasn't quite sure about the dynamics between you and my daughter, but I had a talk with Tamika yesterday, and she was very forthcoming." She sighed to collect her thoughts. I waited for her to finish because I wanted to be certain that Mrs. Matthews was comfortable with how things stood between us. Finally, she said, "When my daughter told me she was pregnant, I didn't ask any questions. She doesn't share much with me when it comes to her relationships...she's always been very private...secretive almost. But Alicia is grown, so I don't ask."

"This is not how I pictured getting my first grandchild. However, he's here now, and I am going to love him regardless. I probably shouldn't say this to you, but I am disappointed in my daughter that she felt the need to gain anyone's attention this way. She's beautiful and smart. This was so unnecessary, but the blessing of my grandson is what I will focus on. You all definitely have an awkward situation, but it is not new. There is nothing new under the sun. Hold your head up, you hear me?"

She was right, our new "family" was not exactly how I imagined becoming a father and a husband. It was what it was though. I appreciated her sentiments, but thinking about the messiness of it all still caused a bit of anxiety, and if I'm honest, embarrassment.

"Yes, ma'am. Thank you for your support," was all I could muster. I hung up the phone, stood up from the bed, and pulled Jaslyn up to me. My chin resting on her head, I wanted her to feel how thankful I was that she was there with me.

On cue, she asked, "You good?"

"I will be."

"What's up?" I relayed the conversation that I just had with Mrs. Matthews.

"That's crazy!"

"I know, right? What made you go up there?"

"I wanted to apologize. Like you said, I didn't want to start a family this way. I know you told me not to go, but I just needed to let her know that I was sorry for everything. When I got there...the fact that she was shivering...and the nurse wasn't trying to help her...it just pissed me off."

"At first, I was mad at you. I thought you were trying to start drama again. I'm glad that you didn't listen to me. My son needs his mother."

"He does," she agreed, but winced and grabbed her stomach.

"Are *you* good?" I could feel my eyes bulging in concern.

"Yeah. I think I just had a cramp."

"Jazz, don't try to be all hard. If you are in pain or having a contraction, let me know! I can't take any more shit."

"I will. I promise." I gave her a side-eye, but she just laughed at me and walked out of the room saying, "It's probably just gas."

I started getting dressed to go see my son, Samuel Matthews Tate was the name Alicia had chosen. Jaslyn and I agreed to name our son Sampson Tate II, but we would call him SJ. She wanted him to be a Junior, but for me, that was too close to Uncle Junior, so SJ was a compromise.

I felt old. Two kids, by two different women, at the same damn time. We would definitely need a few family therapy sessions. My new goal in life was to break generational curses. My sons would know me, and I would know them. I wanted to make sure they were healthy and whole. So, I was determined to make my weird-ass, real-ass family work. All that mattered to me was that my wife and both of my sons knew how much I loved them, and I would die trying to give them the world.

My journey to fatherhood had been rough, and I needed to unwind. A few days after my conversation with Alicia's mom, I was sitting in front of my plasma screen television attempting to take my mind off the pressure that I was starting to feel. Stuart Scott was discussing the impact Hurricane Katrina had on the New Orleans Saints' big loss to the Giants. My attempt to decompress was becoming harder the more I heard how the hurricane devastated the people of Southern Louisiana, Mississippi, and Texas. I was just about to change the channel when Jaslyn called out from the bedroom, "Sam! My water broke!"

I jolted up from the couch and hurried to the bedroom. "What happened?"

"I got up to go to use the restroom, and before I could get there, my water broke. It just gushed out!" She was standing in the middle of the restroom taking off her clothes.

We had taken a few Lamaze classes, and I thought back to what they told me.

"Contractions?"

"Just small cramps."

"How often?"

"Maybe every ten to fifteen minutes, but they don't really hurt. They're just uncomfortable."

"I'm calling the doctor. Get dressed, and I'll get your bag." I was on autopilot. I called the doctor, grabbed her bag, and loaded everything in my truck. I didn't get to do this with Alicia, but I wanted to do everything with Jaslyn. I was nervous and excited, but Jaslyn didn't seem bothered because she was taking her time to get changed. She finally walked back in the room in a fresh outfit and her braided hair, pinned in a bun on top of her head. She'd had her hair braided a few weeks ago because she didn't want to worry about styling it while in the hospital. Her face was fully made-up. She looked like she was going on a shopping trip instead of going into labor. I barked, "What took you so long, and why didn't you tell me you were having contractions!?"

"I needed to shower and get my face together. I'm not going to be looking all crazy just because I'm having a baby. And I thought the cramps might be Braxton Hicks. Like I said, they didn't hurt...plus, I ate those hot wings and ice cream so late last night." She was breathing hard and talking at the same time. She waddled toward me which she had been doing for a few weeks because the way SJ was positioned aggravated her sciatic nerve, at least that is what she told me. It was hard for her to sleep and hard for her to walk.

"Ugh! You aggravate me...let's go!" I grabbed her hand and held it as I escorted her to the truck. I was so excited. I'm sure the traffic cameras caught me ignoring all of the speed limit signs and running through yellow lights. I honked my horn like the Dukes of Hazzard, and Jaslyn looked at me and rolled her eyes. About ten hours later, I had a 7lbs., 2oz baby boy, Sampson Tate II...SJ. I clipped the cord.

After the nurses cleaned him up, he had skin-to-skin contact with his mother, ate, and had a nap. And later on, his uncles and aunts came to see my new king—Uncle Solomon, Uncle Jawaan, and Uncle Malik. Jaslyn's sisters, Caroline, Francine, and Melissa along with her best friends, Shellie and Lisa all came for the party in the hospital room. Tamika came with Jawaan. We had a full house, and I was sure that the hospital staff wanted to put us out. They brought balloons, gifts, fried chicken, and Malik snuck in a bottle of Hennessy with cigars that we didn't light. It felt like a family reunion. SJ took pictures with Jaslyn's parents, Virginia, and his Paw–Paw Leonard. However, the photo...the moment...that touched me the most was the picture with his paternal grandfather, Junior Wilson.

On the day that SJ was going home, I spoke to Jaslyn's attending nurse to see if I could take him to see his brother. I also asked them if Solomon and Junior could visit him as well. She contacted the NICU manager who obliged my requests given SJ was discharging. Jaslyn was a nervous wreck. Even though he was just going to see his brother, she didn't want to let SJ out of her sight, but I gave her a kiss and packed him in his carrier before the three of us took my son to meet his older brother.

We arrived about an hour before visitation hours ended in NICU. The nurse had us wash up and put on hospital gowns. Once, I put on my gown, I took SJ out of his carrier and handed him to Uncle Junior, his grandfather. Then I picked up Samuel and Solomon stood in the middle as the nurse snapped the picture with my camera. Three generations in one photo. It wasn't the perfect family, but it was mine, and for once, I was proud.

Chapter 29
Jaslyn
One year later

"So, Jaslyn, what brings you back into my office?

I sat across from Hope, my therapist. I had completed my community service hours and all of my court-ordered therapy sessions. I still had about six months left to complete my probation, then my record would be clear.

My son was almost a toddler. It was late in August; the sun was high, and the humidity clung to my skin like a warm blanket. In one month, we would celebrate his first birthday, and I wasn't looking forward to planning a kid's birthday in the middle of Texas heat. But SJ was my proudest accomplishment. Maybe, he was what I needed to calm me down. When I looked at him every morning, my heart expanded, full and flowing with love for my son. I knew that I would move Heaven and earth for him.

I was happy.

So, why was I sitting in therapy again when things were going so well.

I sat staring at Hope, trying to get my thoughts together. The silence expanded and grew in the room.

"Jaslyn?"

I let go of my breath and finally acknowledged the question.

"I heard you. I guess I'm trying to figure that out—" I stalled, not sure how to organize my thoughts— "This last year has been a journey..."

"Will it help if I ask questions?"

"Maybe."

297

"Well, let's get right to it. How are things between you and Sampson?"

"Good actually. It's not easy; some days are better than others."

"Tell me about the good days."

"The good days are amazing. He is one hundred percent invested in me, in our family. He's attentive...and romantic! He respects me, and he supports my dreams...he prays for me and with me."

"So, what's the problem?"

"The problem, I guess, is his other son...Samuel...Alicia's son?"

"Explain, please."

"Well—" I didn't want to say what I was about to say, but I needed to admit it— "he never got the paternity test."

"Why do you think that is?"

"After Samuel was born, he said he didn't need it. He loved him, and that was all that mattered to him."

"And that bothers you?

"Yes..." I knew that it shouldn't, but it did.

"Why?"

"I don't know. That's why I came to see you."

"Have you told your husband that it bothers you that he never got the paternity test?"

"No."

"Why not?"

"Because of the fact that Samuel was born early was my fault." After SJ was born, the details of Samuel's birth became a focal point during some of my therapy sessions.

"So, you still blame yourself?"

"Yes! And now, here I am questioning...doubting...asking if Sam is really Samuel's father? How petty and childish, but I want to know, and I think I should know. I think Sam should know."

"And, what if he never gets the test? That's his right. Will you be okay if Sampson decides that he never wants to know?"

"I'm not sure...I guess I have to be."

"The real question is can you fully accept Samuel if you never know?"

"I already accept him?" My response sounded more like a question than a declaration.

"Do you really?"

"Yes!" This time my response was more forceful.

"You don't have to convince me, Jaslyn. You really need to be honest with yourself about how you are really feeling, and then, be honest with your husband."

"I know, but how do I do that without causing an argument or a rift between us. He loves Samuel. He was at the hospital every day, and he took care of Samuel while Alicia was in rehab."

"Rehab?"

"Yes, after her stroke, part of her recovery required her to do rehab. Her stroke is why Samuel was premature. Again, my fault."

"Wow!"

"You see why this might cause a problem? We are still newlyweds. Our relationship started with so much drama already; I'm not sure it would recover from something like this. He loves Samuel! If I tell him how I feel...I'm not sure if he will ever let that go."

"I understand that, Jaslyn, but holding on to your real feelings will cause a problem as well. If you tell him how you feel, you guys can resolve it, repair it, and hopefully, move on from it. But holding all that in, you will never get past it, and eventually, resentment will build up."

I nodded, accepting the truth of what Hope was saying.

"What do I do?"

"As hard as it might be, I think you might need to talk to your husband. Be open, be honest, but most importantly, be accepting if he chooses not to get the test done. Also, you need to forgive yourself for the argument with Alicia. Holding on won't make things better, and now, you are connected to her for a lifetime."

I knew that Hope was right. I thanked her and then left. Walking out of the office, I called Sampson to tell him that we needed to talk. He answered on the first ring.

"Hey, beautiful! What's up?"

"We need to talk."

He sighed. "The words no man ever wants to hear."

I laughed.

"If I get SJ from daycare, will you pick up dinner?"

"Sure. What do you want?"

"I don't care?"

"You say that, but if I pick up the wrong thing…"

I giggled knowing that I could be a thorn in his flesh when it came to deciding on take-out.

"Why don't you cook dinner? You haven't done that in a while. You know that I love everything you make!"

"I'll cook if you do the dishes."

"Fa sho!"

"You and those kids!" Even though I was done with community service, I was still tutoring the kids at church. I actually enjoyed it, and it meant so much more once Solomon convinced me to become a member. I was invested! But working with teenagers was affecting my conversational skills—I sounded like I'd just graduated high school.

"I know! Have you left work yet?"

"I'm leaving here in a few minutes."

"Okay. I'll see you when I get home. Love you, babe."

Sam said, "Love you, too," and ended the call.

I was leaving to get SJ when my phone rang. I was shocked at the caller, but I knew I needed to make this stop before I picked up my son.

I knocked on Alicia's door. Here I was again. Sampson and Alicia had an unofficial agreement for custody of Samuel. For the last year, he spent fifty percent of his time with us. In the beginning, Alicia's rehab schedule allowed her to have Samuel more often. Even though we made the situation work, Alicia and I still had a relationship that was distant. In the words of Virginia Davenport, I fed her with a long-handled spoon. So, I was shocked when she called and asked me to come over. Because although she and I were no longer arguing or fighting—again my fault—our relationship was still icy.

With rehab, Alicia's memory had improved, but she didn't remember all the details of our rivalry. However, she remembered enough to know that she still didn't like me.

With Samuel being with us so often, I tried my best to be a good stepmother, but there was still that nagging feeling in the back of my mind. If I was going to fully open my heart to him, I needed to resolve things with his mother. So, I agreed to come even though I knew Sampson wouldn't want me to come.

Alicia opened the door and stared at me blankly. I couldn't tell if it was the stroke or genuine disdain. Before I could speak, she said, "Come in."

I stepped into the foyer and glanced around before I said, "Thank you."

She walked me through the foyer, past the living room, which was littered with bottles, trucks, plastic blocks, a stuffed giraffe, and pack-n-play. The pristine white decor from my first visit was long gone, replaced with dark leather and soft pillows. *Kids change you,* I thought. Sam and I had moved from his condo into a bigger house with more room, and just like Alicia, our home resembled the yellow brick road to daycare. But it was all worth it.

We entered her kitchen, and I sat down on a stool at the island in the center of the room.

A true daughter of the south, Alicia's hospitality skills were on full display. I'm not sure how long she'd thought of inviting me, but she had taken great care in providing a meal designed to delight the palate—zucchini quiche, smoked chicken sliders, fruit salad, and lemonade were on full display in front of me. My surprise must have been evident on my face because Alicia laughed and said, "Don't worry. I'm not trying to poison you."

I breathed a sigh of relief and then asked, "What's the occasion?"

"I was wondering if we could talk."

"The last time I tried to talk to you, Alicia, things didn't turn out so well. Not just the last time, but every time."

"I know—" she inhaled— "but this is long overdue...and both of our sons are about to have birthdays, and I was wondering...I thought it might be a good idea to plan their parties together, since, you know, they were born so close together. I put Samuel down for a nap, so this is a good time of day."

"A party? Together? Alicia, we barely talk to each other when you drop Samuel off at my house. How are we supposed to plan a party?"

"I know, but I would like to try."

I shook my head in astonishment.

"Would you like something to drink? Lemonade or water?"

"Water will be fine for now."

Alicia walked to the refrigerator covered with pictures of Samuel and manila paper decorated with purple and blue handprints—her son's first artwork.

She pulled out a bottle of water and handed it to me. I accepted the bottle and finally said, "I'm glad you asked me to lunch."

"You are?"

"Yes. I have been trying to apologize to you for a long time, and every time I tried seemed to end in disaster. Before we can plan anything, I want...no, I need to apologize."

"For what?"

"Choking you."

"You choked me?"

303

"Yes. At Sampson's office…when you first told me you were pregnant."

"Yes. I remember some things, and some things I don't. Tamika has tried to fill in the blanks, but it is still hard to hold on to some memories after the stroke. It's like I try to reach for it, in my mind, and there's just a blank."

"I'm sorry, Alicia."

"For what?"

"That you have to go through this…your memory…my part in it...being jealous of you. Everything!"

Alicia held up her hand, "Jaslyn, stop it!"

I thought, *Oh God! I've done it again! She's pissed, and Sampson is going to kill me!* He always told me, "Let me handle Alicia," But, I had to take things into my own hands and show up for this lunch.

I tried to interrupt her. "But…"

"No, stop. Let me talk." Alicia closed her eyes for a moment, and when she opened them, a softness appeared that I had never seen before. "I am the one who needs to apologize. As I said, Tamika has filled in some of the blanks for me, and I have spent this entire year reflecting on everything…everything that I can remember anyway. A lot of how you reacted, I instigated because I was trying to…I don't know…come up, I guess. I've always wanted to marry someone with ambition. With goals and deep pockets. And honestly, I've always been competitive. When I heard you talking about Sam at Tamika's shower and wedding two years ago, I remembered his crush on me, and I guess I made up in my mind that he was my ticket to marrying the type of man I wanted…had always dreamed of. That's it.

It was never about you. You were just in my way. For that—" she shrugged her shoulders— "I'm sorry."

I took a huge gulp of water. Drinking water was easier than trying to get a sentence together.

Alicia continued, "I also wanted to thank you."

I choked on my water, but managed to ask, "Thank me? For what?!"

"Saving my life...and my son's life. Sampson told me the last time he picked up Samuel that you keep blaming yourself for my stroke. And while I would love to blame you, it wasn't your fault. I was supposed to be on bed rest, but I was still working and stressing...about everything! And, truth be told, I wasn't taking my meds properly. There were several days that I missed, and I didn't think that it mattered. The argument we had was just the icing on the cake. If you hadn't come by that day, I could have still had a stroke, and no one would have found me. Not only that, you spoke up for me at the hospital—you made them listen to me. If you hadn't, I could have died. So...thank you!"

And before I could speak, Alicia pulled me up from my seat and hugged me. I hugged her back, and that nagging feeling, the feeling in the back of my mind, was gone. I knew that it was what I really needed.

She looked at me and said, "Now, let's plan that party!"

Chapter 30
Sampson
Doing Life

It was after 7:00 PM when Jaslyn walked through the door. She walked in the house with SJ swinging from her arm, her purse and his backpack dangling from the other. She kissed me, then crinkled up her nose and sniffed before she asked, "What's in the oven? It smells good."

"Just some baked chicken and vegetables. I kept it simple."

I took SJ from her so that she could put her purse and his bag down.

"He's hungry," she said.

It was almost seven-thirty in the evening, and she was later than I expected, so I said, "Put your things down. If you get his bath ready, I'll feed him then bathe him so you can have a minute."

She gave me a relieved smile, "Thank you," before she gave me SJ and put her bags down. She headed upstairs as SJ and I went to the kitchen for his dinner. I put him in his highchair and gave him a Cheeto to hold him off until I could get his favorite food ready, a gourmet meal of nuggets and peas—a strange mix, but he seemed to love it. I should have planned ahead and prepared something for him to eat when he got home, but to be honest, Jaslyn was much better at being a mom than I was at being a dad. She always thought of the little things, everything really. Sometimes I forgot things, like the fact that kids were usually hungry when they came home. I turned on the oven to heat up the nuggets and put the peas in the microwave. I looked at SJ, his brown

307

eyes, a mirror of mine, were wide open with joy as he smashed Cheeto puffs into his face leaving an orange smile of delight. I was tickled, but his mama was going to be mad.

Twenty minutes later, his food was ready, and I started feeding my son who seemed to have an insatiable appetite even at the ripe old age of one...well, almost one. Jaslyn walked in and kissed his face. Then, she walked over to the sink, took a towel, turned on the water, wet it, walked back over to SJ, and wiped his face.

"Why did you give him cheese puffs before he ate his dinner?"

I shrugged my shoulders.

"Sam! He will be sick to his stomach!"

I laughed, "He will be fine."

He giggled and said, "Ju!!" He opened and closed the palm of his hand, a sign the daycare taught him to ask for more. I gave him his sippy cup to keep him happy, while Jaslyn frowned in disapproval. I laughed and took him out of his seat to take him for his bath.

Jaslyn always timed it perfectly so that he could take his bath right after dinner, and the water was never too hot or too cold. Then it was a story, and he was in bed by nine. That was our new normal, coordinating and scheduling, cooperating, and communicating everything around SJ and Samuel when he was with us. There were nights when we were dead tired, but it was all worth it. And it was what I wanted—the family I wished I had as a kid.

After SJ was in bed, Jazz and I finally sat down for dinner. The food had been in the oven, so it was still warm. She fixed our plates and brought the food to the kitchen table. As she walked towards me, I noticed her curves. She hadn't lost all of her pregnancy weight, and late-night dinners left her with a few pounds in all the right places. We were struggling to stay fit, but I found time in the mornings to hit the gym. She was still trying to balance her schedule after her return to work, so she was still hanging on to five to ten pounds, but I didn't care.

She placed my food in front of me, and before she sat down to eat, I pulled her to me and into my arms. I hugged her tight and bent my head down into the crevice of her neck and inhaled the vanilla and jasmine that emanated from her skin. I moved my hand down her back and onto her butt to squeeze and feel her softness. I knew she wanted to talk, but I had other things on my mind. She moaned when I ran my lips along her clavicle and then her shoulder.

I whispered in her ear, "What you trying to do?"

She didn't answer me. Instead, she leaned deeper into my chest and sighed. I pulled her closer to me, so she could feel the need that was rising in me as I pressed against her.

She laughed when she felt me and mused, "Stop being nasty."

I lifted my head and asked her, "A man trying to make love to his wife is nasty?"

Her only response was, "Hmmm..." before she tried to pull away from me. I held her closer so she couldn't leave my arms, but then, her body stiffened. I could feel the tenseness in her body. I placed two fingers on her chin and lifted her face so I could try to see in her eyes what she was thinking.

"Something is wrong. What is it?"

"Nothing."

"Jazz, you called me and said we needed to talk. So... talk to me."

She looked up at me, searched my face, her eyes appealing for something, and seeming to assess me before she finally asked, "Can we sit down?"

"To eat or talk?"

"To talk...I don't really have an appetite, and I want to talk to you before I lose the nerve."

I took her hand and guided her from the kitchen into the family room. We sat down on the only section of the couch that didn't have toys. I pulled her close to me, hoping that she would feel safe, safe enough to share anything and that it would be okay because we loved each other.

"What's up?"

"I went to see Hope today?"

"Your therapist?"

"Yes."

I shook my head in confusion. "I thought you were done with all that."

"I am, but I needed to talk some things out. Things...something I need to speak with you about."

My first thought was, *"What have I done?"* I searched my mind for any issues or arguments that we might have had, wondering what could be so bad that she couldn't talk to me first and instead of going to a professional. It was difficult for me to get my thoughts together, but I managed to say, "I thought we were in a good place?" It was more of a question though.

She put her hand on my knee to reassure me. "We are. Sam, please let me finish otherwise I may never say this...admit this." Before she lowered her eyes, I thought I saw a flash of shame or guilt. I wasn't sure.

"Wait, Jaslyn, what are you trying to say?" I could feel my neck get warm, and my head started to throb at what I was thinking. "Did you cheat on me?"

She drew back from me and twisted her face as she said, "Hell no! Why would you think something like that?"

"I just...because you look..."

"Stop jumping to conclusions and let me finish...and listen! My God!"

I couldn't relax until I knew what this was about. "Finish please!"

"I wanted to talk to you about Samuel."

"What about him?" I was holding my breath.

"Well—" she wouldn't look at me— "I always wondered why you never had the paternity test."

The breath I was holding came out in one question, "Are fucking serious?!"

She finally looked at me with eyes that seemed to be pleading for forgiveness, "Wait! Sam, let me finish!" Her hand was on my chest now. She sat up straight and turned her whole body toward me. "Hear me out. I needed help in finding a way to talk to you because I knew you would be upset, and I didn't want this to come between us. So, I went to Hope."

"You didn't want *what* to come between us?"

"The fact that you never had that test done."

With my jaws clenched, I grunted, "This can't be real."

"Sam, it has always been in the back of my mind."

"I'm not doing this!"

I prepared to stand up, but Jaslyn stopped me. "I love Samuel. I can't imagine our lives without him. Yet, I've always wondered why you didn't want to know, and I

311

needed to deal with that. I'm glad I did because, after my session, I realized that Samuel will always be a part of this family, our family, and I love him because he is my son's brother."

I almost relaxed until she resumed.

"But…"

"But what?"

"Alicia called me, and I still had that nagging feeling. So, I went to see her."

I'd heard enough. "Jaslyn!!" I was furious. It seemed like we were back at square one. "Why the hell did you go over there, and why didn't you tell me?!"

"Calm down! She asked me to come, and honestly, I wanted to finally apologize. Alicia and I never really resolved anything. Nothing will ever be right until we can get along, so I accepted her invitation so I could apologize. I didn't tell you because I knew you would trip out and tell me not to go—" she took a deep breath— "That's it. She wanted to talk, and I needed to apologize. "

I took my hand and ran it across my face in frustration.

"Is that why you were late getting home?"

"Yes."

"You should have told me."

"I knew you wouldn't approve."

"You got that right!" I sneered.

"Sam, I needed to go. Even if she didn't forgive me, I still needed to try. I needed to try so I could forgive myself. I can never really open my heart to Samuel until I let go of the past, and apologizing properly was what *I* needed to do to let go and move on."

I looked down at her contemplating all that she was saying. I finally asked, "So what did Alicia want to talk to you about? What did she say?"

"It was a trip..." Jaslyn shook her head in disbelief. "She apologized...and thanked me!"

"What?!"

"Yes! I couldn't believe it either. She said that she was sorry for trying to come between us, and she thanked me for defending her at the hospital. I was...just speechless."

"Wow!"

"She even hugged me."

"Hugged?"

"Yes! She told me that in the months after her stroke, she had several talks with her mother and Tamika. The talks and, I guess, coming too close to death made her admit that she needed to make some changes."

"Wow!"

"You said that already!"

"Because I'm stunned!"

"Imagine how I felt. Anyway, we talked for a little while and agreed to plan a joint party for our sons' first birthday."

"I'm in the Twilight Zone."

"Sam! I'm serious!"

"Me too! But I love the effort. And I love you. Thank you."

"We will see how it goes. Stroke or not, she's still strong-willed, and so am I. "

"But, back to the paternity test...are you okay now? Can you live with the fact that I didn't have the test?"

Jaslyn leaned in and hugged me, "Samuel is *our* son."

I pulled her close and kissed her deeply, relieved that she accepted my son as her own.

"Thank you. I needed to hear that."

"I'm sorry that the thought ever entered my mind. It was very selfish."

Her words pierced me. I looked at her in gratitude, but there was also some guilt for my own selfishness.

"No, Jaz, don't apologize. I'm glad you were able to open up about it. Frankly, there is something that I need to tell you."

She looked at me confused, "What is it?"

"Wait right here." I ran upstairs, taking each step two at a time. I went to my office, opened the safe under my desk, and pulled out an envelope. I ran downstairs the same way I ran up.

I handed Jaslyn the envelope, and she held it in her hands as she read the address, "Pamela Franks-Attorney-at-Law. What is this?"

"A few months after Samuel was born, Mrs. Matthews called me and asked me what my plans were in terms of custody. I told her about our discussions with Alicia before Samuel was born. She urged me to get a paternity test even though I assured her that was no longer necessary. I just didn't want to add insult to injury after the stroke. Besides, I didn't think Alicia would agree, and it wasn't worth the fight. Mrs. Matthews said she would work on Alicia, and she would agree to the test. 'It's for the best.' A few weeks later, she called me and told me to make the arrangements. I called my attorney, and she reached out to Alicia's attorney, and there you have it... the *test*. The results are in the envelope."

"But you never opened it. Why?"

"Because he's my son."

"So why are you giving this to me now?"

"After you told me about you and Alicia...how you were feeling about Samuel...I don't know...I realized that you weren't the only one holding back. I wanted to be honest with you too."

"Sam..."

"Jazz, don't be mad; I wasn't trying to hold back. I just put the letter in the safe and moved on. I didn't think about it again because it didn't matter. It wasn't important. He's mine no matter what that paper says. My love for him has nothing to do with his mother."

"So, what do you want to do now? You want to burn it?"

"No. Burning it won't change the results."

She asked me, "Did Alicia get results? Her mother?"

"I'm not sure. I didn't ask. I just assumed they forgot about it."

"Do you *really* think Alicia's mother would let it slide if she got results that said you weren't the father? She seems to be trying to do the right thing."

"I guess you're right. I don't know...what do you think?"

"If you don't care, then burn them, but I'll support your decision."

I thought about it and knew what I had to do. "Let's open them together."

"Wait...what? Why would you want to do that?"

"I don't know...I'm just thinking that maybe it could be symbolic. This would be a fresh start, a sign that no matter what, we are in this together—I'm not going anywhere, and you aren't either. Whatever that test says, we will handle it together. Agreed?" I asked because I needed to know that going forward that I had her full support no matter what we faced.

She thought about it for a moment, smiled, and said, "Agreed!"

She handed me the envelope, and I nodded. I could feel the muscles in my stomach tighten. If the results weren't what I thought, then my whole life would change just as it did when I learned that Samuel would be born. This time, though, I would be devastated.

Samuel, my firstborn son, came into this world with a bang. He shouldn't be here, but he was. He deserved love; he deserved a family. I didn't want to abandon him like I had been as a child. What kind of father would I be, if I opened this letter and Samuel lost the only father that he has ever known? Yet, what kind of man would I be if I wasn't Samuel's dad, and I prevented him from learning who his real dad was by not opening this letter? I knew what that felt like. My love for Samuel is what moved me to open the envelope because he deserved to know the truth and, unlike me, I wanted him to know it sooner rather than later. I also knew that no matter what this letter said, I was committed to raising him. He was my son.

I almost cut my finger as I ran it along the edge of the envelope's paper. I loosened the flap and pulled out linen paper with bold, black lettering at the top, my eyes slowly going over each and every letter until the answer was implanted in my brain and stamped on my heart.

If breath was a bank account, then I would be a millionaire because I held on to every one. I couldn't breathe or focus. There were letters and numbers and percentages and words like alleles—my frustration was all over my face.

Jaslyn exclaimed, "What is it?! What does it say?!"

"I'm not sure. I'm trying to figure it out."

Then I saw it—the statement of results and the probability of paternity.

All my breath left me at once, but I was glad that this was all over. I didn't have any fight left in me. I now knew what I needed to know.

There it was, right there in my face: *the alleged father cannot be excluded...tested child...paternity is 99.9999%*

I looked at Jaslyn and smiled. I pulled her into my embrace and held on for life, grateful that she agreed to do this, to do life, with me. I needed her support, her love, and her encouragement. And she needed mine.

"Are you the father?"

"I am the father."

Acknowledgements

I'll try to keep this short because who reads the acknowledgements? I do! And you should too because writing a book takes your whole soul, and you can't do it without a village of people helping you out in small and great ways.

This book took a loooonngg time to complete. Why? Career changes, health scares, grief, fear, and heartbreak all played a part in the starting and stopping and stopping and starting of this book. Well, now it's done, and I need to thank all of the people that supported me in the process.

God–Without Him, I am nothing. Because of Him, I have everything. With Him, I can do anything.

My mama, Patricia Cass–If I don't have anyone else in my corner, I have you. I love you. Thank you for your sacrifice, wisdom, and protection. I'm glad God gave me you.

My sisters, Michelle Cass Hall a.k.a. Tige, Cassandra Cass Curry a.k.a. Sandy, and Adrianne Cass Watkins a.k.a. A–the original "Southside Girls," baddies, beauties, my besties even though we fight like enemies. Thank you for being my second mom (Tige), my protector (Sandy), and my biggest cheerleader (A). I'm trying to get this bag so I can break y'all off a little something.

My nieces and my nephews, Jasmine, Ashlyn, Jonathon, and Adian–Greatness is your blood; embrace it! I'm rooting for you.

My editors, Alesha Price and Angela Ivery–I listened...but then again, I didn't...but then, I really did.

☺ Thank you both for opening your toolboxes to help me produce something that people could actually read.

My beta readers–Misty Tippen and Brandi Washington Johnson, I thought I was finished, but you pushed me further. Thank you! Tonya Tippens, thank you for being my "research" on Labor & Delivery and reading sections of a book without any context. I hope I got it right. Kasandra Chalmers, you are always in my corner! Thank you for being there to get me over the hump.

My hood therapist, Aaron Cato–Thank you for letting me pick your brain on all things male, for gassing me up when I need an ego boost, for giving me the game when I choose to be naïve, and for keeping it real when I need the truth.

My graphic designer, Kiosha Collins–The cover is amazing! Thank you for dealing with my fickle and indecisive requests. I'm looking forward to many more projects!

My friends, my girls, my crew! You know who you are, and you know what it is.

To all of the people that said, "Cass! When are we going to get another book?" To all of my friends that don't like to read but will buy a book anyway, to everyone that allows me to be an interloper in your life and use it for content, to everybody that supports me just because I'm your friend, THANK YOU! There are too many to name, and I am afraid I will miss or offend someone. Just know, I love and appreciate you.